PERILAUS II

PERILAUS II

Mark P. Henderson

First Published in 2021 by Fantastic Books Publishing

Cover design by Reg

ISBN (ebook): 978-1-914060-98-4
ISBN (paperback): 978-1-914060-99-1

For Crunchy

1

The corner seat was secure. The angle of the walls guarded my back, I could see all the other customers, and the conversations at nearby tables seemed innocuous: Gordon Brown had upset multinationals by closing a tax loophole, a woman planned to buy the third Harry Potter book for her grandson's Christmas, and a couple debated whether they should be concerned about the so-called Millennium Bug. I could have answered them, but they were strangers.

Steam from coffee cups, gossiping mouths and wet coats clouded the café window. Through a gap in the mist I watched a tramp shuffle along the pavement shouldering a sandwich board: THE END OF THE WORLD IS NIGH. For a moment I imagined he was Seamus Goldstein, destined to be found with the murder weapon. But Seamus belonged to my embryonic story, the tramp with the sandwich board to the real world. By the time my mind had registered the distinction he'd disappeared. The condensation had coalesced; the window was veiled again.

Embryonic story? My ability to write had deserted me since Linda had gone. To be specific: I couldn't face chapter six, where Peter would be murdered. I'd grown to like Peter and I didn't want him to die, but you can't write crime fiction without a murder. I glared at my laptop. The laptop glared back.

I finished my coffee and sidled out of the café. The rain had stopped; October sunshine graced Edinburgh's streets. Perhaps if I spent the rest of the morning in a green space, breathing fresh air, the channel of creativity might be unclogged. Perhaps. Making sure I wasn't followed, I headed for the Botanic Gardens.

Here was refuge from plot and subplot, conflict and menace, the valley of the shadow. For a halcyon interlude the real environment was more alluring than the shadow-world of my nascent story: lawns and shrubberies and arbours, a haven in the heart of the city. In the middle distance, elderly citizens inspected manicured arrays of rock plants and exotic bushes. Women with squalling children fed squirrels. A football shirt bulbous with abdomen jogged along the path and an anorak surmounted by spectacles appraised the treetops and scribbled on a clipboard. Seated on the damp grass, I let my body recline against a tree: a reassuring chestnut, not the species that had ruined my favourite song: *Am Brunnen von dem Tore* … "Beside the stream at the gate …"

I wonder, I mused, what those two are talking about.

The couple were in their early twenties. They wore jeans and trainers and what I believe are called combat jackets. A piercing – or was it an unsavoury secretion? – sparkled on the girl's nose. The chestnut rustled its bronzed leaves and bestowed an ambivalent smile. A few months earlier, Linda and I had ambled along that path to the water garden.

The laptop reclaimed my attention. Peter and Karen were more important than the young couple. Peter owned property and rents poured in. However, there was another source of money, an unmentioned source, and Karen – brilliant, incisive Karen – bit her lip and asked no questions. This should have been a wellspring of tension. Tension drives a novel. My manuscript was as tense as a soggy napkin.

'Doug, ye English git! Where've ye been?'

Startled, I saved the file, shut down the laptop and struggled to my feet. My jacket shed dead leaves and fragments of bark. George wasn't a threat but it could have been anyone.

'Keeping a low profile. What brings you here on a Friday?'

'Kids' half-term. I'm takin' a couple of days.' He nodded at the laptop. 'New one?'

I scanned the Gardens, made a non-committal noise and asked, 'Sally and the kids with you?'

'Hit squad are with their Granny. Takin' 'em to the pictures later. Sal's in the tea-house.' His head signalled the direction, give or take thirty degrees. 'Coming?'

George led, I followed. He was a hard-bitten accountant who played prop forward, big enough to pick me up with one hand and break me in half with the other, but a gentle giant; too soft with the children, especially Jacquie, who wrapped him round her little finger. Sally, half his size, administered family discipline. They were two of my oldest friends. They'd been life-savers when Linda left.

'Have ye … seen her again, Doug?'

I saw her whenever I closed my eyes. Whenever my hair-trigger imagination molded a passing woman into her shape. A fold in the linen, the murmur of a brook, a fleeting perfume, and I saw her again. Above all, I heard her voice. Speaking. Singing.

'No.'

I lit a cigarette as we walked; awkward for one carrying an inspirationless laptop and a cartload of sadness.

'Aye, well … Sal … we were thinkin' we should invite ye round for dinner again soon.'

Most people I knew in Edinburgh had been Linda's acquaintances before I met them. I no longer wished to see them. I'd known George and Sally before I met Linda. They didn't like her.

'Sally wants me to meet someone new.'

'Maybe.' He gave a slight laugh. 'Guy, lives down the stair from us, artist … Ye've met Guy?'

'No, and I'm not that way inclined.'

'Naw, I didnae mean that, ye daft bastard! He's got a sister, Isabel. Likes yer books. Read all four of 'em twice over. Wonders why the first one's still the best, mind you. Thinks ye need a wee push.'

A *push* to restore the Lost Muse?

'So I've a fan club of one. I'm honoured, but I won't be interested. Dinner would be good, though, thanks. Couple of weeks?'

Maybe that would give me time to transcend chapter six and manoeuvre my characters towards their intended fates. I threw my cigarette into an azalea.

Like the rest of tourist-guide Edinburgh, the tea-house was well-bred and hygienic. The tables were round and white; the chairs matched. Plate glass windows, not veiled with condensation, sustained our contact with artificial Nature. Sally had commandeered a table near the door, red hair aglow from recent re-dyeing.

'Hiya, Doug – thought we'd seen ye, sittin' all alone wi' yer laptop, cheery as a wet weekend. Get yerself a cuppa and come and sit down.'

I queued at the counter and returned with baked potato, cup and saucer and teapot. George had overwhelmed a chair, back to the windows. Sally tilted her head and studied me.

'Gettin' work, Doug?'

'Couple of Russian medical articles to edit. An old colleague in Manchester wants me to run my eye over a PhD thesis.'

Editing work paid most of the bills, and my four published crime novels had paid for luxuries, but there was no pressure. I'd inherited money and I owned my Stockbridge flat outright. Well, technically I owned half of it, but I didn't suppose Linda would claim her share.

'Aye. An' ye're writin' another book. That's good, eh?'

The working title was *The Bronze Bull*. Like its predecessors it was set here in Edinburgh, with Iain McArdle as protagonist. Iain wouldn't appear until chapter seven, after the murder. I'd set up the main suspects and some red herrings and established what ought to become a strong sub-plot. But could I negotiate chapter six?

'Not very. It's as full of sparkle as forgotten beer.'

'Aye, ye'll tell us nothin' about it, will ye? Ye never telled nobody what ye're writing except the Wicked Witch o' the West. Just as long as it's better than yon what's-it-called, *Cold Friction*. Give me the heebie-jeebies, that one, all they old folk in that horrible ward. We both kind o' liked *Artless Dodger*, though, except the ending. That wiz rubbish.'

'Ye're no' the subtlest o' critics, Sal,' said George. 'Ye ken what Doug's books are really about. He's told us.'

We'd had one of those conversations a couple of years earlier – *What I like about your books, what their theme is* – and I'd been drunk enough to be drawn into it. I'd told George that all novels are about people under stress, but in a crime novel, one person yields under the stress and commits murder. The standard objective is to identify and apprehend the murderer, not to focus on the suffering that had led to the crime, the internal conflicts of the perpetrator. However, I always became distracted by those internal conflicts and obsessed with failures of justice. My novels weren't best-sellers.

In *The Bronze Bull*, Karen's mental turmoil, her brilliance, her international reputation, would be ignored by the justice system. In official eyes she'd be the woman who'd aided and abetted Peter; nothing more. And what would it matter that Peter was dazzling, charismatic, a good friend, though not a man to cross, and habitually loyal; though he'd deserted Alison after the miscarriage, and he'd failed to reward David's help? Scottish justice would see only his shady dealings. So it would be for the others: Alison, David, Richard and the rest. The sum of their joys and sorrows, stresses and contradictions, virtues and vices would weigh no more than a feather in the scales of Scottish justice.

DCI Iain McArdle would understand the contradictions and stresses. He'd feel the sorrow. But he was only the instrument of justice. The instrument could be sensitive but the wielder wasn't. And so what? I'd said it all before, four times. I ate my baked potato.

'George tells me I'm invited for dinner, Sally. I suggested a couple of weeks. Would that be OK?'

We talked about their children, and about Guy the artist ('Kind o' wabbit-looking wi' a moustache,' said Sally) and his sister Isabel. There were no children in *The Bronze Bull*, or in most of my novels. I wondered why not.

Sally chortled: 'Och, Doug, get an eyeful o' those two!'

The young couple with combat jackets had entered the

tea-room. I'd been right about the piercing; one of several with which both bodies were mutilated. Tinny pop music leaked from their ear-pieces. I grimaced. George chuckled.

'Modern culture, Doug. Food fer a writer, is it no'?'

'Once upon a time, culture and vulgarity were antonyms. And emetics aren't food.'

I could still elicit laughter, at least when I was serious. I glanced around the tea-room. Nothing obvious, but professional watchers were subtle.

'Ye sound like ye're ninety when ye talk like that, Doug, and ye're no' much older than us. Nae kids, that's what does it. What age are ye now, forty-three?'

'Forty-four, as of August past. I'd have liked kids.'

There was a short silence, but Sally was never slow to speak her mind.

'Ye've been let down by a selfish bitch that wasn't worth yer time or yer love. I ken ye're hurt, Doug, but ye're better off without her. An' ye need to get out more. I'm glad ye're workin' again, bit ye need more stimulation or yer new book'll be rubbish.'

I concealed the palpable hit under a smile.

'I'm out today, Sally.'

'Aye, all on yer tod 'til we tracked ye down and George hauled ye in here.'

'It's good to see you both. You're wrong about Linda, though.' Saying the name stirred the thick silt of memory and clogged my throat. I coughed. 'I'm impossible to live with.'

'Quit beating yerself up, man.' George growled. 'It takes two to make a relationship work, an' don't tell me *you* didn't put heart an' soul into it. Anyway, ye don't need to wait a fortnight to come an' see us in Warrender Park. Drop in whenever ye want.'

We finished food and drink, exchanged farewells and went our separate ways. My spirit was drawn heavenwards by the beauty of the Gardens and the kindness of friends, but rendered flightless by stagnant emotion and the loss of creative drive. I strolled home cradling my laptop; ten minutes to my flat. I resolved that after lunch I'd polish the draft of chapter five and then force myself to attack chapter six.

Blandford Terrace was quiet as ever, but there were no trees there, no one to talk to. I could still smell the chestnut, feel the roughness of its bark and hear the voice of its leaves. But a dryad comforts the living as a fortune comforts the dying: you can't take it with you. I scanned my surroundings. All the cars were familiar, not least my old Ford Capri, pale blue and rusting. There was a flat for sale on the opposite side of the road, a few doors along. The sign was new. No other changes as far as I could see. Except that the young couple with combat jackets and piercings had followed me.

No. Paranoia, I decided. They've just walked the same way. They're not such stuff as surveillance teams are made of.

I hurried inside, double-locked my door, lit a cigarette and set the alarms.

2

The foreboding thumped behind my eyes. It wasn't about the young couple. The state of my flat didn't help but messiness induces anxiety only in OCD sufferers. The black hole of chapter six was contributing but there was something else.

I prepared a cheese and onion toastie and a cup of coffee, copied the morning's work on to my PC and settled to revising chapter five. Linda's portrait watched me eat, drink and study the screen. She was wearing a black business suit, white blouse and gold chain necklace, dark hair freshly permed. Denuded of spectacles, she lost the senior civil servant's authority. Something vulnerable and sly peeped through the curtained face.

My living room doubled as office: sofa, armchairs, television, CD player, laden book shelves, drinks cabinet, desk, computer, office chair. Dust on the surfaces and family photos. Ash-tray half full, cigarette packet half empty. The contrast with Karen's living room in chapter five was stark: neat, tidy, richly furnished and spacious; no ash-tray, and thanks to a daily help, no dust. Yet it could hardly contain the passion of its occupants. It was tricky to convey the anger, the slashing words, without making the reader doubt their love was durable. I knew their future, which I had to hide from the reader, and of course from Karen and Peter.

I put on a CD of Shostakovich's eleventh symphony, the old Leningrad Symphony Orchestra recording with its glorious harsh brass. I needed to capture the progression from eerie calm to shattering violence. However, the music anticipates the grateful tranquillity of its third movement; the next chapter of *The Bronze Bull* wouldn't be tranquil and none of the characters would be grateful. Cutting and pasting, deleting and retyping, I stopped the music when the second movement ended and saved chapter five. It would need further work. The whole manuscript would need further work, and lots of it. But chapter six could be delayed no longer.

I paced from room to room pretending to think. Then, conscious of my folly, I lifted the framed photograph that faced the bedroom wall and turned it towards me: a woodland glade in high summer; sunlight dripping through laden branches like butterscotch, pooling on warm earth. The impact was electric: my heart thrummed, my eyelids prickled, I hyperventilated. Then I heard her singing. *That song*. I dropped the picture and ran to the CD player and put on the Musica Antiqua Cologne recording of Bach's *Musical Offering* at full volume. My hands shook.

After a while the music calmed me. The trembling subsided.

I'd always had a yen for mental pain. Time and again I returned to creepy films and distressing stories. As a boy of five I'd been frightened by a picture-book involving a fairytale wolf, a voracious personification of malice and deceit. Not content merely to re-read the exiguous text, I'd written a laborious copy and added twists of juvenile cruelty beyond the author's imagining. My efforts had intensified the flood of recollection that overwhelmed me whenever the bedroom light was extinguished, washing away the Sandman's blessings and drowning my dreams in terror. Night after night my mother had come to comfort her screaming child. I never told her about the story. No one ever saw my bloodier version, not even the teacher who'd bade me read the picture-book. No one had ever seen that idyllic woodland photograph, either. I should have thrown it away but I couldn't. Memories. Dryads. I rolled a joint, then thought better of it and smoked a cigarette instead.

After dinner, the reheated remains of a chicken curry, I made coffee, drank a glass of Glenmorangie and switched on the PC again. It took twenty minutes to sort through e-mails and reply to a couple. The whisky bottle remained at my side. The joint waited.

Chapter six.

The opening paragraphs flowed easily, but they weren't the problem. Then came the transfer of goods.

Peter's right shoe stroked the leather case beneath the table: black on black. Anticipation tingled from foot to scalp. He sipped his wine.

'Everything in order, Spiro?'

'Perfectly. The linguine alle vongole is excellent. The Piemonte is of course impeccable, since it was your choice.'

The smaller man raised his glass; his spectacles twinkled. His face was lined and scholarly, his hair thin and his suit redolent of mothballs. The piped music was irritating. Something operatic. Peter couldn't place it. He grinned, toying with his baccalà in padella. The accompanying chickpea stew was overcooked.

'You know what I mean.' His eyes gestured towards the hidden case.

'I suggest we use a different language,' murmured Spiro. 'Your Greek would have delighted, I think, the ear of Plato or Sophocles, but–'

'It's now as laboured as your English. And Italian wouldn't be clever in these surroundings. French?'

'D'accord. We shall continue in French. You have the package?'

Peter drew the thick envelope from his pocket and placed it beside his wine glass.

'New euro notes. Twenties and fifties, as agreed.'

His companion winced but went on eating.

'You are – what is the word, Peter? Insouciant? Reckless? As you British say, walls have ears. And eyes. I wished to know, not to see.'

'The walls don't speak French, Spiro, and they're blind. Why don't you count it?'

'Why would I?'

'Trust should have limits.'

Spiro made a deprecating gesture and finished his meal. Peter drew the case towards him. The key was secured to the handle with black elastic. He opened the lock: a sheaf of documents, which he scanned rapidly; all complete. And the object itself: he was sure, quite sure, it was the genuine article. His heart pounded. He extended a hand and then withdrew it again. He re-locked the case, pushed it back under the table and attended to his baccalà and vigneti montessora.

'I didn't ask for the journal reprint.'

'A gift, Peter. It contains details of the discovery, all

our analytical data. Your buyer may wish to know. I suppose you have a buyer?'

'Perhaps more than one. Competition's healthy.'

'Richard Latimer-Brown, no doubt. And Dr Winster?'

'I'd hardly sell to Karen, would I?' Peter seemed relaxed but he was watchful. Had the tension behind those spectacles lessened? 'Though she'll wish to examine it. She's read about it.'

He couldn't be sure; Spiro had learned to control his face. The lone diner at the next table glanced at them again and then looked away; a small man whose features and movements suggested a ferret. He seemed familiar but, like the opera excerpts, eluded recognition. Peter's mind dismissed him.

'I am glad,' smiled Spiro. 'She will be impressed.'

Peter heard 'impressed' as a euphemism for 'envious'.

'Won't the National be upset when they find a major exhibit missing?'

The smile broadened.

'What major exhibit, Peter? Nothing is missing. As I said, everything is in order.'

Peter chuckled.

'What was the trick?'

'Ah. Secrets of the ... trade? Am I correct?' Spiro's expression grew inquisitive. 'Why do you do this, Peter? It cannot be money. I think you are very rich. You need to court danger? Why not climb in the Andes? Why not–?'

'Why do you do it, Spiro? A man of your standing ...'

Spiro spread his hands and shrugged. He drank the rest of his wine.

'Income is not much. A little money for the children. A holiday, a new carpet, a new car.'

'Ah. Not a delight in rule-breaking, then. Or the pleasure of deluding your fellow-experts. Or, as you implied, the exhilaration of danger.'

The two men exchanged smiles. Peter summoned the waiter and ordered black coffee. The talk turned to commonplace matters, in English: literature, music, wine, familiar places. The case remained under the table, caressed by Peter's shoe. The envelope lay beside the wine glass, unremarked. Peter paid the bill. Spiro wrapped himself in a long shabby overcoat and slipped the envelope into its inside pocket. Peter put on his sheepskin jacket and, at last, lifted the case.

At the door they shook hands. It was a blustery night. Spiro stepped into a taxi. Peter walked, the wet wind ruffling his black hair. The ferret-faced diner from the adjacent table followed him.

Midnight chimed.

I was tempted to extend the scene: describe the restaurant in more detail, spin out the conversation. I didn't want to write the next bit.

I swigged whisky straight from the bottle, stubbed out my cigarette and started typing again. The restaurant scene was OK for a first draft.

The name of the club amused him: Loki's. More importantly, he knew the larger of the bouncers; by day, Charlie was one of his rent collectors.

'Awright, Peter? Whit's happenin', then?'

'Not a lot, Charlie. Busy?'

'Friday.' The bouncer shrugged. His tattoos were black under the sodium light. He glanced at his watch. 'Aye, OK, Saturday.' He grinned. Several teeth were missing. 'No' much trouble yet. Goin' in, like?'

'I reckon. Who's on the bar?'

'Graham, is it?' Charlie's fellow-bouncer nodded agreement. 'Aye, Graham. Ken the gadge?'

'Seen him around. Charlie, will you take care of these? Put them in the back?' Peter handed over his jacket and the case, together with two twenty-pound notes. The key was in his trouser pocket, still attached to its black elastic. 'Tell me if anybody asks questions.'

'Whit's in it, like?' Charlie shook the case and listened. He pocketed one of the banknotes and handed the other to his companion.

'Ornament for Karen. And a few papers.'

'Aye, awright, Peter. We'll keep it fer ye. On ye go.'

The noise was deafening, the crowd packed. Peter shouldered his way to the bar. As always, eyes turned to follow him. He gestured for a whisky and soda. Two sparsely-clad girls moved close. He ignored the invitation and nursed his drink, staring at the mirror, watching the reflection of the door. Ten minutes passed before the ferret-faced diner from the restaurant entered. Then came another new arrival, a tall man with a moustache. Recognition was mutual.

Peter beckoned one of the girls on to the dance floor. His body appeared to pay her undivided attention. His eyes tracked the crowd.

The ferret-faced man didn't dance but he didn't leave;

nor did the other newcomer. They weren't together. Separately, they went to the bar. Independently, they kept watch. Two hours passed. The club became less crowded but no quieter.

Peter quit his partner in mid-dance, walked out of the club and summoned a taxi while Charlie went to retrieve his jacket and case.

'Two guys, Charlie. They'll be out in a minute.' Peter described them. 'They're not together. Delay them both, right? Quick search, bit of menace.' He re-attached the key to the handle of the case.

'Askin' a fuck of a lot, mate. Whit's in it fer ...? Aye, awright, then.' Charlie pocketed another twenty-pound note. 'We'll dae what we con. Mind how ye go, Peter. See ye.'

The taxi arrived.

Awkward. He had to walk part of the way or the plot device would fail. Why wouldn't he take the taxi all the way home? Why walk on such a blustery night? Well, he was concerned he might be followed, and if the pursuer discovered where he lived it could put Karen at risk. On foot, he could tell if he was being followed. It would be more difficult in a taxi. And he was confident he could defend himself. And people don't always behave rationally, not even men like Peter.

It wasn't right, though. The passage didn't convince me.

I wondered whether Peter believed in Y2K. No, he was too clever. Too clever for his own good.

I was stalling again. More whisky. Another cigarette. Fingers back on keyboard.

He left the taxi just below the Tron church, crossed the Bridges and strode to the World's End, case in hand. Once, the city wall had stood here. Once, Peter had lived a hundred yards from the spot, with Alison. A few pedestrians traversed the ancient road: lone drunks, a small knot of students staggering from a party, two couples. Taxis hummed past but none stopped. There was little other traffic.

He turned into St Mary's Road and halted in the shadow of a doorway beneath rusted scaffolding, gripping the case. For five minutes he stood motionless. No one passed. He saw no watcher lurking on the Royal Mile. He moved again, down the hill to the traffic lights at the top of Holyrood Road.

There was scant traffic here and no pedestrians were visible. Distant sounds of revelry were disspated by the wind. Peter's footsteps echoed from tenement walls. Black windows stared into the night. Street lights were missing from the bottom of the Pleasance; a supply fault. No CCTV camera nearby. He hesitated at the crossing.

Less than half a mile to go. He glanced up the Cowgate, down towards Holyrood, back the way he'd come. The wind tugged at the black leather case and the key danced on its elastic like a corpse on a gibbet. He began to climb the hill, keeping to the shadows on the left hand side of the road, following the curve to the right. No trees here, no blade of grass, no stream chuckling and gliding. The wind swirled dust and litter, not leaves; it sang among telephone wires, not branches; flapped at old torn posters, not flowers. A door banged. A distant siren sounded.

A car sidled up the hill behind him and stopped. The driver alighted, carrying something. When the voice whispered his name, Peter's reply was calm:

'I'm going home. You should do likewise.'

He turned to walk onwards. The hammer struck him on the back of the skull and he dropped to his knees. Blows fell again and again, shattering his occipital bone and splattering cortex and cerebellum over the wall of what had once been the university psychology department, over his sheepskin jacket. He collapsed face down on the pavement, blood spreading around his head, a shining black puddle. The hammer fell beside him.

He wasn't aware of the hand that took the case from him. He wasn't aware of the presence that picked up the hammer and spirited it away. He would never again be aware of anything.

It was late. I was exhausted and drunk, but against expectation the chapter was drafted. I switched off the screen, dropped the whisky bottle and lit the joint. After a couple of tokes I fell asleep.

3

I awoke fully dressed, half on the sofa, pain gnawing my skull and a cement mixer in my stomach. The Glenmorangie bottle glared from beneath the desk, four parts empty. My computer hummed. Wet autumn light oozed through the yellow curtains and traffic noise penetrated the double glazing, making me resent the blessings of vision and hearing. My eyelids slammed shut.

After a groan or two I sat up and relit the joint. The smoke blunted the headache. Then I ventured to the kitchenette to brew coffee. The Colombian aroma hit me hard but I reached the bathroom in time. Emptying my stomach calmed the cement mixer but sharpened the pain. I cleaned my teeth and stood under a hot shower. Towelling myself dry, shivering, I returned to the living-room, checked the file was saved, switched on the printer, shambled into the bedroom and lay down to ponder traditional hangover remedies. One involved champagne and brandy. I couldn't have stomached it even in homeopathic doses. *Similia similibus non curantur*; no cure by something that causes the same symptoms. Toxaemic slumber subdued my mind before it had time to conjure up further torments.

When I woke again my bedside clock registered midmorning. My head still throbbed. I donned clean clothes, returned to the kitchen and essayed another cup of coffee. The packet of fructose had gone to ground in a wall cupboard; I exhumed it amid a cloud of dust and posthumous condiments. The sweetened coffee was foul but my stomach retained it, Asclepius be praised. Mug in hand I returned to the desk, recovered the print-out, slipped it into my briefcase beside the laptop and the other completed chapters, and attempted one of those relaxation techniques that demand a non-smoker's breath control. It seemed to work despite my lungs. Slouched on the sofa on which I'd slept I began to reconcile myself to existence. Later, I supposed, I might be fit to tackle chapter seven.

Then the telephone rang. I checked my watch: seven minutes past eleven. I lifted the receiver to quell the noise and muttered a 'Hello?' that sounded like an imprecation. And the world changed. With no help from Y2K.

'Hello? Doug? It's Robbie. Have you heard today's news? I'm afraid there's–'

I didn't recognise the voice, yet it seemed familiar: baritone, Scottish, cultivated.

'Robbie who?'

'Robbie Macrae.' The voice was indignant. 'That *is* you, isn't it, Doug?'

Ah, yes, Robbie Macrae. He managed the local branch of a large insurance company. He was fifty-three years old, fit, benevolent and inflexible. He shared a big house in Cramond with his partner, the journalist Niall Ferguson, who was ten years his junior. Robbie was a talented chess player and owned a collection of traditional jazz recordings and some valuable Scottish wildlife paintings. I supposed his voice was like the voice on the telephone. But Robbie Macrae existed only in the pages of *The Bronze Bull*. So did Niall. They had no known resemblance, coincidental or otherwise, to actual persons living or dead. Therefore,

Robbie Macrae couldn't be talking to me on the phone. But he was. *Reductio ad absurdum*. Reduction to any greater absurdity was unimaginable.

To have borrowed a character from real life – even a minor character – is a *faux pas*. Not one I'd make. Yet the voice of a living, breathing Robbie Macrae was burrowing its way into my ear. Had I once met him and retained an unconscious memory? Had my mind recalled him when I started to plan *The Bronze Bull*? Implausible.

'I … Yes, this is Doug. Sorry. You were saying?'

'Have you heard the Scottish news this morning?'

'No. Why?'

'I'm afraid it's a shock. Peter's dead. Peter Wishart. Last night. I'm sorry to be the bearer of such tidings but we felt you should be told.'

The air around me chilled and contracted, stifling me. My legs became powerless. The room expanded; the walls vanished into misty horizons. Family photos and handed-down ornaments blurred on the sideboard. Linda's portrait grinned. My voice, or some vestige of it, asked, 'How?' or 'Where?' or both.

'It was dreadful: he was murdered in the street. Apparently a random assault. The police are questioning a tramp …'

The end of the world is nigh.

True, in the sense that fiction is true. As chapter seven would reveal, the police had found Seamus Goldstein in methylated slumber on a seat in the Meadows two hours after Peter's death, a blood-stained two-pound hammer beside him. The hammer was now in the forensic lab. I'd drafted the report and the CID's inferences.

Anger blazed through me. Adrenalin scared the pain from my head into the shadows behind the filing cabinet, scaly tail waving *au revoir*. Someone must have discovered my unfinished novel and was taunting me. Impossible, of course, because I never discussed work in progress with anyone except Linda, and Linda had gone. I inhaled to prepare a denunciation – *I've no idea who you are, but if you're so lost to all sense of reality, not to mention decency, as to imagine* – but Robbie, or whoever he was, forestalled me:

'We were stunned too when we heard. I don't want to put you on the spot, Doug, but we have to think of Karen. You knew Peter better than any of us – except Alison, of course, and perhaps Richard, but it would hardly … Could you go to see Karen? If the police have stopped interviewing her she'll be alone. She'll need support. Shoulder to cry on.'

Denunciation no longer seemed appropriate. The caller had detailed knowledge of The Bronze Bull's characters. I thought: if I play along, perhaps he'll crack and confess the hoax. Then I'll discover who he is and how he penetrated my security.

'I will, Robbie. Thanks for letting me know. Are you and Niall OK?'

Apparently they were. They belonged to a distant part of the plot and had never been close to Peter or Karen. The caller didn't falter, not for an instant; a consummate actor.

I replaced the receiver and blew on my fingers, wondering whether fear of telephones was a recognised condition. Phonophobia? Lighting a cigarette demanded concentration. I felt violated. I was sufficiently discomposed to look up 'Winster, K. S.' in the directory, but of course she wasn't listed. She didn't exist and the street she lived in, West Arthur Street, wasn't real. I'd checked when I invented her. There's an Arthur Street – off St Leonard Street, abutting Holyrood Park – but it has no named western extension in real-world Edinburgh.

The first response to an outrage of nature or psychopathology is bewilderment. After seconds or minutes, fear ensues, hand in hand with wonder and anger and a sense that the ground underfoot has been confiscated. Pharmaceutical befuddlement, even a partially cured hangover, at once ameliorates and exacerbates the angst. Poseidon was a god of terror in times of volcanoes and earthquakes and wracking storms. It's easy to understand the cult of Dionysus.

I breathed steadily until my heart rate slowed towards normal and the world returned from the far side of the looking-glass. Then the phone rang again. Lifting the receiver was like grasping a spitting cobra.

Karen. The fictional, recently-deceased Peter Wishart's fictional partner, Karen. Inarticulate with shock and grief.

The tone collapsed again in my leg muscles and my pulse hammered. That burning sensation in the soles of my feet had become familiar after Linda left me and I realised she'd never return. Now it was back. The physiological explanation escaped me. Nevertheless, the instinctive urge to console suppressed personal discomfort, overwhelmed mystification and subverted reason.

'Hang in there, Karen. I'm on my way.'

How, though? I could have driven to Arthur Street, or

in view of my blood alcohol level taken a taxi, but there would still be no West Arthur Street, no number 9 West Arthur Street, no Karen Winster.

At least two practical jokers were involved. To judge from their telephone performances, both were talented thespians. Who were they, what was their objective, and how had they learned about *The Bronze Bull*? How had they timed their calls so precisely? Was I being watched? Was my flat bugged, my computer hacked, despite my precautions? I couldn't understand why a surveillance team would ape fictional characters, or what they hoped to gain by doing so.

If I continue to play along with them, will I find answers or walk into a trap?

I sat immobile. Then I lifted the receiver and dialled 1471. The electronic voice recited the number that had called three minutes earlier; not a number I recognised. I pressed 3. Karen answered on the eighth ring, her voice a hoarse whisper. My heart, still racing, plummeted. I temporised: just checking she was at home.

'I'm here. Can't move.'

Fiction develops its own momentum even in real life. I flicked through the yellow pages: taxi services. Third or fourth entry, Acheron Taxis. I booked a cab. Then, mechanically, I shaved, put on jacket and tie, checked that wallet and keys and smokes and mobile were in the customary pockets, donned my coat, picked up my briefcase, set the alarms, left the flat, double-locked the door and stumbled downstairs.

The late morning was dull but it hurt my eyes. Blandford Terrace was quiet for a Saturday but its normality bewildered me. Someone was cleaning a window with single-minded absorption and a chamois leather. Children played among parked cars. A couple of families returned with weekend shopping. A cat stalked timorous movement in a privet hedge. A young crow pecked at the pavement. I lit another cigarette.

The black cab arrived. I said, 'Nine West Arthur Street', and he set off without argument. He couldn't have heard the 'West'.

The movement of the vehicle lulled me into half-sleep. Ordinary, everyday Edinburgh passed by in a haze: cold grey sky, shoppers crowded against the wind, queues of traffic in Frederick Street and the Mound, a scatter of people around the National Gallery, a gang of youths in Hibs colours, buses in simulated Hearts colours. The Royal Mile was chock-a-block. The taxi driver went down George IV Bridge and turned left along Chambers Street. The Museum looked busy, but Karen wouldn't … *Obviously not! Karen didn't exist!*

I jerked myself awake. The trembling and the burning feet were back again. One of Blake's illustrations for Dante's *Inferno* spun across my mind, the one showing a deceased Pope head-downwards in a pit, his naked soles ablaze. By the time I'd regained control the driver had passed the College of Surgeons and turned towards the Pleasance and St Leonard Street. I glanced along the Pleasance; no visible police activity. Two minutes later the cab stopped. The driver turned to me and nodded. I could see neither his face nor the price on the meter; my vision remained blurred. I handed him a ten-pound note and a fistful of change. Without a word he returned nearly all of it.

Out on the pavement I put the money away. The taxi

driver had taken nothing but a small copper coin. I looked up to protest but he'd gone. It wasn't my problem but I felt guilty and had a premonition I'd soon feel guiltier. Right then my dominant sensations were bodily ill, a fogged brain and a dull headache. I buttoned my coat and surveyed the scene.

Arthur Street was unfamiliar; I seldom visited this part of the city. I thought there should be clean new housing around me but I saw no evidence of it. Something – either this part of the city or my recollection of it – must be wrong. I picked up my briefcase and walked westwards like a man with a destination. The pavement was fouled with chewing gum, dog excrement and detritus yanked from wheelie-bins by herring gulls; here and there, for colour and variety, a red plastic bag, a broken green bottle, a beige pool of vomit, a purple sock. The walls were adorned with graffiti: *Bar-Ox 1690; Kylie is a radge; E = mc², true; Niddrie Ya Bass; Young Mental Bureaucrats Rule OK.* This last assertion was written in triplicate: three different spellings of "Bureaucrats", none of them correct. Finding a piece of chalk in my coat pocket, a residue of my talk to the WI in Milton Keynes, I deleted "Rule" and substituted "Administer". Then I resumed my walk to nowhere.

Among the cryptic legends of the graffitists on the blackened stonework of the corner house, a broken street sign hung from rusty bolts: "EST ARTHU". I stared. The soles of my shoes fused to the pavement. Chewing gum. I supposed the sign could be a Latin inscription, but if so either the grammar or the spelling was wrong. The world twisted round, once more out of focus. I'd traversed the looking-glass again.

The first few house doors in Est Arthu boasted lopsided haut-relief numbers and the sorry remnants of paint. Numbers one and three were dismal, dilapidated dwellings, apparently untenanted; five was numberless but a line of clothes from the second floor window implied a resident. Number seven was better maintained and looked clean and healthy. The quality of Est Arthu seemed to improve in proportion to its ordinality. It rose further: number nine was a detached dwelling guarded by discreet hedges. It had grace and charm. Just as I'd written it.

I looked around. Est Arthu seemed deserted. I stalled for time, reaching for my cigarettes.

I squared my narrow shoulders and pressed the door bell. Half a minute passed in silence, inspiring hope of dis-appointment. Then the buzzer sounded and the door was uninvitingly, irresistibly ajar.

I pushed it open and entered, I imagined, the fictitious home of Dr Karen Winster.

4

Karen's home – Peter's home – was twice the size of my flat and ten times better appointed. It only existed on my laptop and my PC's hard drive but now I was inside it, bewildered, scared by its impossible familiarity.

Karen slumped, shrunken and defeated, on a chaise longue framed against the pastel blue arch that opened to the kitchen; as I'd pictured her, but now a living, breathing woman in jeans and sweater and trainers, emitting body heat and despair. She was thirty-two years old, tall and thin, her aristocratic pre-Raphaelite face garnished with freckles. She held a first-class honours degree in archaeology. Her doctoral thesis on ancient Greek metallurgy had evolved into a definitive text. She was a senior curator in the Museum's archaeology department and her gift for recommending objects for acquisition inspired admiration and envy. Her turquoise eyes were wet and swollen. Her red hair would have been in turmoil but she wore it short. Her mouth was taut; from time to time the lips quivered. She had graceful fingers; distracted, manicured nails picked at clothes and upholstery.

If she was an actor she deserved an Oscar. The set designer deserved another. The wide-screen television, switched off at the socket, dominated the corner to my right. The antique brass standard lamp capped with a white parchment shade, one of Peter's acquisitions, guarded my left flank. Serried ranks of books, his and hers intermingled, covered the inner wall from floor to ceiling. The air bore a hint of furniture polish. The mirror above the mantelpiece reflected my face: I was really there. I sank into a royal blue armchair and rested my briefcase on the Wilton. Whispers of a pop music station emanated from the master bedroom.

The house echoed silently with Peter's voice. It smelled of him. Karen's desolation expanded into the enormity of his absence. I'd killed him in the prime of life, knowing it would devastate her. A cocktail of fear, anger and disorientation masked my guilt but couldn't suppress it. I wanted to recollect that Karen wasn't real, that Peter hadn't died because he'd never lived. I wanted to awaken.

If I couldn't, did I have to confess to creating an imaginary tragedy? I stared at the woman on the chaise longue, or the woman I imagined on an imagined chaise longue. Years of remembering lay before her, years of hopeful dreams and sad awakenings.

If this was a stage-set peopled by actors who were somehow conversant with my nascent story, then I'd walked on stage more or less of my own volition; which obliged me to play out the scene. Whatever their motives, the director and cast would demand no less of me. When the curtain fell they'd be satisfied, gods willing, and I could return home.

Alternatively, as I'd conjectured when "Robbie" rang me, suppose I'd once known these people, then erased them from my mind but retained them in my unconscious and begun to write their biographies. This would be contrary to neurobiology and common sense, but suppose it nevertheless. I'd therefore have committed a serious error so I'd owe my victims compensation. Same inference: I must play out the scene. *If the characters prove real*, I decided, *the book must be scrapped.* The thought gave me a hint of relief.

Even more absurd was the supposition that I'd slipped into a parallel universe of my own creation, so the fantasy had become reality; in which case the same conclusion would follow.

I stuffed my critical faculties behind the fraying fabric of reason and recited my lines.

'Robbie Macrae rang and told me what had happened.' My voice was self-consciously gentle. Peter would have sneered.

She nodded, wiped her nose and muttered, 'Thanks for coming, Doug.'

My mouth almost said, 'Least I could do', but my mind resumed activity; Karen's voice, no longer attenuated by telephone acoustics, had shocked cognition into action. Incongruously, I was aware of growing hunger.

'I'm concerned about your being alone.' I'd learned my part and forestalled her retort: 'No, I'm not suggesting you'll harm yourself, though it crossed my mind. But you need someone to help with practicalities. Listen when you want to talk.'

Her face contorted.

'Sure. I'll be great company. I'd just … j …'

I let her sob for two minutes and then asked if she wanted a drink. She continued to sob but conceded a desire for Earl Grey, so I tiptoed through the arch into the kitchen, an enigmatic figure in a Velasquez *Bodegon*. The World Wildlife Fund calendar on the wall was open at October 1999, so if I'd time-shifted it was only by a few days. I knew how Karen took her tea but not which mug to choose. Her favourite bore a quotation from Menander, *ισον εστιν οργηι και θαλασσα και γυνη* (the sea and a woman are equally unpredictable), but it had been a present from Peter, one of the gifts they'd bought each other when they travelled abroad. Its neighbour on the rack was decorated with images of Winnie the Pooh and Piglet. I selected one glazed with an abstract floral pattern and commandeered the E. H. Shepard cartoons for myself.

'I'll stay here.' She held the floral mug in both hands. Steam enveloped her blanched face. Her voice was toneless. 'Work on Monday.'

'The media will lay siege. Robbie called me so I'd come here to facilitate Niall Ferguson's entry. Niall will expect an interview because he knows you. Knew Peter.'

She turned to stone.

'I hadn't thought of that.'

'If you were somewhere they couldn't locate … Your brother's?'

'Eric and I don't mix. He doesn't like … I mean, he didn't …'

Karen and her brother had seldom met after she and Peter became an item. Her mother was in a nursing home: Alzheimer's. Her father had died when she was young. She had no other surviving siblings. I should have considered all this by chapter three.

'Any friend you could stay with? Someone from work?'

She sipped and pondered.

'Beth … But she doesn't know–'

'Shall I phone Beth and explain?'

She said yes; no; it would make her sound feeble. I said

no one would blame her for feebleness and elicited the number. Reaching for the telephone unsettled me, but I delivered a message to Beth's answering machine. Then I studied Karen again.

'You'll need to pack a few things.'

'Christ, Doug, don't bully me.'

'You need to be out of the way of reporters. They'll be after you at the Museum, too.'

She shut her eyes, lowered her mug to the coffee table and turned her face away. My stomach growled. My head throbbed.

'You're right.'

She unwound herself from the chaise longue and sleep-walked, upright and dignified, to the bedroom.

'You need to eat. There's soup on the stove.'

She shook her head, repudiating appetite, and closed the door behind her. I returned to the kitchen and warmed the soup: carrot and coriander with lentils. I dispensed it into two Chinese bowls, found bread and plates, and bore my trophies to the living room on a tray designed like a Spartan shield. I wolfed down my share and made more tea. A lavatory flushed. Karen reappeared, drying her hands and face. She grimaced at the Spartan shield and picked at the bread and soup.

'Did the police give you a tough time?'

She shrugged. 'They were ambivalent. Kind and under-standing, but I'd be their prime suspect if they hadn't ...' She was motionless for a moment and then the tray crashed on to the coffee table, spraying soup over a wide arc, bouncing the bread across the carpet. She no longer sobbed; she howled, writhing on the chaise longue.

'Christ, a drunken fucking *tramp*! Killed *Peter*! For *nothing*!'

My guts threatened to regurgitate the soup. How well I knew the agony of loss: every sight, sound, gesture, every smile, every cloud, every flower, every dropped fork, every bus ticket, connects you with one who'll never again be there. Half of you is amputated. Every nerve jangles, targetless and raw. Frozen, I waited for her spasm of grief to abate. I longed to put my arms around her and hold her, but the gesture would have been hypocritical. In any case, how might she have taken it? And would my arms have passed unresisted through her incorporeal form? The scene could have vanished and left me in unimaginable limbo.

At length she was exhausted.

'Did they *tell* you you'd be their prime suspect, Karen?'

'Ninety percent of murders are committed by family. Partners.' Her voice was devoid of life. After a pause she resumed: 'And I went for a walk last night. Late. Alone.'

'Did you tell the police that?'

She shook her head.

'He was so late. I couldn't sleep.'

Karen had become accustomed to Peter's irregular schedule. His business contacts seldom kept office hours. He'd distanced his dealings from her, but on the night just passed she'd anticipated a gift from him. The anticipation had precluded slumber.

'Had anything been taken? Watch, wallet, cards?'

Of course I knew the answer. Her face grew guarded.

'It's crazy. The bastard didn't even take his wallet. Just stupid, dumb, pointless, mindless *violence*.'

Interesting. Another spasm of pain wracked her but this

time it seemed half-simulated. She knew the gift wasn't in Peter's possession when he was found, so either he'd failed to acquire it or someone had stolen it. If so, who? Not the tramp the police had arrested, that much was clear.

Neither Karen nor Robbie nor any other character in *The Bronze Bull* could imagine how much I knew or what power I had to control developments. This realisation restored a sliver of my confidence; until she cried, with ill-suppressed violence, 'He was with *her*! That's why he was so late!'

Anger at the deceased is common in bereavement but seldom arises so early in the grieving process. I hadn't anticipated this jealous, groundless, rage. The implication shocked me. Until that point everything had passed as I'd written it, or intended to write it, but I'd neither planned nor anticipated this outburst. If Karen had been real it would have occasioned no more than mild surprise. But since she was a product of my imagination, how could she do, or say, or feel anything I hadn't foreseen?

Or *had* I foreseen it, unconsciously? Karen was warm and good-humoured, inspiring friendship and trust and respect, but she was capable of anger. She and Peter had rows, like any couple; they'd had a furious one two nights earlier, in chapter five of *The Bronze Bull*. She was patient with the mistakes of juniors; but management incompetence, carelessness or chicanery by experienced archaeologists, insensitivity and thoughtlessness, all aroused her ire. Her censure was succinct and unequivocal, issuing sharp and cold from the heat of rage. She wasn't afraid to make enemies, though her friends outnumbered them. So perhaps her burst of fury wasn't out of character.

But I was trying to explain it away. Fact: I hadn't predicted it.

'I've known Peter as long as anyone,' I said. 'I'm sure he wasn't seeing Alison.'

I needed a smoke.

'Really?' Her sneer was hysterical. 'Men cover for their friends. Right or wrong?'

So Karen regarded me and Peter as friends. The back of my neck prickled.

'Not in circumstances like this they don't.'

She inhaled, but before the retort could be delivered the door bell intervened. I jumped from my chair.

'Might be a reporter.'

But the visitor wasn't a reporter; it was, I supposed, Beth. Again the chill of disquiet: the scene had shifted further beyond my control. Beth was a friend and subordinate of Karen, so minor a character that my picture of her was vague. But there was nothing vague about the woman on the doorstep: small, plump, black-skinned, decisive, vivacious, cheerful as a geriatric nurse. She sported a bright orange trouser suit and her BMW was perfectly parked.

'Doug Carmichael? Hi – Beth Odombo. I was in the bathroom when you rang. How is she?'

'Much as you'd expect. Come in. Seen any reporters?'

'Niall Ferguson and a photographer pal drove up when I arrived. I said Karen was staying in the George for a couple of nights and I'd come to collect stuff for her. They offered to help. I told them to piss off but they became pressing. Hence the term "press". So I said my boyfriend was here, and he's a South African rugger player who gets nasty if he sees me with other men. Hope you don't mind.'

'I'm flattered. But we're lucky Niall didn't identify the boyfriend, who isn't the kind of Boer you implied. Er … Don't mention Alison Gore. Karen's got it into her head–'

'He wasn't, was he?'

'Unlikely. It's been a couple of years. But he was out late last night–'

'Obviously. Does she know they've released the tramp without charge? What's he called? It was on Radio Forth news.'

'Seamus Goldstein. Not surprising he's an alky. With a name like that he's a walking identity crisis.' I frowned. 'I suppose his prints weren't on the murder weapon, and he'd no motive, and neither the strength nor the speed. Peter was strong and seriously fit. Better not tell Karen yet.'

Beth gave me a quizzical glance and rushed indoors. I followed at a more sedate pace and found the women locked in the hug I hadn't dared bestow: tears, comfort, soothing phrases. I waited 'til the contact dwindled to hair-stroking and then said:

'Karen, tell the police where you're staying and say it's to avoid the press. It wouldn't be smart to let them believe you're hiding. Anything else I can do?'

Nothing. The scene was played. Beth offered me a lift home but it was the wrong direction; she had to take Karen to Penicuik. Karen thanked me with a peck on the cheek. Her lips felt shockingly warm. They trembled like a real person's. So much for my fear of touching her.

I left Est Arthu and strolled to St Patrick's Square, gulping cigarette smoke. No sign of Niall or his photographer; maybe they'd gone to the George. I caught a bus to the city centre. The rain was holding off so I decided to walk home from Princes Street, then prepare dinner and decide how to cope with the day's experiences.

I executed the first part of this plan, but when I reached Stockbridge there was a snag. I'd lived in the upper villa flat of 17 Blandford Terrace ever since I'd moved to Edinburgh, seven years earlier. Drunk, sober, stoned, day and night, summer and winter, fog and snow, I'd always been able to find my way home. Today, search as I might, I couldn't locate Blandford Terrace, let alone number 17.

I asked directions. No local resident had heard of Blandford Terrace. One of them checked her A to Z: there was no Blandford Terrace in the index. She gave me the exact locations of four streets with vaguely similar names in different parts of town.

I'd played out the scene but my tormentors weren't satisfied. I couldn't go home because home wasn't there. Even my ageing Ford Capri, it seemed, was no longer of this world.

5

My briefcase was heavy but it was an anchor of normality. Encased in invisible glass I returned to the centre of the familiar alien city. The castle and the Bank of Scotland building were illuminated, as always when daylight fades. Everyday streets and shops bustled with everyday crowds. I surveyed them from a galactic distance. I met no acquaintance. I sought direction for my thoughts, which were undergoing Brownian motion, and for my feet, whose forward progress simulated intent. I lit another cigarette as they walked. I bought a copy of the *Evening News* and put it into my briefcase.

The shelves of Waterstone's on George Street held copies of *Artless Dodger* and *Bushman's Holiday*, price £6.99, but neither of my other novels was there. None of the four had sold well. They'd disappointed Linda. Privileged to enjoy high status but perforce anonymous outside the corridors of power, she'd hoped in vain for her partner to lap up accolades and prizes. However, I'd established that Douglas Carmichael was a published author in this world as well as the world I called home.

I left Waterstone's and bought a small radio. The salesperson accepted my credit card, which gave me an idea: the ATM at the Royal Bank in Princes Street recognised my PIN and delivered two hundred pounds without a murmur. There was plenty in that account. Linda had emptied the other one when she left.

What I'd told Karen, or Robbie had told me, was true: in times of trouble everyone needs friends. A number five bus took me to the top of Marchmont and I walked down the hill, briefcase dragging on my arm. Warrender Park Terrace looked just as it did in the everyday, real world, and so did George's flat, but the people who inhabited it weren't George and Sally. Whoever they were, they claimed they'd lived there for five years and had never heard of Sally or George. My reaction alarmed them; after a couple of minutes I apologised and left before they called the police.

I was on my own, somewhere near the orbit of Pluto, my soul close to absolute zero. And I was hungry again.

Drifting towards Newington I discovered a small hotel called *The Brigadoon*, a converted nineteenth century merchant's villa in darkened sandstone approached by a wrought-iron gate, a gravel path and three steps ascending to an imposing front door. On the left of the portal was the bay window of the dining room, on the right the sash window of the office. Door and window-frames were emerald green. James Merriman, the manager, had dark curly hair and looked absurdly young. I secured a north-facing en-suite room overlooking a small back garden that boasted a tired autumnal lawn and an overgrown laburnum. There was a sundial in the middle of the lawn, and in the far corner, close to the laburnum, a defunct fountain capped by a concrete naiad clad in moss and algae.

I dropped my briefcase on the bed and used the shower. The hot water washed some of the tension from my muscles, such as they were, but failed to restore me to my home planet. The face in the steamed-up mirror was still mine: undistinguished, brown-haired, approaching middle age. I had no clean clothes, no toothbrush and no razor. *Tomorrow, Sunday*, I decided, *I must go shopping, unless my flat and the world that contains it return from limbo overnight.*

The thought gave birth to inspiration. I dressed, ran downstairs and borrowed the yellow pages from Mr Merriman. Taxi services: A2B, Abbot, A Cabs, Adler… A2B, Abbot, A Cabs, Adler… *No Acheron*. I inspected the cover. Yes, these were the current yellow pages. I checked the main directory; no Acheron Taxis. I trudged back to my room and slumped on the bed, head in hands. My tormentors weren't disposed to relent.

After a while I took the radio out of my briefcase. At least I could have music.

The front page of the *Evening News* carried Niall Ferguson's column about Peter's death: "Local Businessman Murdered". Peter Wishart, 35, of West Arthur Street, Edinburgh, had been found in the Pleasance in the early hours, *et cetera*. A police spokesman had said, 'We are treating this as a case of murder', and appealed for witnesses. Seamus Goldstein, 67, of no fixed abode, had been detained for questioning but later released. Mr Wishart's partner, Dr Karen Winster, 32, a museum curator, had not been available for comment. A couple of sentences at the end of the column mentioned Peter's "varied and successful international marketing enterprises" and conjectured a police investigation of his commercial contacts. That would have worried a few people. The article held no surprises, except the murder weapon wasn't mentioned. Typical of DCI Iain McArdle: he wouldn't have wanted the owner of the two-pound hammer to be alerted.

I ran a comb through my hair and phoned for a taxi.

There were plenty of taxi services, just not the one I wanted. I supposed that my favourite Italian restaurant in Edinburgh, the one featured in chapter six of *The Bronze Bull*, would exist in both worlds, and I believed my protagonist would call there this evening. I was curious to see him in the flesh.

The taxi deposited me in an untransmuted Lothian Road. The rain had started. I turned up my jacket collar and trotted to the restaurant. It was Saturday evening, but Festival Season was behind us and I was early enough to find an unreserved table in the corner furthest from the door. The windows were curtained, the lighting subdued. A floor-to-ceiling wine rack dominated one wall. Maps of Italy showed the principal wine regions. On each table stood an empty, wax-clotted bottle in a wickerwork holder. The muzak comprised excerpts from Puccini. The music Peter had failed to recognise? Wouldn't Rossini have been more apposite for a temple of gastronomy?

I ordered a Pizza Napoli, a portion of garlic bread, a conscience-salving green salad and a half-carafe of house red, and watched the waiters bustle. Customers arrived in twos and threes and fours with umbrellas and parkas, laughing, chatting, animadverting about the weather. Peter had often dined here with business contacts. The staff would remember him; the way I'd written him made him hard to overlook. A reader of *The Bronze Bull* would picture of a man in his thirties, around six feet tall, thick dark hair swept back from a high forehead, prominent cheek-bones, deep brown eyes, determined jaw, muscular frame, and an air of latent menace laced with ironic humour and a hint of stag weekend. His back-story had been integrated into

41

the draft manuscript: Classics degree from Oxford, ferocious squash player, fluent in six languages. Women found him irresistible and he exploited them, though he'd established two relationships during each of which he'd almost been monogamous. The first had been with Alison Gore, a maths teacher and sports fanatic. They'd renovated a flat in the Old Town and lived there until she suffered a miscarriage, whereupon their relationship had fallen apart. The second had been with Karen. Men had respected Peter, and most had been in awe of him, but a few had become lasting friends. Richard Latimer-Brown had been one. Much of Richard's private collection of archaeological treasures had owed its acquisition to Peter.

While I was planning *The Bronze Bull* I'd sketched a scene in which an acquaintance asked Karen whether she was proud of having taken another woman's man. Karen had smiled and said, 'I spend my life transferring items of value to more suitable surroundings'. The retort had pleased me but I'd decided the scene was redundant. Quality of writing depends on how much of it you scrap.

My dinner arrived. As I finished the last of the salad and wine and awaited coffee my expectations were confirmed: two CID officers in plain-clothes uniform entered the restaurant. The senior member of the duo was Iain McArdle. He looked just as I'd written him: big and overweight with greying hair and world-weary jowls. While his faded eyes surveyed the diners, his subordinate, DS Bob Williamson, summoned the manager and the wine-waiter and showed them a photograph. They nodded and began to answer questions.

Bob interested me. As with Beth Odombe, I'd formed

no clear picture of him. In the flesh he proved to be tall and athletic with grey eyes and receding black hair. He didn't look in my direction. However, Iain's gaze lingered on me, which was unsettling. After a while, hands in raincoat pockets, he joined Bob, who scribbled while the manager gabbled and gesticulated with stereotypical *brio*. Soon, the two officers departed in grave but excited colloquy. I drank my coffee.

The chain of events was clear. Post-mortem examination had revealed the contents of Peter's last meal. Therefore, the police knew he'd eaten Italian food a few hours before he'd died. This narrowed the search to Italian restaurants in Edinburgh, and, as expected, Iain and Bob had struck oil. They now had a description of the man who'd dined with Peter the previous night, though they'd yet to identify him. I could have told them that Spiro Andropoulos had amassed a small fortune by selling irreplaceable archaeo-logical relics to foreign buyers. He'd frequently conducted business with Peter, who'd acted as middle-man for Richard Latimer-Brown and other collectors, including a few private museums. But the police must be left to unearth this in-formation themselves.

There was much else for Iain and his team to discover. They hadn't learned that Jimmy Farquhar had dined at the table next to Peter and Spiro, overheard their conversation and then followed Peter to Loki's. The manager and waiters might have noticed ferret-faced Jimmy but they'd probably forgotten him. Moreover, Iain and his colleagues knew nothing yet about the existence, nature, provenance, de-sirability or current whereabouts of the bronze bull. But the case had only just opened. Iain would need time.

Crime fiction always boasts a brilliant law-enforcing protagonist – private detective, pathologist, forensic psychologist, priest, journalist, amateur sleuth or professional police officer – with personal problems to enrich his or her character. They all share an unswerving commitment to truth and justice, and an infallible ability, requiring astonishing cleverness or at least one flash of intuition, to identify the perpetrator in every case. The dénouement is presented in the penultimate chapter. Iain McArdle paled into mediocrity beside those paragons. He was conscientious, capable, experienced, a good organiser and an effective people-manager; but he relied, with only occasional idiosyncrasies, on routine police methods. He became embroiled in the corruption endemic among criminal investigation departments, and, least forgivably, he was fallible. In *Cold Friction*, which had upset at least one critic by its treatment of geriatric medicine and euthanasia, Iain had arrested the wrong man. A miscarriage of justice had ensued. In *Bushman's Holiday*, Iain had nailed the killer, but only by supervising a diligent and painstaking routine investigation. The critics' notices had been damning. In *Artless Dodger*, the killer had again been identified by Iain and his team but had vanished without trace, leaving him on the "wanted" list. It was easy to see why I'd won no awards, and why sincere, assiduous, imperfect Iain McArdle would never be the focus of an eponymous television series. He simply wouldn't *do*.

A radio interviewer once asked me why. It had been a short interview so I'd offered a short answer: policemen are people, and people are flawed, and justice is flawed, and fiction should tell the truth.

Let me explain. I was English by birth, Scottish name notwithstanding, but I loved Scotland. I loved her varied and romantic scenery, her people, her sometimes glorious and often tragic history, her contribution to world culture, so disproportionate to her population, her traditions, her music, her legends, her seashores and her wildlife. I loved her national pride. But her pride was sometimes misplaced, not least in supposing her criminal justice system to be perfect. When I'd decided to set my crime novels in Edinburgh I'd used Linda's contacts to research the justice system: lawyers, a one-time High Court judge, retired police officers, a couple of prison governors, prison officers and chaplains. I'd also talked to some current and former inmates of Scotland's penal institutions. My informants' collective insights had disturbed me. They'd suggested that some five percent of people serving custodial sentences in Scotland were innocent of any crime and a further ten or twenty percent, though certainly criminals, hadn't committed the offences for which they'd been convicted. I'd heard accounts of fabricated and distorted evidence, forensic incompetence, false professional testimonies under oath, defence advocates bought off by the Crown, deals struck with tabloid reporters and swindles involving Legal Aid. Officially, Scottish justice assured the public of its unstained probity, and red-top tabloid accolades precluded doubt. But the system was a long way from perfect.

There was a risk of overstating the case. Well over seventy percent of Scotland's prisoners were guilty of the crimes for which they'd been brought to trial. Justice might hide an inconstant heart under a self-regarding and sanctimonious façade, but the façade didn't lie as a matter of routine.

Nevertheless, the system's infelicities were well known within the relevant professions, and those infelicities were hard to correct: the country lacked a truly independent appeals court, and Scottish criminal cases, unlike English ones, couldn't be referred to the House of Lords. Alarmed by those observations and my research findings, I'd set out to reveal the clay feet of Scottish justice through fiction.

I knew that many individuals who worked for criminal justice in Scotland were honest and well-meaning. Several were competent. I'd begun to consider the existential plight of a decent individual who soldiered on within the blemished structure, hoping his commitment and integrity would evoke fairness from defective institutions. The thought had given birth to Iain McArdle. I admired Iain; he'd almost become a friend. I wished him success even while I engineered his failures.

Did I wish him success in the present case? Peter was dead. The person who'd killed him had killed at my instigation. People I'd grown to like during the previous two months had been destroyed in a night's drunken writing: one had been murdered, one was his murderer. At least two had been bereaved by his passing. I'd been relieved when Iain withdrew his gaze from me.

My mind lurched again: *was I right about Peter's killer?* Of course I'd decided the murderer's identity when I started to plan the novel. However, so much had diverged from my intensions and expectations – Karen's reactions, the three-dimensional realities of Beth Odombo and Bob Williamson, indeed the whole bizarre situation – that maybe I'd been wrong. Perhaps someone else had killed Peter. Someone I hadn't considered.

When had my pattern of thought undergone this meta-morphosis? Maybe when I'd found my flat had vanished, or when I'd tried to visit George and Sally. No matter: at some stage I'd accepted the parallel-universe hypothesis. Peter had lived and was really dead. Karen and her grief were real. The murderer was real – whoever he or she might be, my original choice or otherwise – and Iain was on the case. And I was stuck inside my own creation, unable to return home. What was I to do?

I ordered a Drambuie and another coffee.

The first option, I decided, savouring the Drambuie, was to use my laptop to control events. Since I'd created this situation by writing I could manipulate it by writing. What were the limits of my power in this world of my own making? *Perhaps I could write myself back home, if I wished.*

The second option was to participate directly, as I might in the real, accustomed world. I'd already visited Karen and, in a limited way, provided support. I could do the same for others, especially those who'd been most affected by the murder. And I ought to visit Robbie Macrae because he'd been the first to contact me.

I finished the Drambuie and relished the coffee.

There was, of course, the question of the bronze bull. I'd yet to decide how, or even if, it would be retrieved from the hands that currently held it. Should I solve that problem by writing or by action?

I'd consider the possibilities the following day, or the day after. In the meantime I needed sleep. Stress and the after-effects of alcohol had dulled my brain and exhausted me. Perhaps when I awoke – in the morning, if the gods allowed – the world would have returned to normal. Today's events would have been a dream. I wouldn't need the help of a non-existent taxi service. This hypothesis, objectively more plausible than others I'd entertained, seemed oddly unlikely.

I paid the bill, put on my coat and left the restaurant. The rain was heavy now and the wind gusted around the Usher Hall and the corner by *Shakespeares*. I started towards the taxi ranks at the West End. Had Linda been beside me, my umbrella would have shielded her against the assaults of wind and rain and we'd have walked sedately. Having neither Linda nor umbrella, I ran.

But before I'd sprinted a dozen steps a hand gripped my shoulder and froze me in my tracks. A man's voice, clipped, precise and hostile, pronounced: 'Douglas Carmichael. I want a word with you.'

6

I recognised David Michie from my description in chapter four: ramrod-straight, hard-eyed and intolerant, still an army officer at heart. He even wore a moustache. Stereotyping; I'd need to rewrite him. At that moment I'd have preferred more distance between us. He spun me round so I was face to face with his old school tie. His grip on my shoulder hurt.

'Where is it?'

His voice hissed like tyres on wet tarmac. Sodium lights and passing headlamps glittered from the droplets on his Barbour. The rain plastered his short brown hair to his skull; the effect was a little absurd. Pedestrians ignored us, rushing to avoid the rising spray and the swirling downpour.

'If you want to talk, David, I suggest we get out of the rain.'

He gritted his teeth, bit his tongue and pushed me into the shelter of a close, a narrow stone tunnel between tenements, litter-strewn and stinking of urine but mostly dry. The wind swirled, seeking entry, but the traffic noise was muted.

'Right,' snapped David. 'Out of the rain. Now: Peter Wishart had it with him last night before he was killed. So where is it?'

'You accusing me of something?'

'Did you kill him? Look at me. Was it you?'

It might be argued that I'd had every right to kill Peter, having created him, but I could neither accept nor reject the claim without reservation. I had the right to manipulate my own creation as I pleased, but only within the bounds of ethics and literary plausibility. Then it occurred to me that if David Michie were the murderer he'd behave as he was doing, pointing the blame at someone else. My mouth twitched.

'Look at *me*, David: half Peter's size, not combat-trained, reactions a tenth the speed of his. You think I could have crept up on *him* and smashed his skull with a blunt instrument?'

'What blunt instrument?'

'What indeed?'

He exhaled, frustrated.

'I'll spell it out. According to reliable sources, Wishart left the restaurant last night carrying a suitcase. It contained an ancient artefact, a bronze bull, with authenticating documents. You were there. You saw him. When his body was found there was no suitcase. So the murderer took it. Therefore, I need to find the murderer so I can recover the bull. You're the likeliest suspect. You've been in the same restaurant tonight, revisiting the scene. So *where is it*?'

Yes, he'd have confronted the murderer. He was no coward; he'd been mentioned in dispatches as a junior officer, an explosives expert, during the Falklands Campaign. No doubt he could still design booby traps. I frowned and uttered a judicious grunt.

'Yes, I saw Peter leave the restaurant with the suitcase but I didn't see him afterwards. And it might not have been the murderer who took it. Or Peter might have stashed it.'

'Don't try to be smart. Common sense–'

'–can mislead. You can't be certain. But you presume you've the right to recover the bronze bull. Why?'

'For Richard, of course!' He spat. 'The bull was promised to him. It's partly paid for. It's his. So I *do* have the right.'

I'd devised a curious relationship between David Michie and Richard Latimer-Brown. The back-story was as follows. When David had resigned his army commission he'd taken the rental of a cottage on Richard's estate. Within a fortnight, Richard had started to exploit his tenant's craftsmanship to help him restore the antique clocks, scientific instruments and other devices he'd collected and to catalogue his archaeological treasures. Richard was a fine craftsman, but his eyesight being no longer perfect he'd begun to delegate decisions to David, who was now running Richard's workshop with military precision. He accorded his employer the loyalty and respect due to a superior officer. The Inland Revenue was unaware of their financial arrangement. David had other sources of income, too; Richard turned a blind eye to them.

'In some sense of "right", maybe. Peter's expenses would have to be defrayed in advance. But the bull could have been promised to other recipients.'

'Hah! Karen Winster. Wishart was a shark.'

'No, David. Animal metaphors won't get the bull back. Peter wanted to do business with Richard. He also wanted Karen to handle the bull and restore it to its rightful home in order to enhance her reputation. It's known as a moral dilemma. Peter was a decent crook with the interests of those he liked at heart.'

'Decent?' David gave a bark of laughter. 'A man who reneged on his obligations? Of course, you were his *friend*.'

'So were you, once.'

David released his grip. I rolled my shoulder. He glared, breathing heavily. His aversion to hitting smaller men saved me from a beating but his fists were clenched.

'So the Museum has it.'

'No, David, the Museum doesn't have the bull and wouldn't want it. It doesn't fit their acquisition policy and they'd have no title to it. If it reached them they'd send it to Greece or Sicily. Karen doesn't have it, either. She was expecting it but Peter was killed before he got it to her.'

'So who *does* have it?'

'How the hell should I know?'

His distaste for punching lesser mortals was almost overwhelmed but his discipline was impeccable.

'You – always – know.'

This conversation was strange. No one in this fictional world could know where the bull was or who'd killed Peter. No one except the thief, that is, and most people would suppose the thief to be the murderer. And despite his posturing, David didn't believe it was me. The world's creator knew, or should have known; but if David had identified me as the creator, how had he done so, and why did he show so little respect for his maker?

'Thanks for the compliment, but I'm not omniscient.'

'Peter Wishart told you everything. Most of us were less informed.'

An explanation of sorts, perhaps.

'I suppose there's no point in suggesting you leave it to the police?' I said.

If the bronze bull fell into Iain's hands it would be retained as evidence. After the thief was arrested, tried and convicted it would be dispatched to Athens or Agrigento, or perhaps Palermo. David wouldn't want that.

He pushed his face towards me. His voice sounded like the swish of a cloak.

'I'll find it.'

It was supposed to be his exit line. As he turned on his polished heel and strode into the rain I called after him: 'Tell Richard I'll call in the next day or two. I'll phone first. Any news of Alison?'

'No.'

'Peter's death will have hit her hard. I thought her sister might have told you something.'

His moustache writhed.

'The less I have to do with Lydia Gore, the better.'

A far superior peroration. He turned his back on me and marched into the night. The downpour stood to attention and saluted.

David wasn't a misogynist; he and Alison had been friends before the miscarriage, before Alison had learned of the fallopian injury, before Peter had left her and, independently, earned David's enmity. But it seemed he neither liked nor trusted Alison's sister. There must have been tension at Abbey House. I wondered about Lydia's childlessness. Perhaps she was infertile, too. Maybe it ran in the family. Tubal phimosis or hydrosalpinx, perhaps; the predisposition can be hereditary. Or common or garden endometriosis. I hadn't needed to decide.

I lit a cigarette, trembling, then left the shelter of the close and found a taxi. In my room at the *Brigadoon* I took off my clothes, set them to dry and powered up my laptop.

I conducted a few experiments to test my capacity to

manipulate events, but the results were discouraging. The most carefully-wrought sentences brought neither razor nor toothbrush into existence; I'd still have to go shopping. I wrote a short description of my humble abode in the familiar world, including the phone number, but the number proved unobtainable; typing hadn't reincarnated my flat. I tried the weather: *The rain ceased and the clouds slowly parted. A half moon gleamed on the rooftops. Stars glittered cold and clear in the velvet dark above the city.* Then I took chapter four of *The Bronze Bull* from my briefcase and re-wrote the description of David Michie, despoiling him of his moustache. I walked to the window and opened the curtains. The clouds hung thick and heavy and the rain slanted before the rough westerly. So much for meteorological intervention by computer.

I closed the curtains and switched off the laptop and climbed into bed. Put out the light, and then put out the light. Merciful sleep, which I'd feared I'd murdered, came quickly, but the dreams were confused and disturbing; small wonder, but small comfort. Peter was entertaining a hazy group of male acquaintances in an anonymous bar. The table was packed with full and half-full glasses. He was telling a hilarious story about a tiger catching fire in a castle banqueting hall. Everyone laughed and applauded, ignoring the handle of the hammer protruding from his battered skull. I shouted above the laughter: 'He can't be talking to you, there's a hammer in his head,' but no one heard and the effort woke me, unable to identify my surroundings. By the time I'd recognised my bedroom in the *Brigadoon* I was asleep again, dreaming of Alison, supine and motionless on the bed of a clear mountain stream, eyes open, surveying the passing clouds through the curtain of flowing water. 'You mustn't lie there, you'll drown,' I told her. 'I must,' she replied, 'otherwise I can't stop crying.' Poor Alison; your tears were my fault too.

Then, inevitably, I dreamed of Linda. We were in the Berwickshire dell we'd visited so often during our first summer, beside the clear burn that trickled among woods and fields and wildflowers down to the Tweed. But the clearing under the broad trees where we made love beneath the July sun was dark and disfigured. Linda's face was dull and she turned her back on me. She didn't speak, but I feared she might sing, the lovely mezzo-soprano I heard so often in solitude. I followed her, pleading, consumed with misery and desire. We passed through rooms I couldn't recognise in a house I'd never visited. She'd come here with him after she left me. I sensed his presence. Then we were outside, in the darkness near the foot of the Pleasance. 'Why do none of your women look or talk like me?' she demanded. It was an accusation of infidelity; groundless, unjust. I opened my mouth to protest, but then I looked down and Peter was lying dead at my feet, his head smashed, and Linda had gone.

I awoke, heart hammering. After a while I lay down again, enforcing relaxation. My dream-Linda had been right; I'd never realised it. Consider *The Bronze Bull*: Karen, tall and skinny and crowned with short red hair; Alison, big and muscular with blue eyes and fair hair closely cropped; her sister Lydia, lively and shapely, blonde waves curtaining a coquettish face. It was even true of my minor characters; Beth, for instance, was black. But Linda, my wonderful, callous, faithless, unforgettable Linda; how different! Petite, dark brown hair, brown eyes; forty years old, but a 34C-24-34 figure. Her unspectacled face, sly and submissive, subtly East European; her mouth, wide and expressive; her speech, educated southern English; her musical taste, close kin to my own; her delight in horror films; her jewelled ear-rings …

I climbed out of bed and helped myself to the nearest bottle in the mini-bar. Anaesthesia once more. Oh Linda, Linda.

I opened the curtains again and looked out into the night. The rain had ceased and the clouds had parted. A half moon gleamed on the rooftops. Stars glittered cold and clear in the velvet dark above the city.

7

On the face of it, my symptoms suggested schizophrenia. If schizophrenics inhabit a world with aberrant but internally consistent rules of thought and behaviour, as R. D. Laing had proposed, then the previous twenty-four hours had admitted me to their ranks. Some schizophrenics believe they're endowed with superhuman powers: they're God, or Napoleon, or they're guided by saints. I'd attributed quasi-celestial qualities to my laptop, and the almost total failure of my experiments (the weather change was probably coincidental) hadn't entirely destroyed my faith in it. Nevertheless, most of my mind disdained the label "schizophrenic". As Linda's intolerance of me had burgeoned she'd dubbed me "schizoid" and I'd considered the insult absurd. Despite recent events, I still did. However: when you plan a crime novel you know from the outset that X will be the murderer, but *The Bronze Bull* had started to develop in ways I hadn't foreseen, not least by ingesting me. So could I still be sure that X was guilty? Perhaps Y would prove to be the murderer, or maybe Z, and X would be innocent. Those thoughts, along with others, had unleashed my ruminations about schizophrenia.

The morning's normality was skin-deep; whether or not I was sane, everything around me remained crazy. My flat's phone number was still unobtainable. Karen's name was now in the directory; "Acheron Taxis" wasn't. I showered and dressed as though nothing were amiss, consumed a full breakfast, put on my coat and sallied forth into the fictional world. The sky was blue, the October sun made a valiant effort to warm me and the air felt washed by the rain. However, the need for shopping trumped my appreciation of the weather. I took a bus to Leith Walk, examined the selection of vehicles for hire in a garage and opted for a navy-blue Toyota Land Cruiser; knowing Richard Latimer-Brown, which in a sense I did, I needed to prepare for a visit to Abbey House. My decision constituted evidence for rational thought. I drove to Asda.

My relationship with the Land Cruiser encountered teething troubles. Its controls were in unaccustomed places. An elderly Sunday driver in a hat, nodding dog in the back window, challenged my patience. Irritated by her adagio manoeuvres I bruised my fist on a part of the steering column that was innocent of horn and then washed my windscreen at her. However, by the time I returned to the *Brigadoon* with my purchases I was comfortable with the controls and I'd learned how to engage the four-wheel drive.

The pleasures of a clean shave, clean teeth and fresh clothes are hard to exaggerate. A light luncheon of supermarket sandwiches and two cigarettes sufficed to launch me into the afternoon. However, to be consistent in the world I'd created and entered I needed to inquire about Karen. I'd lacked the foresight to note Beth's number, but Odombo wasn't a common name in Penicuik.

'Hi, Beth. Doug Carmichael. How's Karen?'

'Hi, Doug. Asleep. Had a terrible night but my GP's seen her. Signed off for a week.'

'Not without a fight, I trow.'

'You trow rightly. She keeps half-saying something about

an ancient bronze that might come into the Museum. It's tormenting her as much as the more obvious matter. Doug, any idea what the police are doing?'

I had my little radio but I'd bought it for music not news.

'No. Have you?'

'They've detained a fifty-three-year-old Greek man for questioning.'

So Iain's team had identified and located Spiro Andropoulos. Disturbing; I hadn't yet written that passage. Spiro couldn't have heard about the murder or he'd have been more elusive. It was now certain that Iain would learn about the bronze bull before the end of the day. Why had I created such a competent detective?

'I've an idea about the bronze. Tell Karen I'm trying to locate it for her.'

There was a moment's silence. Then: 'You know more than you're saying, Doug. The bronze has something to do with this Greek man, right?'

'Indirectly.'

Another silence. Then: 'Do you know who killed Peter?'

'How could I?'

'I've no idea, but you seem to know a lot. Anything you ought to tell the police?'

That was an interesting question. If I'd had equivalent knowledge of a serious crime in the everyday world I *would* have told the police. Should the disjunction between planes of existence make a difference? Didn't the moral imperatives of World One apply in what I suppose Karl Popper would have dubbed World Three? However, I refused to be interrogated by someone I'd invented. I'd had enough of that with David Michie.

'If there were, I would.'

'Yeah. OK. Look, Doug … I'm not sure I should mention this, but did you know Karen and Peter had a massive row the other day?'

Of course. I'd written it. Peter had told Karen he might sell the bronze bull to Richard. She'd exploded.

'I'd gathered. But we needn't mention it to the police.'

Beth sighed.

'I suppose not. I mean, it hardly seems likely–'

'No, it doesn't.'

'But she did go out alone, late.'

'No law against that.' But I was being unkind; this was a strain on Beth. On me, too; Karen's very existence was a strain on me. I infused conviction into my voice: 'Forget it. No way did Karen kill Peter.'

'You know that line from *The Ballad of Reading Gaol*, "Each man kills the thing he loves"?'

'Karen isn't a man. All right?'

'OK, no need to bite my head off!'

There wasn't, but I had to stop Beth's train of thought before it ran over all of us. Karen had suffered enough and would suffer more. So had I.

'Sorry. I hate Oscar Wilde. Listen, Beth, you're doing a great job. Karen needs you. But suspicions won't help her. Agreed?'

'Yeah. Agreed. Sorry, Doug. Being stupid. But once the idea got–'

'You needed help to extirpate it. Task accomplished?'

'Accomplished. Extirpated.'

I conveyed kind thoughts to Karen, rang off, lit another cigarette and started to ponder. World One, World Three.

Did I truly have more control over World Three, the world I'd created, than I had over the "real" World One? Was X still the murderer, not some unidentified Y or Z? I thought I was being disingenuous when I told David and Beth I didn't know who'd killed Peter. Maybe I wasn't.

I phoned Abbey House and then drove to the city bypass and the A1. The leaves were turning but the afternoon remembered summer. Despite the weather the Sunday traffic was lighter than usual and the new road had cut journey times. Twenty-five minutes from the *Brigadoon* I jolted along the drive of Abbey House and parked beside the studded oak door. Richard sprang out to greet me, a vision in frayed jeans and work-boots and a sweat-shirt that had seen more shapely days. His handshake was crushing.

This was beyond doubt the Richard Latimer-Brown I'd written, which meant I retained some control over World Three. He was in his mid-fifties, medium height and build, hair and beard seasoned with grey. His voice and sense of humour emanated from public school. I'd made him intelligent, eclectically learned, a hyperactive workaholic with fine manual dexterity, shrewd business sense and a colossal though selective capacity for patience. Loud, charismatic, generous to a fault, he had the tact and the laugh of a hyena.

'Doug! Good to see you again! What's this, Japanese? I thought a Ford was all you could afford! Ha-ha-ha! Ford, afford! Slug! *Slug!* Come and look who the Jap's brought in! Come *on*, Slug! You'll have it dark! My God, Doug, *Japanese*! Ha-ha – afford a Ford! Afford a Ford!'

He drove a silver-grey Mercedes E220 with a personalised number plate and a sticker in the back window reading *Save Our Songbirds.*

'Hired, Richard. Mine's out of commission.'

The doorway was transmuted into the frame of a living portrait. Lydia Gore, known in the village as Mrs Latimer-Brown, was self-consciously picturesque. Seen through a tumble of blonde waves, her smile of greeting simulated pleasure.

'Oh, Piggy, why didn't you tell me Doug was coming?' Richard ignored her, lost in droll vehicular ruminations. She continued: 'I wish I'd known, Doug. Would you like a cup of tea?'

Her black ankle-length skirt flowed ahead of me into the house, up the spiral stone staircase with its slit windows and yellowing prints of Scottish scenes, and along the corridor between metre-thick, tapestry-clad walls to a small kitchen graced with state-of-the-art appliances. Richard entered the house in our wake and on some impulse, or maybe it was planned, vanished into the workshop, an erstwhile cellar. I thought I heard him talking to David, but the conversation was absorbed by the massive stonework and masked by Lydia's prattle.

Seeking new bearings at every step I was in a state of elevated anxiety, chronic subliminal dysphoria. I felt like the survivor of a shipwreck, cast up on an island I'd imagined but never seen, rescued by beings of whom tall tales were told, who accepted me as though I, too, belonged in those same legends. Or my creations were flesh and blood; I, the creator, was a phantom. *Was* this schizophrenia? And why had I left my laptop at the *Brigadoon*?

'… writing anything new?'

Her smile invited an answer.

'A rough plan. Don't know if it'll work.'

'Piggy likes your books. I don't read much, not like Ali. Oh – I got this new Playstation game, it's a hunting game, you have to track a bear or a boar or whatever and you can have dogs and guns, and there's cover – Is the tea OK, Doug? I'm sorry, I don't know where the sugar is, Piggy's put it away – Oh, do you remember Nutty? He came back! Last week, about ten days ago, or – no, eight days, I remember, it was Saturday, when Hearts drew one-all with Rangers – Piggy said he wasn't the same squirrel, but he was, he wanted chocolate chip cookies just like when he lived here …'

The kitchen window commanded a view over lawns and flowerbeds to a panorama of fields and trees. There were oaks and beeches, pines and bird cherries, and tree species I wouldn't name; an oasis of wildlife and dryads in the East Lothian agri-desert. According to chapter four of *The Bronze Bull*, Lydia had found the baby squirrel two summers earlier, fallen from his dray not far from the house. She'd hand-reared him. The animal had learned to accept food from human hands but still craved freedom. She'd called him Nutty, and delighted to watch him scrabble at window-panes, rush around the walls or climb curtains in his quest to surmount the barrier that separated him from the grass, the trees, the open air that were his birthright. Her merriment had betokened an all-too-human inability to comprehend that living creatures aren't toys and imprisonment is torment. I'd deleted the account because it hadn't seemed relevant to the story.

'Seen Alison lately?' I asked. 'Peter's death must have affected her.'

Lydia's effort at sincerity presented as a kind of awed

prurience: Peter's death was dreadful, really shocking, who could have done such a thing? She hadn't seen Alison for a fortnight, though a few days earlier they'd chatted on the phone about their mother's health, a holiday in Istanbul, a protest march in Birmingham and clothes prices in Princes Street.

'Ali goes jogging on the beach at lunch-time when it's fine, before afternoon classes. It's a super beach near the school, especially when the tide's low, so it's nice for a jog if you like jogging, though it's a bit shingly and rocky, and there are lovely rock pools, lots of hermit crabs and starfish–'

Richard's boots resounded in the corridor and he burst into the kitchen like the north wind. His voice preceded him, swathing me in excitement. He'd acquired an early nineteenth century chemical balance with almost all its brass weights, which I must see, and an original Davy lamp, and a piece of surgical equipment, probably late eighteenth century, on which he wanted my opinion. His charisma lifted me from my chair like a fallen leaf and blew me downstairs to the workshop, tea half drunk. He took the stairs three at a time. David had returned to his cottage. I offered my opinion on the surgical device.

Richard said, 'Why did you give up medicine? I've often wondered.' But without pausing for an answer he paraded before me an Edison phonograph that he and David had restored to pristine condition, and an ivory-inlaid Georgian music box, its mechanism rejuvenated.

I'd given up medicine years earlier. A junior doctor in A and E, I'd worked seventy hours non-stop when four traffic accident victims were admitted: a man, D.O.A.; a boy and a girl, D.O.A.; a woman, unconscious. After I'd dealt with her injuries and she was awake again I had to inform her that her husband and children were dead. She asked whether I had children. I said I hadn't. She struck me in the face and wept. I left the ward, bought a pizza with olives and pepperoni, slept until my next shift and then quit medicine.

The workshop walls were adorned with safety notices and tools hung in precise order, each in its place; though one was missing. I didn't mention the lacuna because Richard's manner had undergone one of its sudden shifts. The grey eyes behind the half-moon spectacles fixed on mine. His motive for arranging a *tête-à-tête* became clear.

'Doug, do you know a James Farquhar? Lives in Leith?'

To be precise, Jimmy Farquhar lived in a single-bedroom flat, non-existent in World One, in the maze of tenements between Leith Street and Easter Road. I inferred he'd contacted Richard; again, not something I'd written.

'I know *of* him. Does a lot to raise money for Save the Children and the Children's Hospice in–'

'You know him personally?'

Did I know *Richard*? Or Lydia, or David, or Karen, or any of them?

'Met him. I believe his wife left him a few years ago. Their little boy had died. As far as I know, Jimmy makes money any way he can: heroin user, small-time dealer. He's had convictions for assault.'

'Dangerous chap, then?'

'I wouldn't trust him.'

Richard grunted.

'Could he have killed Peter Wishart?'

I noted that Richard showed little overt distress about the murder of a friend.

'I doubt it, though a surprising number of people seem capable of murder.'

'You think the number's surprising? Hmm? Ha-ha!'

'Maybe not. But why *would* Jimmy Farquhar kill Peter? Why do you ask?'

Richard paced to and fro, fingering a nineteenth century church organ pipe, reviewing his decision to confide, picking his words.

'This is between you and me. Lydia doesn't know. Lydia *doesn't* know. Even David doesn't know all of it.' He allowed me a moment to signify compliance. 'Peter had acquired an item of Greek antiquity. Seemed convinced it was authentic. Paid a lot for it. A lot. I was willing to buy it and allow him a fair profit subject to proof of provenance. James Farquhar phoned yesterday evening and said the item had fallen into his hands. He demanded a hefty price. Less than Peter's, mind you. Less than Peter's. So I need to know about James Farquhar. If he *does* have the item, he killed Peter.'

Richard was in the same dilemma as David. He was morally obliged to share his suspicions with the police, but that would have put the bronze bull for ever beyond his reach; and aside from his compulsion to possess the unique and irreplaceable, he'd paid a retainer for it. I temporised.

'Not necessarily. James Farquhar can be vicious, but he's small and heroin slows him down. It's straining credulity to suppose he could have killed Peter Wishart, even if he knew about the item you mention and decided to–'

'David traced Peter's movements on Friday night. James Farquhar could have done the same.'

'That doesn't follow. He *might* have the item you mention, though. If you meet him I'd recommend somewhere public.'

Richard waved his arms.

'Of course, Doug. Of course. Ha-ha-ha! You'll stay for dinner?'

Another abrupt shift; the topic was closed. I demurred because it was short notice for Lydia, but my objection was dismissed: Lydia would be delighted. I insisted on driving into the village to buy wine. Lydia came with me to purchase milk, chattering without pause. Evidently Richard could shut out white noise. My irritation mounted to anger when she extolled the colours of the leaves on certain trees lining the drive. I'd refused to notice them. The song echoed in my head, and I had to hum the third movement of the trio sonata from the *Musical Offering* to suppress it.

Dinner was iced melon, then lamb with aubergine and a great deal of garlic, followed by lemon sorbet and coffee. Lydia's love of cooking was second only to her passions for hunting and football. 'Not bad, Slug,' said Richard; 'I could eat more of it.' Throughout the meal he dominated a discussion ranging over Europe's economic prospects, the Y2K nonsense, the desirability of private as against public museums for preserving relics, Peter's untimely death, global threats to wildlife, and the care of guinea pigs. His pronouncements were punctuated by the hyena laugh. Even Lydia hardly spoke.

By the time I left I was exhausted. It was dark; there was frost in the air. My hosts stood beside the oak door while I climbed into the Toyota, but Richard dived back into the workshop with an abrupt farewell and left his partner to administer a more lingering adieu.

A hundred yards away, discreet activity was visible at the door of David's cottage. David sometimes entertained ladies of questionable immigration status. He had many contacts. Lydia giggled.

'Career army officer. Never grew up and never will. A thing of duty and a boy forever.'

I doubted whether the pun was original but I smiled. David's antipathy to Lydia seemed to be reciprocated. Predictable though she was, she had the capacity to surprise, albeit artlessly. Reiterating her giggle, she said: 'He looks more boyish than ever now he's shaved off that silly moustache.'

8

Inhaling cigarette smoke, I studied the invisible garden behind the *Brigadoon* and tried to order my thoughts. Mahler's eighth symphony squeezed through the speaker of my radio.

I'd driven too fast on my return from Abbey House, overtaken on the bypass only by a presumably off-duty hearse. I was dismayed by what I'd achieved, excited by the new evidence for supernormal power, appalled by the responsibility. I'd switched on the laptop as soon as the bedroom door closed behind me but my fingers had frozen over the keys. How to begin? I echoed the ancient prayer that Mahler had set to music in the first movement of his symphony, invoking the spirit of creation: *Veni, creator spiritus.*

Like Karen and her graceful home in West Arthur Street, Abbey House and its residents were just as I'd written them. Nevertheless, my reactions had been at odds with expectation. As author of *The Bronze Bull* I'd distanced myself from Richard's bulldozer qualities and sympathised with Lydia. However, Richard had proved more congenial in the flesh, his overbearing manner a facet of his energy and passion, while Lydia had annoyed me. It would have been hubristic or inhumane to rewrite her, though I wanted to. She was bright enough to transcend the silly girlie act. Perhaps it attracted Richard. Or perhaps she'd been nervous; but if I was an old friend, why would she be?

The most striking feature of the afternoon had been Abbey House itself. It was precisely as I'd envisioned it, yet its baronial solidity, its unequivocal assertion of the right to exist, its four-square rootedness in East Lothian's bedrock, had filled me with awe. Surely such a monument was too massive to be founded in one man's imagination. Like the surge of sound that ends the first movement of Mahler's eighth, its weight seemed too great for a single mind to bear. It was hard to accept that Abbey House was fictional.

I needed to address three interrelated questions. First, what was happening in *The Bronze Bull*, the plot of which had advanced beyond my partial draft and sketches for further chapters? Second, what could and should I do about those advances, by writing or participating? Third, how could I escape from World Three and return to World One? How could I get home?

This third question was paramount but unanswerable; the phone book remained innocent of "Acheron Taxis". If I was a plaything of the gods I'd no choice but do their will until they turned to other toys. If I'd slipped into a parallel universe I must return, if at all, by means unknown. But did I wish to go back to World One? The company of people who seem to like and trust me was pleasurable. With the sole exception of David Michie, the characters in *The Bronze Bull* had welcomed me. Also, I felt no urge to check my room for bugs as I did in World One, and I could walk or drive without looking over my shoulder. Moreover, if I could rid David of his moustache by writing, I could surely expunge anything disagreeable from World Three. Nevertheless the sense of unreality was discomfiting. The glass wall that separated me from this fictional place was unbreakable and had no door. Karen's kiss on my cheek, David's harsh grip on my shoulder and Richard's vigorous handshake had testified to the solidity of my creations, yet the characters, even the buildings, remained in my mind a celluloid light-show. I craved World One as the exile craves his native land, whatever dangers lurked there. However, there was no obvious resolution to this dilemma.

The first of my trinity of questions was straightforward. Jimmy Farquhar had obtained the bronze bull and hidden it in his flat. Richard's name had been mentioned during Peter's dinner with Spiro; Jimmy, seated at the next table, had heard it. Now he was trying to sell the bull to Richard. Did he know about David? No matter: he must have realised that the bull was integral to the murder investigation so Iain would be seeking it, putting him at risk of arrest, so he'd be keen to offload it.

As author of the story I had to decide the provenance and fate of the bronze bull by literary judgment, but as a participant in the story my judgment had to be moral. Here, my first and second questions overlapped: there was no clear boundary between the development of the story and my literary and practical actions regarding it. The issues were tangled. I already carried a burden of guilt: Peter, Karen, Alison, even Spiro.

The sensible approach was to ascertain what *could* be done before deciding what *should* be done. Synthetic necessary truth: the acceptable is circumscribed by the achievable. As far as action was concerned, World Three appeared little different from World One. My limitations were evident: I was a middle-aged male, neither strong nor fit nor in any way remarkable. On the other hand, I boasted a detailed understanding of the situation and the people involved, having created them, which on the face of it gave me a big advantage over both Iain and the murderer. Moreover, I believed I was good at listening to people, empathising, eliciting information.

An interesting question arose: what would happen if I died in World Three? More broadly, I thought, suppose I were to remain in World Three for decades. In time, old age would beset me. My death in an alien universe could unleash a classic science-fiction paradox and must therefore be forbidden by the laws of nature, so the dislocation of my existence has made me immortal. However, I wasn't disposed to test that hypothesis. The world might be abnormal but it behoved me to exercise normal caution.

The potentialities of writing, I decided, might be eluci-dated by further experiments. I sat before the laptop and typed a summary of what I knew:

Items that pertain directly to me aren't translated from the written word to actuality. For example, I couldn't write a toothbrush into existence. I had to buy one.

In particular, I can't write myself back to World One, or find my flat.

I can sometimes alter external events, but only in ac-cordance with the natural scheme of things. For instance, if the change in last night's weather did result from my typing, it happened long enough afterwards to seem un-exceptional.

Changes I write aren't effected retrospectively. The world accommodates itself to my alterations as best it can but normal chronology can't be distorted. In World One, I could have decided against David's moustache and edited the draft text so he never had one. In World Three, David did wear a moustache but he shaved it off. Therefore I don't, for example, have the power to bring Peter back to life, or eliminate any of the information that Iain and his team have gleaned.

I stopped typing, rolled a joint and smoked it. The small lump of hash in my pocket grew smaller. The ethereal sounds of Mahler's Faustian fantasy eddied in my mind. As the final notes of the symphony filled the room I started to type again, praying for Apollo's guidance.

The barman of the Brigadoon dropped a bottle of vodka and swore under his breath. James Merriman emerged from his office and entered the bar and glared at him. I sat at my table drinking a glass of red wine, mulling over the contents of my next chapter, watching the barman clear up the debris of broken glass and spirits under the cold gaze of the manager. The young woman who'd been drinking at the bar came to sit beside me, but my attention was fixed on the accident and its aftermath so I didn't notice her until she murmured, 'You seem preoccupied. Would you like to go to bed with me?'

The paragraph was neither golden prose nor gripping fantasy but perhaps it would serve its purpose. I saved it, turned off the laptop, extinguished the joint, silenced the radio, which was now broadcasting an interview with an actress of whom I'd never heard, and went down to the bar. It was quiet: at a corner table, two elderly men in venerable suits were drinking pints and chatting softly. One of them nodded to me. A young woman was seated at the bar drinking vodka and tonic, Linda's customary tipple.

I noted her presence, implicit in the paragraph I'd just composed, and wondered whether I'd seen her arrive at the hotel before writing her into being. She wore a smart business suit, but sensible shoes and thick red socks. The suit contained an attractive figure but she was facing away from me. I looked around. There was no one in the bar apart from me, the young woman, the two old men and the barman, who seemed taciturn if not hostile.

Buying a glass of red wine, I thought, shouldn't prejudice the outcome of my experiment. I moved to an unoccupied table, lit a cigarette, sipped the wine and began to consider my next chapter. *Should I visit Jimmy Farquhar, assuming his flat is where I wrote it? Should I call on Robbie Macrae and Niall Ferguson, who'll be disappointed at failing to interview Karen? Should the focus be on the police investigation, or on Karen, whose grief cuts me so deeply I can't staunch the flow of guilt?* Perhaps I could assuage her misery, as I'd half-promised Beth. An idea began to form. But I had to remember I wasn't a character in the story; I was only the author.

The crash of the falling vodka bottle startled me. The barman swore under his breath. One of the old gentlemen in the corner made a comment and his companion laughed. James Merriman emerged from his office and glared at his subordinate, who returned the look, half cowed, half defiant, and sidled away to find mop and dustpan and brush. Young Mr Merriman watched his exertions coldly.

My heart thumped and pins and needles exploded in my extremities. Did excitement alter the blood calcium level? I ought to have known; but the afternoon's revelations, accumulated emotional exhaustion and cannabis had impaired my powers of recall. However, it was now beyond reasonable doubt that I could influence World Three by writing about it.

'Dr Carmichael? Douglas Carmichael?' Her smile was crimson. 'Ye look preoccupied. Can I have a word with ye?'

I stared across the table until the smile dimmed.

'You have the advantage of me, as they used to say. A word about what?'

The smile re-ignited. She *wasn't* like Linda: her eyes were hazel, her hair mousy brown, her chin determined, her nose too long. She proffered a business card.

'Emma Menzies, *Daily Record*.'

She pronounced the surname traditionally: "Minghies".

'Ah. You know Niall Ferguson. You want to talk about the Wishart murder.'

'Mphm. Niall said ye were quick. But ye looked a wee bit stunned when I spoke to ye.'

I contrived a leer.

'You didn't say what I expected you to say.'

'What did ye expect me to say?' She studied my face and her mouth twisted. 'Och, ye're kidding! Ye thought I'd walk up to a stranger in a hotel bar an' offer sex? Aye, right.'

I shouldn't have been talking to this woman. Tabloid reporters do no one any good. But the excitement of proving my power over World Three had suspended my judgment, and the hash hadn't helped.

'Do you want to talk about the Wishart case, Ms Menzies, or are you trying a novel chat-up line?'

'The former. I can find better targets fer the latter. How's the late Mr Wishart's girlfriend?'

'Bereaved.'

'Aye, right. So what's she saying about the murder, like?'

'Nothing in my hearing. You probably know what she's told the police, which is more than I do.'

Red-top reporters buy information from police officers, in addition to official police press briefings. Without breaching the law, they can use that information to influence juries, helping to ensure convictions, particularly in high-profile cases. After the verdict, they demonise the convicted person to ensure his, or occasionally her, effective elimination from the human race. The Scottish gutter press is a cog in the guilt-manufacturing machine of the justice system. It also fulfils something of the social role that public executions served during the eighteenth century.

'When'll ye next see Karen?' said Emma.

'After she's fit to return home and to the Museum, I suppose. Meanwhile she's staying out of everyone's way. Don't ask me where.'

'But ye ken where. Ye ken fine where she is. And ye know what happens to folk mixed up in criminal cases that dinnae co-operate wi' journalists?'

'*Far* more serious consequences than obstructing the police, I imagine.'

'Ye'd better believe it. Ye'd be surprised how much we ken about Douglas Carmichael and how much mair we can find out.'

It was empty menace but it chilled me. What *had* she learned about me? I drank the rest of my wine, disguising the hit, and laughed in her face. I offered her a cigarette; she gestured manicured disgust.

'Another drink, then, Emma?'

'I'll get them. If there's any vodka left sin' yon wanker dropped the bottle.'

She snapped her fingers and the taciturn barman responded. Drinks acquired, she resumed her interrogation. This time she leaned towards me and lowered her voice.

'Dinnae mess me around, Doug, right? I want to know whit Peter Wishart got frae Spiro Andropoulos in the restaurant on Friday night, a few hours afore he was murdered.'

'I'll tell you what I've heard but you'll know already: it was a suitcase. My informant didn't see what was in it. Didn't the police divulge the contents?'

'They didnae. The guy leading the investigation kens whit was in it but it seems he's the only yin whit does. Exceptin' you, maybe. And Karen.'

So David wasn't the only World Three inhabitant to attribute near-omniscience to me.

'Iain McArdle. He isn't telling?'

'He's no' even telling his ain minions. He's fannying 'em aboot and they're fannying us aboot. You know whit they tellt us? "The suitcase is believed to contain an item of archaeological value." Who dae they think they're kidding?'

In terms of revenue and police interest, international trafficking of stolen art treasures and antiquities was second only to the illegal drug trade, though people-trafficking ran it close. I chose not to enlighten Emma.

'Not you, evidently. But if *you* can't elicit the information, what makes you think I can?'

'You knew Peter and you know Karen, and folk tell ye things. So I'm sure ye know. Dinnae worry, I'll no' use yer name. And I pay plenty o' cash if the information's good. Nae questions asked.'

My smile was almost involuntary.

'You'll tempt me to invent something plausible, Emma.

But Peter did deal in "items of archaeological value", and I suppose Spiro Andropoulos does, too. Have the police released him?'

She took a petulant swig of vodka. Mr Merriman returned to his den.

'Aye. Weird, eh?' She wiped her mouth with the back of her hand, smearing the crimson lipstick. 'Come on, Doug, ye ken as well as I do, it's got to be drugs. International traffickin', big time. McArdle couldnae prove Andropoulos was a courier; nae intelligence, nobody grassed; so he couldnae charge him. He couldnae even keep him in the country, for all the Advocate Depute will summon him as a witness when there's a trial. Bad luck, eh no? Everybody wants to know who took Wishart oot and nicked the suitcase. What *I* want to know is whit was in it.'

So much for control of World Three; this conversation was running wild. Building a cathedral of matchsticks is the business of conspiracy theorists, not hard-nosed reporters, and Emma's fantasy hadn't enough matchsticks for a side-chapel. So why the mad conjecture? Frustration at the lack of police information might have been an efficient cause but hardly a material or formal one. She'd divulged one new fact, namely that Spiro had left the country, but the chain of argument was missing a link. Something had happened that I didn't know. And this was supposed to be *my* story.

'I've no contacts on the drugs scene, Emma. In any case, Peter didn't deal drugs. And if it *is* just another drugs case, why won't McArdle say so? Police appeal for information about drug gangs.'

'Correct. So whatever this stuff is, it's new and dangerous. Peter Wishart was a contact fer Andropoulos and his cronies. Their main outlet in Scotland. Come on, Doug, it's no' rocket science. The public has a right to know whit sort o' drug Andropoulos and Wishart were dealing and whit it does tae its users. All I want is the information. I'll keep yer name quiet. That's a promise.'

Her eyes were dreaming of national press, banner headlines: New Drugs Menace, another threat to vulnerable youth. Her soul was incandescent with lust for fame; the final cause. I shook my head.

'It doesn't ring true, Emma.'

She could recognise a dead horse when she'd flogged it. She banged her glass on the table and stood up.

'OK, Doug, so ye won't tell. Remember, I warned ye.'

She marched away, gutting her handbag for car keys. At the exit she turned and grinned. The keys dangled limply from her fingers. Long nails. The varnish matched the lipstick but clashed with the socks.

'Maybe ye've no' heard, Doug. An hour after Spiro Andropoulos disembarked at Athens airport he wiz shot dead i' the street. Fer spiriting an item o' archaeological value out o' the country? No, I dinnae think so. The Greek polis are hunting the gunman. Now, want me to hint tae *our* polis that ye ken more aboot this drug consignment than ye're telling? Or will ye phone me i' the press room afore noon the morrow?'

The barman ignored the exchange. The two old men seemed uninterested, but they admired Emma's departing figure. They resumed their *tête-à-tête* and chuckled.

Emma's speculations were groundless, her threat hollow. But she'd given me her business card, and her exit line was better than David Michie's.

9

Grey chill oozed from the asphalt Firth under a wet Monday sky. I'd lingered over breakfast, reviewed my notes, and then followed the coast road through Prestonpans and Longniddry and parked opposite the Gosford Estate. Linda and I had come here soon after we'd started to live together. She'd never shown any wish to return.

My shoes were unsuited to the terrain so I chose to wait rather than walk. I lit a cigarette in the lee of the Toyota, hoping fresh air and nicotine would clear my head. There were aromas of salt tide and seaweed, decomposing guano and molluscs. Gulls cried. A few other cars were parked: nature lovers, dog lovers, lovers. Clumps of sea buckthorn dripped. Pale droplets formed on withered marram and sea-lime. Cockenzie power station was a ghostly presence beyond the bay to my left, wet sands curved towards Aberlady on my right, and the Isle of May was barely visible through the mist. The scene was indistinguishable from its World One counterpart. I might have slipped back into reality since the previous evening, in which case there'd be no Alison. The thought evoked unexpected dejection.

Who'd shot Spiro Andropoulos? My ignorance of his killer's identity and motive might imply his death had nothing to do with *The Bronze Bull*. But it might not. On the other hand, *was* he dead, if I was still in the world in which he existed? My only evidence was the word of a tabloid journalist. Those questions had kept me awake during the night but no answers had vouchsafed themselves. However, the restless hours had yielded plans for the next two days. Little writing would be involved. The written word could be crucial, but I'd learned to fear its sometimes uncontrollable consequences. Scrupulous command over one's manuscript is essential. I might have envied Emma and her kind, whose profession required no such assiduousness, but one can't envy what one desires not to emulate.

The corner of my eye glimpsed a rat, dark and wet as the sky, darting along the foreshore and behind the rocks. Burning pain pierced my right temple and I grunted and jerked, dropping my cigarette. Tiny ripples shivered over a rock pool that reflected the undifferentiated greyness. I leaned on the side of the Toyota and controlled my breathing.

A steady jog of trainers on shingle approached from the west. I stepped around the vehicle and raised a hand in greeting. Alison trotted towards me: white tee shirt and shorts, muscular arms and legs, flushed face, perspiration. Saving her breath to pay off the oxygen debt, she nodded to me and sneered at the Land Cruiser.

'Gas guzzler. Rich little woman's car. Takes the kids to school. Can't see over the dashboard.'

'You stereotypers are all the same.'

She gasped amusement, but I sensed a diatribe rising behind her dam of reticence. There was anger in her eyes. I wondered why. However, her next words were innocuous.

'Ecologically unsound, Doug. Where's the Capri?'

She had a blue Fiat Uno, economical on fuel. But she'd revealed that she, like Richard, knew what car I drove in World One.

'Out of action. I hired the beast for driving on ground like this. And to Abbey House.'

She tilted her head. I continued:

'I went yesterday. I gather Lydia hasn't been in touch since Saturday. Maybe you weren't around.'

'Think she'd have called if I had been? Iddy's the most self-centred bitch in Creation. Has big sugar daddy, big money, big house; why bother about big sister? Maybe she's got what she deserves. He's too old for her. Treats her like shit.'

"Iddy" had been the infant Alison's attempt at her baby sister's name. As a teenager she'd infuriated Lydia by suggesting she buy a yacht and call it "Iddy".

'That's harsh. Of course, Lydia isn't my sister.'

'And Richard's your mate.'

According to the manuscript, Alison's relationships with Richard and Lydia were more amicable than she implied. Few of their communications and visits erupted into animosity.

'Climb into the gas guzzler,' I said, 'before you catch pneumonia. I'll get you to school in time to shower and change.'

'Destroy my street cred.'

But she opened the passenger door and sprang into the seat. My ascent to the driver's seat was painstaking. I closed the door, felt for cigarettes and decided against.

'As a matter of interest, Alison, where *were* you yesterday?'

She gave me a considering look.

'Why's it a matter of interest?'

'Just being a friend. Wanting to know you're OK.'

She stared out of the side window, not unleashing the pent-up fury I'd sensed. I started the engine. She shrugged.

'The dell you told me about in Berwickshire. Amazing, you *telling* me something.'

So Alison knew about Linda, and about our dell. My mind's eye saw the gate, the burn springing from the soil, the rough track winding downhill among the trees, the sunlit clearing. Peace and solitude. *Am Brunnen von dem* … A photograph turned to the wall. *I'd told Alison? How?*

'Yes. Peace and solitude. They're great. And you're tough, Alison. But sometimes we need a friend.'

Disingenuous, Doug. I only wanted to know whether her mental state matched my description. She laughed without humour, took two deep breaths and asked me to drive her to school. She was silent most of the way.

As I negotiated the gates she said, 'I'm fine, Doug. I was bereaved in advance. I grieved for twelve months after we split up.' I concentrated on parking the overlarge vehicle in a tight space. She continued: 'He never wanted to be kept on the straight and narrow so he chose someone who didn't care what risks he took. I knew she'd be the death of him.'

'You think Karen killed him?'

She shrugged again. After a moment she added: 'You know how we met? I was in an athletics tournament in East Berlin, just before the wall came down. There he was among the spectators, stunning-looking guy gabbing to the officials in German, doing deals. I came second in the discus and he took me to a restaurant where the Party members went. String of Mercs outside. A few days later he drove a van full of art treasures out of the country and flogged them around Western Europe. Got home, phoned me to ask me out. He made several runs like that, lifting stuff from Eastern Europe and selling it in the west. Invested his profits in housing. Raked in rents. Then he got into stealing archaeological treasures and selling them to collectors. That was how he met Richard. Then Richard came to dinner and met Iddy. It was how Peter met bloody Karen, too.'

A long speech for a private, self-contained woman; but about Peter, not her. The school grounds were turbulent with children, high voices whirling and bouncing, skipping and wrestling. The Toyota shook as though it were sobbing.

'The papers would love that story.'

She snorted.

'Niall Ferguson's been after me. But we were kids together and Robbie's a friend so I know him too well. Mind you, I'm going to Cramond–'

'I've encountered one of Niall's pack, too: Emma Menzies, *Daily Wreckage*. She said Peter and his Greek contact were drug-running.'

'Bollocks.'

'My sentiments exactly. Emma was struck by the coincidence that Peter and the Greek were killed within two days of one another.'

She gave no overt reaction, though she looked away. I asked whether the police had talked to her. She said she was cold and must shower and change. She shivered, then pecked me on the cheek and opened the door. As she alighted from the car she asked, 'How about you, Doug? Coping?'

'Like you. I talk when I have to.'

'That'd be a first. Try to remember: friendship cuts both ways.'

I sat, window open, watching her. As she walked across the school yard she was accosted by a thin bespectacled woman with short dark hair.

'Good jog, Ali?'

'Fair to middling, Jan. Shelves still attached?' She pointed at my maligned vehicle. 'You know Doug, don't you?'

'Of course. Hi, Doug, nice to see you again. You been jogging too?'

I nodded through the window and conjured a smile.

'No chance. Causes unhealthy hypertrophy of the ventricular myocardium.'

'You took the words right out of my mouth. Shelves are brilliant, Ali, you're the perfect man about the house. Except you don't leave any mess.'

I closed the window, manoeuvred the Toyota out of its parking space, avoiding the maelstrom of juvenile bodies, and drove back to town. Once again I was unsettled; who was Jan? Obviously a fellow-teacher, but ... No matter, she probably didn't figure in *The Bronze Bull*. My watch told me I'd missed Emma's deadline. She'd be devastated. I was more concerned about Iain McArdle's movements.

I located Radio Three and listened to a recording of the Brahms fourth; not the best performance but I needed music. Instead of following the bypass I drove into Musselburgh and stopped for a late lunch and two cups of coffee. Then I returned to Edinburgh.

There were roadworks around Jock's Lodge so I cut through Duddingston and Holyrood Park. Easter Road was solid with traffic, as always, but I found a parking space in a side street. I bought a tartan sports bag, paying cash, and took the five minute walk to a flat that didn't exist in World One. Within little more than forty-eight hours I'd have met all the obvious murder suspects except Seamus Goldstein: Karen, David, Richard, Alison and Jimmy. Maybe Lydia, too. Therefore, I seemed to be ahead of Iain. But I lacked the resources of Lothian and Borders Constabulary.

Perhaps there'd be other suspects, reflecting deeper and darker conspiracies, when the plot of *The Bronze bull* developed further.

The common stair of the tenement stank of neglect, misuse and disinfectant. The dark brown paintwork was dusty and peeling. The doors were innocent of names. Surprisingly, his bell worked. I stood three feet back from the threshold. Suspicion radiated from the spy-hole. Then bolts and safety chains were unfastened and the door half-opened.

'Whit the fuck *you* wantin'?'

David wasn't my only detractor in World Three. Alison's unspoken anger haunted me, but Jimmy Farquhar's animosity was unequivocal. He was small, unshaven, red-eyed, clad in vest and jeans, barefoot and unwashed, arms festooned with tattoos. His teeth were brown and sparse, his hair thin. The air of the flat was redolent of uncleanliness and narcotics.

'I want a word, Jimmy.'

'Whit aboot?'

'You have something for sale. I can match Richard Latimer-Brown's price.'

'Whit the fuck ye talkin' aboot?'

'Richard's getting cold feet because the police are looking for it. You'll need to drop your price if you want to sell it to him before they catch you with it. But you can sell it to me, right now.'

He stepped back. A jerk of the head invited me in. I took a deep breath and stepped into the hallway. My skin crawled. I dropped the sports bag.

'Whit ye wantin' it fer, like?'

'Once it's off your hands, will it matter? Just don't tell anyone you sold it to me.'

'Who sez I've got it? Some cunt grassed me?'

'Work it out for yourself, Jimmy. How many people have you offered it to? How many others have *they* told? Richard told me you'd contacted him. I don't think he's mentioned it to anyone else, but other people aren't as discreet.'

His overheated eyes calculated.

'Three grand. Cash up front.'

'Think I'm daft, Jimmy? Two grand. And I want to see the goods first.'

He glanced behind him: shadows, dirt. The floor was bare wood. His feet risked splinters and infection. My heart thumped in my ears. Why was I afraid? This flat, this man, this situation, were fictions. Fictions couldn't harm me. Yet I had to treat them as real.

'Listen, I didnae kill the cunt, right? He wiz deid when I got there. That's the God's honest truth. An' I ken whae *did* kill 'im, I seen–'

'That's what they all say. But they'll find your prints on the murder weapon.'

'They'll no'! I never touched it wi' ma haunds!'

'What, carried the hammer all the way to the Meadows

and never touched it? Not even while you were placing it beside the sleeping tramp?'

'Fuck's sake! Ye werenae there! Who telled ye?'

'You'd be surprised. I want the bull, Jimmy. Two grand.'

But I'd pushed him too far. His, 'Aye, right, whitever' was overly casual, and as I followed him along the hall he spun without warning, knife flying at my rib-cage. He was left-handed. My adrenalin level, his heroin intake and the goddess of Fortune conspired to his disadvantage. Reactions faster than usual I kicked hard, landing a blow on his shin, and grabbed his arm with both hands. I couldn't have held it long, but as he staggered, stigmatising me as a fucking bastard, I kicked again and connected with his scrotum. He gasped and collapsed and I kicked him three times on the head, vicious with fright. He lay still, not even swearing. Blood trickled from his nose and mouth. The knife remained in his fist.

Shaking, I dashed into the nearest room; the bedroom. Sheets tangled and filthy. Nothing under the bed but trainers and boots. I flung open drawers, emptying the contents in armsful. Then the wall cupboard. Nothing hidden among the clothes. A high shelf, empty. *Zeus help me, where is it?* A long mirror from a junk shop stood on the floor. Nothing behind it except dust and fluff. On the dressing table, a grimy photograph smiled from the past: Jimmy's vanished wife, Lesley, and little Shaun, who'd died. I peered through the doorway. The architrave was chipped. He was lying where I'd left him. Sweat broke on my palms and forehead.

It's fiction. It isn't real. It's just a story and I'm telling it. But repeating those words had no effect; I went on sweating and shaking. What kind of story isn't affected by words?

I scuttled into the living room. There was a children's cartoon on the television, sound muted. Maybe the carpet had once had colour. I threw cushions aside, upended chairs, checked for loose floorboards. I scanned the window ledge, under the television, behind the gas fire. On the mantelpiece was a thank-you card from the children's hospice: 'Thank you Uncle Jimmy for our lovely presents'. It was a mass of coloured crêpe paper stuck in random, brilliant patterns on a cheap cardboard base.

I couldn't find Peter's suitcase. Contents of shelves crashed to the floor. I couldn't find it. Heart in mouth. Pounding. Throat parched. Hard to breathe.

The bathroom stank. My stomach heaved. The case wasn't in the lavatory cistern. Nor under the bath; no room. Nor in the airing cupboard. The floorboards were solid. *Oh Zeus.*

Had he moved? Was his knife hand closer to his side?

I dived into the kitchen, my whole body sweating now. A floorboard was loose. I grabbed an unwashed carving knife from the sink and prised it up, the handle slipping in my grasp. It took two hours, though my watch made it twenty seconds. There was nothing beneath but lath and plaster and rubble. No suitcase among the clutter on the table, no bronze bull. *Well, it would hardly be out in the open, would it, Doug?* Wall cupboards: packets of food and unused plastic utensils, and the heroin stash, worth a few pounds on the street. Did he use the washing machine? Not for storing archaeological treasures. No bronze bull in the fridge.

Then I froze. My eyes stared at a rubber band hanging from the work surface.

Movement in the hall; groans, muffled obscenities.

Why is there a rubber band …?

The carving knife was still in my hand but I needed another weapon. I crept backwards, staying at floor level, sneaked the sink cupboard open, felt inside with my free hand. Stared towards the kitchen door. Sweat stung my eyes. The sounds continued. What was he doing? My breathing was spasmodic. My left hand slipped on the waste pipe; found a bucket, a floor cloth, a brush, the edge of a shelf. *Good, I could jam the bucket over his head and hit him with the brush. Oh, and a dustpan. A veritable armoury.* I heard him stagger to his feet. He knew I was still in the flat. He was starting to quest for me. It wouldn't take long, though his movements were sluggish. My hand discovered a plastic bottle; too light and fragile. But there was something bigger beside it: solid, leather-clad. Peter's case. Shock leapt up my arm and into my throat and stomach.

Zeus had answered my prayer. But the gods take even as they give. It was too late. Only seconds remained before he entered the kitchen.

The doorbell rang, three times. Peremptory.

Police? They could save my life. But then they'd charge me with assault to the endangerment of life, attempted robbery, perverting the course of justice … perhaps other offences. I stifled a giggle.

Jimmy faced the classic existential dilemma, the either-or moment. Should he locate and eliminate his assailant, who knew too much about him, or answer the door? My heart rate climbed and climbed. I listened. Dragging footsteps traversed the hall. Which way were they going? The carving knife shook in my hand. Sweat soaked the handle.

The front door opened. So loud, so rapid was the pulse in my ears that I couldn't identify the voices or hear what they said. But there were angry words. Someone tried to enter. Jimmy had a knife. There were sounds of a tussle; grunting; a soft, heavy bump. The door slammed. Footsteps galloped down the common stair and disappeared. Silence fell.

My heart thumped. My watch ticked. No other sound.

Minutes passed. Slowly, very slowly, I rose from my foetal crouch, holding the edge of the sink. My legs were not to be trusted. My right foot was bruised from Jimmy's cranium. At length I tiptoed to the kitchen door, avoiding the hole where I'd lifted the floorboard. I maintained my grip on the carving knife. It was no longer shaking as much.

Jimmy lay on his right side, four feet from the front door, motionless. The handle of his knife protruded from between, at a guess, his fifth and sixth ribs. The entire blade had penetrated vest, skin and intercostal muscle. His eyes were open. Not blinking.

With sudden calm I picked up my sports bag, returned to the kitchen, replaced the carving knife on the sink, washed my hands (*why?*), lifted the suitcase from the cupboard, put it into the bag and left the flat. Stepping over Jimmy was the hardest part. It required a major effort of will. I'd seen and handled corpses, including recently-dead ones, but I wasn't there in a professional capacity. I was sure that as I stepped over him he'd return to life, seize me and bear me to the ground. Happily, my certainty was misplaced. His eyes remained open. He didn't move. I kept watching him as I fiddled the door open and sidled on to the stair. Then I ran.

Half-way down the street I dropped the bag, doubled

up and vomited my lunch over the pavement. An elderly woman walking a black poodle said, literally, 'Tut-tut,' and hurried past. No one else seemed to notice.

I recovered the bag with its precious contents and, legs trembling and vision clouded, found my way back to the car. Twenty minutes elapsed before I dared to drive. I stayed well below the speed limit and took the greatest care.

10

My skin had passed naked through a car wash. Tremor locked my body. My stomach was knotted. My heart wouldn't resume its normal rate. My senses registered random fragments. My mind could formulate no action. My foot hurt.

The noise from Jimmy's flat must have alerted the neighbours. They'd have kept watch. Seen me leave. Described me to the police. The woman with the poodle would have known from which stair I'd fled, loot in hand. The lines must have been jammed with reports of my driving. Police headquarters would have collated the information and sent cars to the *Brigadoon*. I knew they'd be waiting for me. Before the Toyota reached Grange Road I'd formulated four disparate accounts of what had happened.

But no one was waiting. I sneaked into the hotel. Why hadn't I been challenged? Surely my face, my hands, my clothes, stank of Jimmy Farquhar's death? They were playing cat-and-mouse. Mr Merriman, passing through the lobby as I entered, smiled and said, 'Good afternoon, sir, will you be wanting dinner this evening?' Shock of realisation: it *was* still afternoon. I croaked out a negative.

Too much had occurred in the tale I'd created that wasn't of my making: Karen's outburst about Alison, the appearances of Beth and Jan, the death of Spiro Andropoulos, the hiding place Jimmy had chosen for the bull. I'd never imagined, still less written, the crude fight, or planned

Jimmy's death. Had Peter been in my place he'd have over-powered Jimmy in minutes, ascertained the whereabouts of the bull and departed with it. There need have been no bloodshed. On the other hand, Peter might have sought vengeance for the theft. I saw him rising from the mortuary slab, replacing organs set aside by the pathologist, marching with shattered skull and indomitable purpose to Leith, confronting Jimmy at the door, stabbing him with his own knife.

But would Peter have left the killing unreported? Wouldn't he have checked for residual life, hope of resuscitation? At least closed the dead man's eyes? Those tasks had been beyond me. Peter would have stayed cool. He'd have selected and followed the best course. He wouldn't have been immobilised with shock, incapable of decision.

What I'd planned for *The Bronze Bull* could no longer be trusted. It had become irrelevant whether, in my conception, Jimmy had murdered Peter. Some would see gratuitous denial of a crime as tantamount to confession. One thing was clear: Jimmy had tracked Peter from the restaurant or intercepted his homeward route, otherwise he couldn't have acquired the bronze bull. So if he hadn't killed Peter he'd witnessed the killing. Indeed, he'd told me so. Had he resorted to blackmail and met his end at the killer's hands? On the other hand, his death might have been unrelated to the case. Violence clings to the coat-tails of the heroin trade.

I returned to his flat. He lay where I'd left him, staring and unseeing. Taking care not to hurt him I withdrew the knife from his side. He sat up, eyes unblinking, and extended his left hand. I placed the knife in it and closed his fingers around the handle. The movement of the blade towards my rib-cage was hypnotic. I made no attempt to avoid it. A tramp shuffled past the high window, sandwich board over his shoulders: REPENT, SINNER, FOR Y2K IS AT HAND.

I awoke on my bed in the *Brigadoon*. A stabbing pain in my ribs restored my capacity to move. Still shaking, I sat up. My injured right foot was swelling; tenia synovitis, I presumed. With a stupendous effort I shook off my clothes and stood under the shower. I remained there for a long time. The pain eased, though my skin remained raw.

A semblance of vitality returned. I put on clean clothes and drank whisky from the mini-bar. My skin burned and my proprioceptors were knocked off balance. Food was necessary but impossible. I had to dispose of the clothes I'd worn and then report Jimmy's death without drawing further attention. And decide what to do with the bronze bull.

Several Classical authors had related the story of the Bull of Phalaris. Versions differed but overall they probably encompassed a grain of truth. Perhaps the gruesome instrument had never been used, notwithstanding the claims of Lucian and Cicero, though if Phalaris *had* tormented the creator in his own creation he'd have acted in character. No surviving Classical text reported a scale model of the Bull. A master metalworker could have made one, but the "bronze bull" of my novel-in-progress was my own invention, and any evidence I could adduce for or against its authenticity would also be my invention. The object in Peter's suitcase, in my sports bag, had no known counterpart in World One.

I lifted the fictional bull from the case. It was heavy, almost a foot long, uniformly green, and it seemed to shimmer. Its antiquity, genuine or feigned, quivered along my forearm nerve-tracts. Hair rose on my scalp. I wouldn't have cared to scrape away the verdigris to expose the ancient or not so ancient bronze. The tiny pipes set into the flared nostrils were delicate. If this object was indeed two and a half millennia old their survival was miraculous. I placed the creature on top of the television like a sacrifice on an altar, relieved to set it down.

There was an A4 folder in the case. It contained a receipted invoice in Greek, a reprint of an article from the *European Journal of Archaeology*, a sheaf of analytical data, various writings in Italian, Greek and French, and a few numbered labels. Those items might during the course of the novel prove the bronze bull to be authentic, as I'd intended, but the story was no longer following the path I'd planned. From the World Three perspective, what I believed about the bull mattered little; I was no archaeologist. The model and the documents could have been forgeries. Expert opinions were needed, detailed analyses. Karen was far better qualified than Richard in that regard and she could access the necessary resources.

But this was absurd. The bull existed, along with the documentation, only because I'd conceived it. I could make it genuine or fake at a literary whim. Moreover, I could, indeed must, decide who'd receive it. However, a voice below the veneer of reason whispered that since it had reached the *Brigadoon* it had grown. Standing atop the television it glowed, dominating the room. I forced my hands around it, thrust it into its case, shoved the case into my sports bag, hid it in the wardrobe and jammed my briefcase in front of it. My mind heard it bellowing, craving freedom.

Suppose I gave it to Richard. If it were genuine he'd become the possessor of another unique, perhaps priceless, treasure. But from a literary perspective, so what? I could contrive another theft, perhaps another murder, but there had been too many already. Surfeit cloys the reader's appetite. Otherwise, options would be limited. Dramatically speaking, to give the *genuine* bull to Richard would prove a dead end. However, if the bull were a fake, Richard and David would move mountains to trace the genuine article, if such existed. Many possibilities for plot development would open: *inter alia*, the traffickers would be exposed and the murderer or murderers identified.

The opposite would follow if Karen received the bull. If it were proved a fake it would be scrapped, or consigned to an unvisited store-room, buried under the dust of Lethe. The story would descend into bathos. However, if the bull were authenticated, the plot would grow hydra-headed: reconstruction of the image's creation and its convoluted history, arguments about the culture of Akragas, current and future ownership, tracing of the traffickers: limitless possibilities. The murder story would become part of a larger, more intricate whole. I'd planned such a development when I sketched the novel. I'd wanted the bull to be the real protagonist, hence the working title. The text had been drafted with that in mind until Saturday morning.

To change objectives part-way through a project is unwise, so I decided I should give the bull to Karen. I'd promised as much to Beth, *ergo* my motive for visiting

Jimmy. But unless the bull was authenticated the story-plan would fail, and in World Three I couldn't be confident of authentication. Also, Richard had paid a retainer for the treasure, so if I didn't deliver it to him I'd be an accessory in its theft. However, if I gave it to Richard I'd change the scheme of the novel, and the story would flop unless the bull was *not* authenticated. Therefore, I faced a dilemma both literary and moral. Could I choose, and then write well enough to justify my choice?

My head spun: emotional overload, mental confusion; probably hypoglycaemia. I shouldn't have drunk the whisky, much though I'd needed it. I didn't dare use my mobile to call the authorities. I didn't dare drive. Several minutes passed before I summoned a taxi and went to the Caledonian Hotel. From one of their public phones I called 999 and reported a stabbing at Jimmy's address, not giving my name. I left before the call could be traced. After an exhausting limp to Tollcross I bought a Chinese takeaway and returned by taxi to the *Brigadoon*. It was a relief to have reported Jimmy's death, though the potential conse-quences were scary. I ate some of the food and ditched the rest.

There was a stain on my right shoe: blood. I'd been in a crowded hotel and walked along a busy road with a blood-stained shoe. Everyone would have noticed. Everyone now knew I'd kicked James Farquhar on the head and drawn blood. I thought I'd freed myself of evidence but perhaps I'd never be free. Me and Lady Macbeth. I rushed to the bathroom and scrubbed the shoe with soap and water. Dye leaked into the washbasin. I'd never remove the forensic traces. The shoes, too, would have to be thrown away.

There was a text message on my phone. I panicked, but the sender was Alison. How had she learned my number?

'Thanx 4 meeting me 2day. Great 2 c u again but wish u would talk. Going 2 Robbie and Niall 4 dinner Fri. U r invited. C u there?'

They wanted to question me about Karen. At least Niall did. But in front of Alison? I'd have expected more tact from Robbie. Of course, Niall wanted to question Alison, too, yet she seemed undeterred. I located Robbie's number in the directory.

'Yes, Doug, we'd love to have you. Sevenish, dinner at eight? Niall's cooking.'

'Thanks, Robbie, I look forward to it. Would a game of chess be unsociable in the company of Niall and Alison?'

'We'll ask. Until Friday.'

'Robbie, before you go … remember you rang me last Saturday?'

He paused.

'Of course, and I'm eager to know how things are, but I don't think we should talk on the phone. Rumour has it that Peter was involved in shady dealings. The police are digging.'

'Quite. Just to let you know, Karen's being looked after by friends. But I've had a confusing time. I'm trying to remember, did you ring me at home on Saturday? Sorry if that seems trivial.'

This time there was no pause: 'I rang your mobile, your land-line being ex-directory.'

'Ah. It doesn't matter. See you Friday.'

Was it my land-line or my mobile that had rung at 11.07 on Saturday when the world had changed? I was no longer sure. I texted a reply to Alison: 'Great – see you then'.

I was making social plans as though life were normal; as though I had not, a few hours earlier, or minutes, or days, stolen a priceless antiquity – or a fake – from a heroin dealer, who'd stolen it from a murder victim, and then fled another murder scene. The thought took root in my mind. I looked at the wardrobe. The door was shaking: a slight draught, or a trick of disturbed vision. I saw a rat scuttle from it into the shadows. A sharp pain stabbed my right eye socket.

I'd imagined it. The rat, not the pain.

The thought grew and sent out shoots. Through how many hands had it passed during its long or not so long history, this simulacrum of torment? Within three days it had gone from Spiro Andropoulos to Peter Wishart, then to James Farquhar, like (how apposite the cliché!) a hot coal. Now it was in my hotel room, and I had to give it to someone I was bound to consider a friend.

I was weary beyond measure. The insides of my eyelids were sandpaper. I went to bed and dreamed I was standing in the room staring at my own body. 'Too bad,' said Linda. 'You won't get away with it this time.' She was stroking the bronze bull, which was purring, an eerie, melodious paean. 'You should have hidden him.' She was right; I should have put Jimmy into the tartan sports bag and shut him in the wardrobe. No one would have found him there.

The bull's purring transmuted to a tinny, high-pitched tune, familiar and irritating. I half-wakened and recognised the pleading of my phone. The room was dark. My hand groped for the mobile and my heart hammered. How quickly could I escape? I gained control over the instrument and grunted, 'Hello,' remembering the phone call that had changed the world the previous Saturday, half a lifetime ago.

'Doug! Oh, Doug, I'm sorry, I didn't know who else–'

'Beth? What's wrong? Hell, what time is it?'

'Half past six … Doug, they've detained her under Section Two. They've just left. Two police cars. All the neighbours staring … They're going to charge her, I know they are. Oh, Doug, you have to tell me, you have to be honest with me, is she guilty?'

11

My head pounded: too little food, too little sleep, too many shocks. Showering and shaving demanded a marathon effort. I drank water from the tap and devoted a few minutes to self-pity.

Early arrest of an innocent party is a trope of crime fiction. However, since cliché must be avoided and I had scant regard for the conventions of my genre, Beth's near-hysteria may have been justified. Nevertheless, Iain must have had good reason to swoop so soon, since he was meticulous as well as fallible. I'd have to invent the good reason.

Sunrise and two cups of coffee restored my capacity to cope, though my head thumped, my foot throbbed, and the bits in between weren't much more comfortable. The morning was clear again, frost in the air. I locked my room, loaded briefcase and sports bag into the Toyota and drove to Penicuik, where I inflicted a supermarket breakfast on my stomach, swallowed two ibuprofen tablets, drank more coffee and smoked two cigarettes. I didn't know my way around Penicuik so the rush-hour had peaked before I located Beth's address. There was a police car outside, together with press and a crowd of spectators. I parked in a neighbouring street and limped back to Beth's.

'Hello again, Doug. I see ye didnae call me like I telled ye.'

'Your powers of observation are impressive, Emma.'

'How do ye feel about yer pal Karen now?'

'Like a friend in need. How do *you* feel about her?'

'Like a reporter in need. Ye dinnae look so guid. No' been sleeping, like?'

'I'm surprised you of all people can't recognise a hangover.'

'Och, aye, very wounding. Close to Ms Odombo, are ye?'

'No, but she'll prefer the company of an acquaintance who isn't nosey to the prurient inquisitiveness of the hoi-polloi and the callous intrusions of reporters. I'm sure you can relate to that.'

'No' really. Yer syntax is too convoluted.'

'My syntax is straightforward. Perhaps my vocabulary's too precise.'

The police were leaving as I approached the door, two young constables carrying Karen's property. They asked my business. I explained. They exchanged glances and allowed me passage, then trudged down the path to their car. A volley of questions rebounded from their shield of taciturnity.

Beth was slumped on a sofa, staring at the wall. She barely acknowledged my presence. The house had a freshly-searched air of disarray. There was a faint aroma of spices and strawberries.

'Does she have a lawyer?' I asked. 'One she can instruct in her defence?'

'Expect so.' The words were *sotto voce*.

'If not we'll find her one.'

'She did it, didn't she?'

I told her "innocent until proven guilty" might be a joke in practice but it was the right principle. The police make mistakes, I reminded her, and they hadn't charged anyone yet. I asked whether they'd taken Karen's house keys.

'They left them. Why?'

'Someone will need to restore her house after the police have searched it. They'll be invasive.'

She looked round. Her eyes were devastated.

'Will they break in?'

'They've got Peter's keys.'

She wanted to know when she could see Karen, whether visits would be allowed, and what could be done about the reporters congregating outside.

After six hours of detention, I explained, the suspect must be either charged or released unless the police are granted an extension. 'If she's released they'll bring her back here. If she's charged they'll keep her in a cell overnight. Then sheriff's court in the morning and she'll be remanded in custody. If that happens we'll visit her tomorrow lunchtime.'

'Won't she get bail?'

'Not on a murder charge. Not in Scotland.'

She shut her eyes and appeared to pray. I allowed her two minutes and then tried to sound both gentle and confident.

'She didn't do it, Beth. Now, about the reporters. Can we leave via your back garden and through a neighbour's house? My car's round the corner.'

It was possible; she had a friend whose garden abutted her own. They went to the gym together. While she sneaked away to inquire I switched on my mobile.

'Richard? Doug Carmichael. The police have detained Karen Winster. They've got wind of Peter's dealings so they'll go through her house with the proverbial fine-toothed comb. If they find anything linking Peter to you and David, you'll receive a visit.'

A moment's silence hung.

'Right, Doug. Not surprised. Thought it was her. Thought it was her from the start.'

'I think it's implausible. She loved him, and she hadn't the–'

'Oh, come on. Vigorous young chap like Peter, bags of money, away from home half the time? Hell hath no fury, Doug. Hell hath no fury. Need to understand people better. Still driving that Jap monstrosity?'

I conveyed love to Lydia and ended the call as Beth returned, bolting the door behind her. Her friend would be at home until she went to collect the kids from school.

'What now?' she said.

'You phone the Museum and tell them you'll be in later. Then I help you tidy up. Then we escape via your friend's house and I take you for lunch.'

Compliant, she phoned a colleague. I brewed coffee.

'Thanks, Doug. For coming. And everything. Sorry I'm a zombie. It was a horrible time to phone you. Please, sit down and rest. I'll sort the place out. You don't look well.'

'Hangover. I'm OK. Tell me if you want a hand.'

I hoped domestic activity would be therapeutic. While Beth bustled around restoring items to their places, making beds, plumping cushions, I fell asleep on the sofa. Deplorable manners, but my sleeping mind punished me; dreams accused me of creating characters and then destroying them on an industrial scale. I'd no defence. I woke when the Dyson approached the sofa. Beth was sorry to disturb me and managed a smile. She went for a shower. I called Robbie. Niall would know the story but courtesy was in order, even to persons of dubious reality.

We evaded the press and reached my car. The pain-killers and the short sleep on Beth's sofa had alleviated the headache but my foot hurt. While I drove, Beth recalled memories of Karen, as friends and relatives do after a funeral. My heart went out to her. I empathise more with characters in novels than World One acquaintances.

'The evening after I got the letter telling me I'd been accepted for the research studentship, she phoned to invite me to a pub lunch so we could get acquainted. I said, "You'll recognise me – I'm small and black and I'll wear yellow – but how will I recognise you?" Know what she said?'

Of course. I'd written it.

'I can't guess.'

'She said, "I'll be the tall redhead holding a pineapple".' Beth's laugh was feeble. 'The following day I went to the pub, and lo and behold, there's this regal woman in a navy blue suit sitting alone with a half-full glass and holding a pineapple. She'd bought it specially. How to get a nervous M. Phil. student to relax: buy a pineapple! I knew then I'd fallen on my feet. I fell on my feet even more when I got the job with her. She's formidable, scary, dedicated, quirky, witty, understanding–'

'I suppose she was made that way.'

Beth was quiet for a while, then asked: 'Doug, she *didn't* do it, did she?'

'No, Beth, she didn't.'

I crossed my fingers.

We were in Edinburgh by one o'clock. I parked in

Chambers Street and took Beth to an Indian restaurant. She denied appetite but ate her lunch.

'I don't want to drag you through it again, but briefly, what did the police ask and what did you tell them?'

Nothing unexpected, she said: had Karen gone out alone during the past three days, had she been back to the Museum, had she had visitors, talked on the phone, confessed to killing Peter? Had she had anything in her possession that might belong to the Museum?

'Do you think they were talking about the bronze she kept mentioning?'

I nodded and told her that if the police believed Karen hadn't left Penicuik, and the Museum staff hadn't seen her, the Museum probably wouldn't be searched. Beth ingested a mouthful of lamb Madras.

'Doug, you said you might be able to locate the bronze. Can't you tell the police what you know? To help Karen?'

Fictional or not, she deserved honest answers. Up to a point.

'There's little they don't already know.' I explained that I'd seen Peter and his contact in a restaurant on Friday evening, and he'd gone to a club after the meal so he could spot anyone tailing him. 'He was carrying a little suitcase, which he left with the bouncers. Seems the bronze was in the suitcase together with authenticating documents. He left the club in the early hours and walked part of the way home. Someone was waiting for him in the Pleasance. He was killed and the suitcase was taken.'

'So if *Karen* had the bronze–'

'The police would believe they had her bang to rights.' They'd know Peter was planning to sell the bronze to a private collector, I continued, hence the row with Karen the previous week. His real intentions would never be known, but if the article was genuine it was archaeologically important. From the police standpoint it was material evidence that they needed to link to Karen. 'They didn't find it in your house so the search is on. They'll soon learn I'm Karen's friend and I knew about Peter's dealings. So if *I* turn up with the bronze or reveal its whereabouts, *I'll* be arrested for the murder. Or for perverting the course of justice by ensuring Karen isn't caught with it. Neither alternative will help. And before you ask, *I* didn't meet Peter in the Pleasance and bash his head in.'

'I wasn't suggesting–'

'No blame if you were, Beth. One possible suspect has accused me to my face.'

She seemed abashed but she recovered. Since I'd mentioned Peter's "dealings" and his "contact", she asked, did I know what he was doing, and did the police know? I told her the police knew more than I did.

'Peter took art and archaeological treasures from poor countries and sold them in rich ones. He was a link in an international network. Many of his recent deals involved Iraq.'

'A lot's been published about thefts from Iraq since the Gulf War,' said Beth. 'The history of ancient civilisation: Sumeria, Assyria, Babylon, Persia–'

'Thanks to Peter and his associates, much of that material is now in the west.'

'Jesus. He was involved in that? Did Karen know?'

At what level might Karen have known? Sex killers' wives might find bloodstained clothing and other evidence, hear police appeals, but never voice their suspicions even to themselves. Some remain in denial for the rest of their lives. Others crack and do something unpredictable. I explained the analogy to Beth, who connected the pieces, pushed her meal aside and stared at the table.

'I believe that's one strand of police thinking,' I said. 'But there's more. Does the name "Spiro Andropoulos" ring any bells?'

'There's an archaeologist called Andropoulos. Works in Athens, National Archaeological Museum. Karen doesn't like him.'

'He was the contact I mentioned. Peter got Spiro's name and e-mail address from Karen's computer. They'd been dealing for eighteen months. She'd told him Spiro wasn't above the occasional breach of professional ethics.'

Beth asked whether I was sure.

'Yes, but there's a saving grace. Iain McArdle, the guy in charge of the murder investigation – you met him this morning, though you might not–'

'Big fat fellow, going bald. He was OK. One of the other men recited all the formal stuff to Karen. Then this fellow and a woman officer had to be with her while she got dressed.'

So Bob Williamson would conduct the formal recorded interview. Iain was grooming him for promotion, but did he have other motives? I explained standard police procedure to Beth: the officer who detains the suspect has to remain with her until she's been interviewed. It was designed to humiliate and unsettle the detainee, to soften her up for questioning.

'Hence their arrival at an ungodly hour of the morning,

too. Anyway, I was saying: Iain McArdle knows this case opens a can of worms. Think of all the organisations set up to prevent thefts of archaeological treasures and art works: S.T.O.P., the SALVO web, Trace and ACTS, Getty's OBJECT ID, COPAT, Art-Protect, all the stolen art databases … Every national police service has a specialist department for the purpose. In Britain it's part of New Scotland Yard–'

'I know all that, Doug! I see your point, though: once the lid comes off Peter's dealings, Scotland Yard will take over McArdle's murder inquiry. But surely McArdle could still claim credit for exposing the network?'

He couldn't, I told her, unless he charged a relevant person with killing Peter and did so soon. The team investigating the trafficking network would see the murders as a crucial lead. Iain needed to recover the missing bronze, too. 'That's why he's had Karen detained even though his case isn't watertight. It's also why he allowed a subordinate to detain her. If the interview proceeds according to plan the subordinate will arrest and charge her. If the case goes pear-shaped, Iain won't shoulder all the blame for wrongful arrest.'

She asked how much of what I'd said was guesswork.

'I deduced much of it this morning,' I said. 'Iain McArdle is too careful to make premature arrests, so I had to reason out why he'd had Karen detained.'

'If you're right,' said Beth, 'he'll have to charge her even if she *is* innocent.'

'Yes, but watch your wording. At present she's either innocent or guilty; I believe innocent. If she's charged she becomes either convictable or not convictable.'

'Same thing, surely?'

'Not when the case is argued adversarially in front of a jury.'

Her fingers gripped the edge of the table. Her eyes closed. She said her head was spinning.

'Doug, did you say "murders", plural? Has there been another?'

'A little bird told me that Spiro Andropoulos was shot dead in the street when he returned to Athens. The Greek police are investigating.'

She shook her head, over and over again.

'So the *traffickers* could have killed Peter. What's Karen got herself into?'

'Nothing directly. And both deaths might be unconnected to the network.'

She stared towards the window. I glanced in the same direction but saw no cause for alarm. After a minute she said, 'I must go to work. Everyone knows Karen's been staying with me since Saturday so I'll run a gauntlet of questions.'

I took a pencil from my pocket and scribbled on a table napkin, then amended the draft and handed it to Beth. She almost smiled.

'Right. E-mail that round the staff and then shut my office door. You're brilliant, Doug.'

'I try not to let it show. Beth, Karen's going to be on the news this evening; be prepared. If the worst happens we'll visit her tomorrow. If it doesn't, does she have a key to your house?'

'Yes. But that's a thought; I'd better go home early.'

'I'll run you back. I'll feed the meter now, and then I'll

spend the afternoon in the Museum. You'll find me in the science and industry section. Or text me when you're ready and I'll come to your office.'

We entered the Museum side by side. There was a low-key police presence. Reporters shadowed the officers as fleas accompany dogs. Beth and I ignored both species. They returned the compliment. As we parted she asked where the mysterious bronze had originated; the Museum wouldn't acquire anything from Iraq. And where *was* it? Did I know? Was it anywhere the police could link to Karen?

'Not Iraq; it's from southern Europe. It's best you know nothing about it for the time being, Beth. But you're right, we don't want it near the Museum.'

A sensible precaution in principle. However, it was just a few yards away, in the back of my car.

12

I followed Beth to the Museum's "Staff Only" area, entered an unoccupied office, obtained an outside phone line and delivered an anonymous message to Police Headquarters for DCI McArdle: *The bronze bull was taken from Peter Wishart by James Farquhar around 3 a.m. on Saturday.* I added Jimmy's address and rang off, sneaked out of the office and went in the science and industry section to await Beth. Either my tip-off failed to reach the chief inspector or he ignored it; Karen was arrested and charged despite my efforts.

I was annoyed with Iain McArdle. He'd compelled me to rush a facet of *The Bronze Bull* that I'd wanted to develop step by step.

Beth cooked dinner while I read the *Evening News.* This gender role stereotyping would have amused Linda and me in happier times. Karen's arrest filled the front page. Niall's lead story condemned her without flouting the letter of the law. He was a skilled journalist. No doubt Emma would reveal further details, with less subtlety, in the following day's *Record.* Further selective information about Karen, Peter and the Museum occupied pages 2, 3 and 5 of the *News.* Niall's photographer had been busy. Jimmy Farquhar's death had been accorded three column inches on page 4.

My headache had subsided and my foot wasn't throbbing as much, but a worry had been added to my collection:

Beth had assumed a significant role in the story. As she cooked, her speakers relayed a CD of Eastern European folk music arranged for soloists and choir, and I was embarrassed to find myself enjoying it. If I'd needed to specify her musical taste earlier I'd have guessed a preference for heavy rock. Also, since she was only a minor character, I'd foreseen no need to describe her house – 1950s, semi-detached, on the outskirts of town – or consider questions of family or partner. As a result, I had no clear perception of the fittings and décor around me, and I'd devoted our homeward journey to eliciting details of her life. At least my questions distracted her from Karen.

Beth had obtained an upper second in archaeology from Edinburgh University and then undertaken M. Phil. research on Scottish Bronze Age discoveries with Karen as supervisor. She'd been Karen's assistant in the Museum's archaeology department for three years. All that was in my sketches for *The Bronze Bull,* but I'd created no personal information about her. I now knew she'd been born in Nottingham of a Kenyan immigrant family, who'd supported her financially. Her father and elder brother ran a clothing business and her younger brother was studying for an MBA. She'd had several boyfriends, none current, and she lived alone except for a lame black and white cat called Harmony, who was sulking in the garden to avoid me. She suffered nickel dermatitis so she eschewed most jewellery. She hated cigarette smoke. In view of her distress about Karen, the Director had given her the rest of the week off work.

I'd ensured she was less informed about me, but I'd smoked scarcely a cigarette since the morning. If a woman who only existed at the periphery of a fictional tale had influenced my behaviour I'd have been exasperated.

At six o'clock she emerged from the kitchen with plates bearing pork chops in an aromatic sauce, boiled potatoes and a lightly-fried mixture of mushrooms and courgettes. In culinary skill she rivaled Lydia; in all other respects, save pretension to the porcelain brand of femininity, she excelled her. I opened a bottle of Provençal red and dispensed it into lead crystal glasses drawn from an antique cabinet. She silenced the music and we watched the television news. While we ate we assimilated reports of a devastating earthquake in China, a hurricane in Central America and another crisis in the Middle East. We dined in comfort while we watched and listened. The urbane urgency of the reporters, the familiarity of format, our capacity to stem the flow of shocking images at the touch of a button, distanced us from the faces and voices of the bereaved, homeless and starving, the enumeration of dead and missing. The last item before the weather forecast described the arrest in Athens of a forty-one-year-old Iraqi, Ibrahim Youssef, for the fatal shooting of Spiro Andropoulos. This touched our emotions more than the reports of disasters.

My brain echoed with the clash of existences. Most of the news would have been identical in World One. I'd watched the same newscasters and reporters on the dusty television in my Stockbridge flat five days earlier. Only the item about the Andropoulos murder belonged to World Three. The barrier between reality and fiction seemed thinner than cigarette paper, yet I couldn't breach it.

Karen's arrest was the lead item on the Scottish news. There was a brief interview with her line manager, the

Museum's Director of Collections, who lauded Dr Winster's reputation, expertise, integrity, popularity and undoubted innocence; and a comment by a Detective Chief Superintendent, whose evaluation differed. Beth shed tears. I took our plates to the kitchen and brewed coffee, the food in my stomach transmuted to lead. Guilt saturated me as it had in Karen's house on Saturday.

By the time I returned to the living room Beth had regained her self-command. Harmony returned and submitted to stroking on her mistress's lap, glaring at the intruder. Feline contact calmed Beth more than my unspoken words of reassurance. I refilled our glasses.

'Karen will be in a bad way when we visit.' I cleared my throat. 'On top of her grief about Peter she'll be disorientated.'

'I expect her to be furiously fucking angry.'

'We're more likely to see bewilderment, confusion, inability to focus. However she speaks or behaves, don't take it personally.'

'I just have to see her.'

'You will. What are your plans after we're back from Stirling?'

She shrugged. I suggested a walk along the coast if the weather remained fine. She met my eyes for the first time since dinner. Deep dark eyes in a kind East African face.

'Don't you have other things to do?' she said.

'Nothing that can't wait.'

She was silent for a long moment.

'Karen said you were a good guy. I felt rotten phoning you at half six in the morning but I couldn't have coped without you.'

I said I was glad she'd phoned and she was coping splendidly, but the accolade stung. How many Spanish heretics had deemed Torquemada a good guy? Silence stretched between us. Harmony sank into slumber. I knew I should leave. I offered to wash the dishes but she said she had a dishwasher. Then she added:

'You said her house will need tidying after the police search. If you're really free tomorrow, could we …? No, we'll have to ask Karen. Doug, I know what you're saying, a walk by the sea would … but I have to *do* something.'

I paused for thought.

'You could write to her.'

'But if we're going to visit–'

'People who've been in prison say both visits *and* letters are beyond price. Write about anything. You'll find the prison address online. Everyone who cares about Karen should do the same. And somebody needs to coordinate visits; a prisoner can't have more than three visitors at a time. You'd be ideal.'

The prospect of action raised her spirits. I lifted my coat but she asked me to stay. Something else was troubling her.

'The bronze, Doug. You said it was southern European. The Museum won't acquire anything from south of the Alps unless it's Egyptian.'

'It isn't.'

'Peter must have known that. Did he tell Karen?'

'Karen knows what it is, or purports to be.'

She nodded.

'So it's important or controversial enough to merit her judgment, and if she authenticates it or proves it a forgery

117

… But after she's evaluated it … Sorry, thinking aloud. I'll ask her. If she's up to considering …' Her voice tailed off. Then she forced out the question, 'Do *you* know what it is?'

'Peter told me it's a model of the Bull of Phalaris, conceivably made by Perilaus himself. Know the story?'

'It rings a … No, not really.'

'Akragas?'

'Old Greek city state in Sicily, where Agrigento is today. I read something about a bronze bull but I can't recall details.'

I told her it wasn't my subject but I'd studied the legend when Peter told me his latest ploy. According to Aristotle, writing two hundred years after the event, Akragas had been founded in the early 6th century BCE by Greek colonists from Gera. Phalaris was the son of a nobleman from Rhodes. He was commissioned to build a temple for the new city but he took over the citadel and gained control. He ruled Akragas for seventeen years.

'Builder and workers taking over the city is a common story,' said Beth. 'It's how half the tyrants in Classical legend gained power.'

'Yes, but Phalaris was a real historical figure, and an effective ruler despite his alleged drunkenness and cruelty.'

I recounted what I'd read: Phalaris had founded impressive buildings, installed an aqueduct, strengthened the city walls, adopted an expansionist policy, developed trade links – not least with Carthage – and established festivals including athletic contests. Akragas had remained prominent and sophisticated for a century after his death. Empedocles had lived there.

'Eventually it became another Roman colony, but the ruins look Greek–'

'Ah. The penny drops.' For the first time that day, Beth smiled. 'Excavation two years ago, paper in the *EJA* by Andropoulos and others–'

'So you recall the story.'

Beth remembered Karen's response to the reports, excitement mingled with scepticism. She asked whether the model bull had been among the finds.

'Allegedly.'

'Hot property, then. Should be in Athens.'

'Or the Regional Archaeological Museum in Agrigento, or the Agrigento Archaeological Museum, or the Salinas Museum in Palermo?'

'The Paolo Orsi in Syracuse might have a claim, too. They hold several important Greek bronze pieces.'

'I bow to your professional knowledge. I suppose there was enough argument about acquisition for Spiro to have relieved the National Museum of the bull. But is the bull Peter bought from him the original or a fake?'

'Good question! Karen could authenticate it and then advise on custody … Or if it's a fake, she'd stir …' Beth nodded. 'I get why she's keen to see it. Model bull of Phalaris–'

'If it's authentic.'

'Check. What *is* the story?'

'Legend, told in different versions over centuries. Most authorities think there's a historical basis. I'll regale you with it tomorrow. Right now I should leave, especially if you're going to write letters and e-mails. I'll ring in the morning, we'll go to Stirling, and we'll have a walk when we're back.'

She still didn't want me to leave but I was adamant. The conversation had helped us both: guilt hadn't overwhelmed me, or sorrow Beth, and the prospect of the morrow was comforting. Harmony escorted me off the premises. As I manoeuvred the Toyota towards the main road I felt an unaccustomed lightness of being; my chronic foreboding had subsided. I reached the Bush roundabout feeling almost happy. No sooner had I realised this than Linda started singing to me from the rear of the Land Cruiser.

The car ran into the verge and the engine stalled. The song ceased. I knew there was no one in the back but I was shaken. I stepped out into the night, grateful for street lighting, and smoked a cigarette. At length I opened the rear door: nothing there except my briefcase and the sports bag containing Peter's suitcase. I stared at it.

The rest of my drive to the *Brigadoon* was hesitant. Fortunately, traffic was sparse; more fortunately, the voice I loved remained silent. The soundless laughter behind me was the product of overheated imagination. I reached the hotel's diminutive car-park without accident and lit another cigarette. I needed a drink.

I left my briefcase and sports bag in the car. Perhaps, in this, the gods smiled on me. As I entered the hotel, James Merriman told me someone was waiting for me in the bar. I'd been on my way there but I was disconcerted. Who was it? Emma again?

The two old gentlemen were seated at their corner table. They nodded to me. A young couple in the far corner exchanged laughter and intimacies. They ignored me. The taciturn barman was polishing glasses. He ignored me, too. In Emma's place sat a large, too-familiar figure. He rose as I approached the bar and turned to face me, smiling, hand extended. The hand held an open warrant card.

'Dr Douglas Carmichael? DCI Iain McArdle, Lothian and Borders CID. Can we have a chat?'

13

We sat like old friends, drinks before us. His eyes, faded blue, betrayed both chronic and acute weariness: years of gazing into the darkest recesses of humanity had accoutred them with the whole armour of cynicism, and it had been a long day. They also betrayed a hint of uncertainty; he'd made an arrest but he wasn't satisfied. What he saw in *my* eyes I preferred not to imagine. At least he didn't plan to detain me; this was informal. There was no other officer with him. Also, he was drinking beer.

'I suppose you want to ask me about Peter Wishart and Karen Winster, since I'm friends with both.'

'Aye, something like that. If you don't mind me saying so, sir, you don't look too good.'

'I was thinking the same about you. I suppose today's been exhausting for us both. And I drank more than was good for me last night. Haven't slept much since Saturday, when I heard about Peter.'

'I can imagine. Aye, I could do with my bed. But there's a few questions will keep me awake unless you can help me answer them.'

'I will if I can.'

His large head nodded acknowledgement. He lifted his pint and took a long drink, then fixed his eyes on me again. He could stare without blinking. It unsettled suspects.

'You spent the day with Elizabeth Odombo. You went to her house this morning, had lunch with her in

Edinburgh, accompanied her to the Museum, then back to Penicuik. You left her house half an hour ago. What's your relationship with her?'

Which of us was being watched? Reason said Beth; gut feeling said me.

'I first met her on Saturday. She was the only person Karen was willing to stay with so I phoned her to make arrangements. After Karen was detained this morning she rang me because she needed company. So I spent the day with her.'

'Considerate of you, sir. Plenty to talk about?'

'Karen, mainly. And Peter. Reminiscences. Planning prison visits. Incidentally, Beth and I believe Karen's innocent.'

That was a half-truth. I wasn't sure what Beth believed. Nor, I suspect, was she.

'Aye, so she is until the jury decides otherwise.' Iain took another swig of beer. 'Did you discuss the late Mr Wishart's business dealings with Ms Odombo?'

'I told her a little. She'd suspected some of it.'

'Aye, she would have. She's in Dr Winster's confidence, is she no'?'

I took a deep breath and swallowed my drink. I needed another. I put a cigarette into my mouth and paused, lighter in hand.

'Do you mind?'

'Not at all, sir. I'm a passive smoker every working day. Interesting to see a doctor who smokes, though.'

I lit the cigarette.

'I haven't been in practice for fifteen years. Anyway, it's no odder than a clergyman who keeps a mistress.'

'Right enough. I've met a few of those.'

He was outwardly relaxed but everything about him was watchful.

'Peter told me what he'd planned to buy from Dr Andropoulos,' I said. 'Apparently several collectors were interested. Beth had no idea what it was until I told her this evening. All she knew was Karen had expected to receive an allegedly ancient bronze and hadn't stopped fretting about its whereabouts. I'd treated Peter's information as confidential. I've only repeated it to Beth, and now you.'

I was drawing fire, but what choice had I? There was an edge to Iain's voice as he leaned forward to menace me; exactly, I noted, as I'd have written it.

'Confidential? You knew his dealings weren't kosher! Did you no' think of maybe telling the police?'

'Not about this supposed model of the Bull of Phalaris. Why would a business deal with a distinguished Greek archaeologist interest the police?'

His lips curled. His eyes remained cynical.

'Which of us are you trying to kid, Dr Carmichael?'

He was goading me. I accorded him partial success.

'When you said you wanted a chat, Chief Inspector, I assumed you meant a civilised conversation. I'm a law-abiding citizen. If you think I've committed a crime, say so. If not, please be less confrontational.' I indicated his empty glass. 'Want another?'

'Aye, thanks, just the half.' He leaned back in his chair and his smile seemed genuine. 'Have you, sir? Committed a crime?'

'I'm not going to admit to any.'

The visit to the bar allowed me too little time to collect my thoughts. Too soon, I returned with drinks. But Iain was now affable and confiding.

'All right, Dr Carmichael, maybe I owe you an apology. Like you said it's been a long day. Thing is, we need to find this bull. We know it's in Scotland, probably not far from where we're sitting, but we don't know where. Dr Andropoulos told us he'd sold it to Mr Wishart on Friday night, and like you said, he had documents to prove he'd come by it legally. But Andropoulos had a shady reputation and Dr Winster knew it.'

I crossed my fingers and said Spiro's reputation was news to me. Iain drank more beer.

'We think Dr Winster *did* get the bull from Mr Wishart, but he'd decided to sell it to one of the collectors you mentioned, so they had a wee argument. Having got her hands on the bull she had to hide it. It isn't in her house, so she probably got someone to take care of it. Ms Odombo seemed a likely bet, but it wasn't in her house either, and we can't find it at the Museum. So who has it? Well, sir, you were the first person to visit Dr Winster on Saturday, the police forbye, and you've spent today with Ms Odombo. If you were in my shoes, what would *you* be thinking?'

I nodded. My heart thumped again. Soundless laughter rang in my ears and the first line of that bloody song repeated itself over and over: *Am Brunnen von dem Tore ...*

'I see. Emma Menzies has talked to you. Emma didn't like it when I refused to confirm Peter's alleged involvement in drug dealing. She did her best to persuade me.'

His eyes narrowed: surprise, appreciation, subdued mirth, renewed suspicion. I went on:

'Karen didn't give the bronze bull to me for safe-keeping. Nor did anyone else. Feel free to search my room. Or should I act like a criminal and insist you obtain a warrant?'

'Och, come on, sir, *now* who's being confrontational? I'd never get a warrant for that and I wouldn't try. If you believe Andropoulos got the bull legally and sold it to Wishart legally, and you didn't know it was important to our investigations, you wouldn't knowingly have done anything wrong by keeping it for Dr Winster. But if you *do* learn where it is I hope you'll let us know.'

The ostensible escape route: I could give the bull to Iain and I'd be in the clear. This irritated me. He'd just been presented with evidence of my reasoning powers but he still believed me gullible. I smiled and assured him. He changed tack, scratching his head and studying his drink.

'Trouble is, I don't know much about archaeology or how museums work. The Director of Collections at the Museum – is that her title? – Aye, I think that's it … Anyway, she told me an object from Classical Greece or Sicily wouldn't fit into their collections. Forbye, there's a law prohibits the Museum acquiring anything unless they can prove a valid title to it. I gather Dr Winster's had a lot of latitude in her research because of her reputation, but what would she want with this bull if it's no use to the Museum?'

'I'm sure you asked her and I'd be surprised if she didn't answer. Explaining her interest in the bull wouldn't incriminate her, would it?'

'Quite right, sir, it wouldn't have. What's your take, though? You know her.'

I didn't know where he was leading me. I couldn't see a

trap in the question but his persistence was puzzling. However, when in doubt, tell the truth. So I reminded him that Karen was a world authority on ancient Greek metallurgy. If she'd received the bull she could have ascertained whether or not it was authentic. If it was authentic it was major discovery. She'd have been able to say where it was made and where the copper had originated. She'd have been able to date it. The results could have provided new insights into the 6th century BCE Mediterranean world.

'On the other hand, if the bull's a fake, she'd blow the lid off a scam. If you're right about Andropoulos's reputation she'd be glad to expose him. She can't tolerate cheats. So I understand why she was keen to get hold of it.'

'Mphm.' He drank the rest of his beer. 'So you're telling me it's genuine. Andropoulos knew it would fall into her hands if he sold it to Wishart so he wouldn't dare try to pass off a fake. Right?'

'Probably, but Andropoulos might have seen it as a challenge. He could have manufactured a convincing replica to pull the wool over expert eyes.'

'Mm. Bit of a risk, do you no' think? But if the bull's genuine, it's something any museum director would give their eye-teeth for, right? So how come the Director of Collections was adamant about not wanting it?'

What was his agenda? Was he trying to implicate the Museum in the illicit trade in antiquities? Or trying to exonerate them, protecting his nation's pride against Scotland Yard interference? Or was this, in some indecipherable way, about me? I chuckled.

'I'm sure there's nothing you don't know about bureaucracies, Chief Inspector. I haven't grasped all the ins and outs, but it goes something like this. For any public museum in Scotland to make an acquisition, the Director of Collections has to be convinced and must then persuade the Head of Corporate Planning and Performance and the Director of Finance. Then they have to convince the Director of the National Museums of Scotland and the rest of the Corporate Management Team. Then *they* have to persuade the Trustees that the acquisition's worth funding, and if the Trustees agree they have to find money from the National Fund for Acquisitions. The National Fund for Acquisitions comes from a government grant, so the Trustees might have to apply to the government for a top-up. So unless the proposed acquisition accords exactly with the Museum's official policy there's not a hope in Hell of jumping the hurdles. Even if there was it would take forever.'

Iain gazed at me in seeming admiration.

'Ye know the system inside out, so ye do. You've told me more about its workings in a minute than the Museum staff did in three hours. You must have had good reason to learn that much detail.'

Another couple of steps and he'd have implicated me in the international trafficking network. So much for handing over the bull with impunity. I shrugged, the epitome of nonchalance.

'Picked it up from talking to Karen, or rather from being talked at by Karen. She's been responsible for many of the Museum's recent archaeological acquisitions and the bureaucracy drives her nuts. Frustration causes harangues. I'm sure I don't need to explain.'

He appeared to relax, laughed a little, conceded the

point. Then he thanked me for talking to him and apologised for taking up my time. He put on his coat and gloves.

I pocketed my cigarettes and stretched my arms over my head and yawned. Linda's singing sounded in my ears. I watched Iain walk to the door. He looked untidy. He raised a hand in farewell, then turned again and asked:

'By the way, sir, do ye happen to know a man called James Farquhar?'

My heart skipped. I frowned, seeming to concentrate.

'It's a common enough name, but I don't personally know a James Farquhar. Why?'

'Just wondering. A James Farquhar who lived in Leith was found dead in his flat last night, and this afternoon we received an anonymous tip-off about him. We're trying to trace the caller. We've got the message on tape, and voice analysis is good these days.' His smile was warm. 'Good night, Dr Carmichael. Thanks again for the chat.'

14

In order to convey something of Iain's *modus operandi*, I'd planned at some point in *The Bronze Bull* to put a remark about Tigran Petrosian into Robbie Macrae's mouth. Petrosian, the world chess champion, used to make innocuous-looking moves with no evident plan, shifting a piece here, a piece there, seldom seeming to attack. Then his opponent's game collapsed and he won, for reasons revealed only by subsequent analysis. Iain hadn't attacked me directly but his informal chat had left my game collapsing. I'd created a grandmaster of detection.

Or should I have compared Iain with the former Prime Minister Harold Wilson? Wilson's parliamentary colleague George Brown once remarked, 'Harold couldn't cross an empty room in a straight line'. Iain hadn't left the almost-empty bar of the *Brigadoon* in a straight line, and our conversation had turned several corners.

However, Petrosian lost games and ultimately the world title; Wilson lost elections and ultimately the party leadership. Subject to certain restrictions I could step outside the game, change the rules and alter the board. Petrosian's opponents had had no such advantage, nor had Wilson's. Iain didn't know my power.

Two sleepless hours passed before I reached that conclusion. I rose from bed, threw on some clothes and braved the rear of the Toyota. Midnight chimed. I snatched my hand back from the sports bag, rescued my briefcase and returned to my room. My laptop toiled through the small hours, the light from my room struggling towards the sundial in the *Brigadoon*'s garden, while the radio graced my ears with Richard Strauss's *Metamorphosen*. Provided the exclusion clauses covering alteration of personal circumstances didn't apply, three things would happen: Bob Williamson indisposed by a gastrointestinal infection; the tape bearing my anonymous message mislaid; Iain summoned to London to discuss the trafficking network with New Scotland Yard. Having done all I could to change the future I fell into bed and slept. I awoke at breakfast time, rang Beth to tell her I'd be late, and then slept again until 9.30.

Refreshed, though my foot still hurt, I dressed in clean shirt, jacket, tie, new trousers and new shoes, and dumped their predecessors in a skip in Mayfield Road. Daylight rendered the sports bag and its contents innocuous and I drove without alarm. In Penicuik I invested in boots, walking trousers and a thick sweater and reached Beth's at five past eleven. She'd prepared coffee and early lunch. Like me, she'd had a bad night and slept late; like me, she'd been busy at the keyboard. E-mails had been exchanged and the beginnings of a visit-coordinating system were in place. She'd written and posted a long letter to Karen.

I seemed to have made one of my characters feel good without manipulating her by laptop. Nevertheless, although Beth wore her orange trouser suit and forced a spring into her step, she was twitching. People always do before their first prison visit. She tried to hide her tension, but I'm aware of my characters' moods even when I'm talking to them rather than writing them. I dumped my new walking gear in her living room; we'd change after we were back from Cornton Vale.

On the way to Stirling I broke speed limits; visits to remand prisoners started at quarter past one.

'I promised I'd tell you about the Bull of Phalaris. Or have you looked it up?'

'No.' She gave a tight smile. 'I await a rendition from the master raconteur.'

'Anyone in mind?'

'Always the optimist.'

'My offering's second hand and not in mint condition.'

'I'm a sucker for bargains provided I can inspect … Oh – you meant the story.'

Laughter helped.

'Are you sitting comfortably? OK: background. The best-known versions come from Roman sources. Lucian gives what seems to be a full account, but he's writing seven centuries after Phalaris. It's like people today telling Robin Hood tales, or Malory writing about King Arthur.'

'Worse, isn't it?' Beth had tuned in to the topic. 'A modern Brit might see Robin Hood as a national hero. A second-century Roman writing about a long-dead Hellenic tyrant wouldn't be complimentary.'

'Fair comment. There are versions from Cicero and Diodorus Siculus, too. They weren't as far removed from the alleged events, but there was still a gap of centuries and they were still Romans writing about Greeks. They don't paint rosy pictures of Phalaris, but how much credence do they merit?'

'My estimate would be sod all. But a story told by several different authors *could* have a historical basis. Maybe.'

'Better evidence: Pindar wrote about the Bull as though it was common knowledge. He lived less than a century after Phalaris, and he was Greek.'

'Wow, Doug, the revelation! Pindar was Greek!'

'Want to hear this story, sarky bitch?'

'Yeah. Get on with it.'

'OK. There was Aristotle's reference as well, and a dry report by Scipio ... Anyway, the story. The version I know best is Lucian's. A skilled metal-worker from Athens, Perilaus by name, sought to gain the favour of Phalaris by offering him a gift suited to his tastes. As you may have inferred, the gift was a life-sized bull made of bronze.'

Beth saw problems. A bull-sized quantity of bronze? Expensive. How would even a skilled metal-worker get his hands on that much? And what about the logistic issues – transporting the raw materials and the finished article, which must have weighed tons? And the risk of piracy?

'The Bull was hollow,' I told her, 'which reduced the logistical problems and is crucial to the story. Also, Perilaus could have made the Bull *in situ* in Akragas. Phalaris was engaged in public building projects so he'd have hired top-flight metal-workers as well as masons, *and* provided materials. Anyway, this Bull was a masterpiece: lifelike, full of power and grace. Even Lucian admits that Phalaris was so struck by its beauty he ordered it to be offered as a gift to Apollo.'

Beth awaited the twist in the tale. I said the twist was in the metal-worker.

'Perilaus stayed the tyrant's desire to present the Bull to the god by pointing out its real use. In its back he'd hidden a lockable trap-door. He said: "If you wish to punish anyone,

Phalaris, make him climb into this contrivance and lock him up, then attach these flutes to the nose of the Bull and have a fire lighted underneath. The man will groan and shriek in the grip of unremitting pain, but his cries will make you the sweetest possible music on the flutes, piping dolefully and lowing piteously; so while he is punished, you are entertained by having flutes played to you." Unfortunately for Perilaus, he'd misjudged his employer's taste. Phalaris was cruel but Perilaus sickened him.'

'Not a music lover?'

'Phalaris pretended not to believe the inventor. He said a few pipes couldn't turn shrieks of agony into soothing music. Thus he persuaded Perilaus to attach the flutes as specified and then climb into the Bull to demonstrate the sound effects. As soon as the creator was inside his creation, Phalaris locked the trap-door and commanded a fire to be lit. Sure enough, the sounds that emanated from the flutes were musical, albeit loud. However, the Bull was so beautiful that Phalaris wouldn't allow the death of a wicked man to defile it. So he had Perilaus taken out while he was still alive, albeit singed, and thrown over a cliff to perish on the rocks below and lie unburied and unmourned. Then the Bull was purified by the priests and presented to the god.'

I started to tell other versions of the tale but Beth had stopped listening. While I was still talking she said, 'Aren't you going to ask whether I believe the story?'

'Do you believe the story, Beth?' I grinned.

'Roman debasement of all things Greek. I'm sceptical about the historical basis. Isn't this a human sacrifice story mutated by repeated oral transmission? The folk process?

Carthage and Western Sicily offered human sacrifices in pre-Classical times.'

'Isn't a hollow bronze bull an unusual device for human sacrifices?'

'Is there a usual one, Doug? I believe Sicilian rivers used to be represented as bulls, often with human heads. And wasn't Akragas named after the local river? Maybe the tale of a bronze statue representing the river god became conflated with folk memories of human sacrifice.'

'It wouldn't explain the Pindar reference. Or Aristotle. Or Scipio.'

'I don't know, Doug. Internal evidence can't prove the story's true, even with multiple sources. But the model bull that's caused the present troubles, if it *is* contemporaneous …'

She fell silent again. Four feet behind us, the bronze bull watched from within the case within the sports bag. I concentrated on the M9 and pressed the accelerator. It was almost ten to one when we reached junction eleven and headed for Bridge of Allan. I nearly missed the turn into Fountain Road and over the level crossing, but we entered the prison car park as the Toyota's clock passed the hour mark.

Cornton Vale dates from the 1970s and its architecture is atypical of prisons. At first glance it's a collection of oversized holiday homes set in well-kept grounds. There's desultory building work. Then you notice the electronic gates, the security fence, the barred windows, the cameras, the uniformed staff, and the illusion evaporates. This is no home for holidaymakers but for damaged, vulnerable, dangerous women, and for innocent women whom it damages and renders vulnerable or dangerous.

The officers on duty were as welcoming as circumstances allowed. We gave our names and declared whom we wished to visit. One of the officers located Karen on her list and telephoned Ross House, where most remand prisoners were lodged. I asked if I could pay fifty pounds into Karen's PPC.

'PPC?' whispered Beth.

'Prisoner's personal cash,' I said. 'I want to be sure she can buy necessities. We can bring stuff for her – books, papers whatever – if she requests it.'

The officer gave me a receipt for the fifty pounds. We sat in the bleak waiting room among other visitors. The chairs were stained. Our attire didn't match the norm; we'd have attracted less scrutiny in our walking clothes. Notices around us specified rules, outlined the counselling and other services available to inmates, and enumerated the consequences of importing drugs and weapons.

The visits were called. A door was unlocked. Keys, wallet, cigarettes, lighter, loose change and Beth's handbag went into a locker. We passed through a metal detector. The personal search wasn't much worse than you suffer at airports. We waited again, in line, until all the prisoners with visits had assembled. Finally, another door was unlocked and we were admitted to the visit room. It was small, depressing and in need of renovation.

Karen was a dignified, authoritative woman with lively wit and strength of character. The woman awaiting us, staring at the floor, looked twenty years older than Karen. There was little evidence of dignity, less of authority and none of wit. Life and strength had collapsed. Perhaps the transformation would be reversible but scars would remain.

We sat at her table and greeted her. She didn't answer. She'd suffered the worst of culture shocks and the fault was mine. I'd rather have been anywhere else in the world than facing her in that visit room.

Private grief isolates us. Sartre was wrong: Hell isn't other people. In times of despair, Hell is oneself. Shared misery brings people together, a group segregated from the world by unscalable walls of emotion; its members comfort each other. The intense bonds generated by such comfort fracture when the crisis is resolved, yet at the time it's a blessing. Personal, unshared misery is different. It feeds on itself and allows no consolation. Like chronic severe pain, it robs you of the power to think beyond yourself or empathise. It precludes the grace of receiving empathy. Prison officers and managers know the risks. They don't want suicides.

I improvised an opening gambit.

'Karen, it would be stupid to ask how you are and I can't begin to guess how you feel, but we all know this is a ghastly mistake. Beth and I will do everything we can to help. All your friends are behind you.'

Her glance was unreadable. Her lips moved without sound. Beth stared, full of Karen's despair. I ploughed on:

'There's fifty pounds in your PPC so you can buy stuff at the canteen. Tell us when you need more. We'll bring whatever books and writing materials you want. Just post a pro form to Beth.'

No response. Clinical depression can set in rapidly after a shock but seldom like that. Beth took over, her voice bright.

'Everyone at work will write to you, Karen, and they'll

visit whenever they can. You'll have at least one caller every day.' She listed a few names.

'That's down to Beth, Karen,' I said. 'She's been busy.'

Vestigial acknowledgement. Beth took Karen's hand, which wasn't withdrawn but didn't respond. One of the officers told us not to sustain physical contact. Beth apologised and relinquished her hold. She and I talked about trivia but failed to elicit interest. We asked about Ross House and prison life. The responses were whispered monosyllables. The hour ticked away.

It was asking for the moon for Karen to be more responsive, but the bull had – so to speak – to be taken by the horns. I leaned forward and whispered.

'Karen, this is confidential. I know what was in the package you were expecting from Peter last Friday. I've told Beth but no one else. The police know what it is because Spiro Andropoulos told them, and they're searching for it. They believe it will lead them to an international trafficking network, so they're not telling the press. If information leaks, the smugglers will vanish.'

At last, Karen responded; the wet turquoise eyes fixed on me. I continued:

'I've recovered the package. We need your instructions. But in the names of all the gods, don't breathe a word about it here. Prisons leak confidential information faster than Whitehall.'

She shook her head.

'To be more precise,' I said, 'I have the object itself *and* the accompanying documentation. Beth could probably assess the documentation but I guess she'd rather you did it. Right, Beth? If you send out a pro form requesting papers from work, we'll photocopy the documents, put them into a folder and hand them in next time we visit. You can authenticate them when you feel able. But what about the object? I suppose metallurgical analysis is needed, but I've no idea how to go about it or what to do with the results. And if the police get a sniff of it in the meantime they'll seize it and the consequences will be disastrous. It's urgent, Karen, or I wouldn't bother you right now.'

'You've got the bronze bull? You?' Her voice was a cracked whisper. 'What is it …? A photo. Photos.'

'Right, we'll get photos to you along with the photocopied documents. But please tell us who can do the analysis and will *guarantee* discretion.'

Karen stared at her knees. I sensed mounting anger in Beth. Then, at last, Karen stirred again, blinked at Beth and whispered:

'Tom. Tom MacIntyre.'

'Thought he'd retired, Karen,' said Beth.

'Still goes to the lab. Call him. At home.'

Karen withdrew again. I tried to solicit suggestions about disposing of the bull, but in vain. Beth glared at me. Too soon, or not soon enough, the visit was over. We were shepherded to the exit. Karen and the other prisoners were taken through a different door to be searched for contraband. I voiced my concern to the nearest officer.

'Aye, we ken aw about her, sir. She's on sui. watch, two'd up in Ross Hoose with a German lassie. Nuclear protester. Bit cracked, but clean enough and a carin' soul.'

Reassured, I stepped outside and turned to Beth, supposing she'd be distressed. She was furious.

'What in Christ's name were you doing, Doug, battering

Karen with those questions? And you're a bloody *liar*! You told me you knew where the bull *was*, not that you had it. So where is it? Or are you pretending?'

She'd no business to speak to me like that.

'Stop shouting. We're not discussing it here. Get in the car. I'll tell you as we drive.'

'I'm not getting in any bloody car. I want answers. Now.'

'Don't be stupid. In the prison grounds? Get in the car, then I'll tell you.'

'I'm *not* getting in the car. Not 'til I know what's–'

'Fine. The station's two miles that way. Then you'll need to get the bus from Edinburgh to Penicuik and then walk. And your questions won't be answered.'

I opened the driver's door. Beth punched the rear of the Toyota and recoiled with a yelp. I stared. She was doubled over, clutching her arm.

'Jesus,' she gasped. 'Didn't *you* get a shock? That wasn't static. There's an electrical fault on this thing. Check the battery leads.'

'Get in, Beth. Let's take a look at you.'

She got in.

15

Arms folded, lips compressed, she glared through the windscreen. I let the silence hang until we reached the M9.

'I didn't lie. On Sunday, I said I'd a hunch where the bull was. The hunch proved correct so I now have the bull. Satisfied?'

The diatribe was uncorked.

'Satisfied? Sure. Like, you've explained your hunch, how you got the bull, where it is now and why you didn't tell me. Fine. You don't *need* to tell me, but you *can't* not tell me and then pretend you have. And you didn't check the battery leads. Typical man. Know best about bloody everything.'

I said that if there'd been an electrical fault *I'd* have got a shock because I'd touched the car first.

'Oh, so I imagined it? Hysterical woman?'

I let the point pass.

'The only thing I didn't tell you was that I *have* the bull. If you'd known, and the police had questioned you, it would have been awkward. I *should* have told you, though. Sorry.'

Her arms partly unfolded and then she resumed her scrutiny of the motorway. *Ισον εστιν οργηι και θαλασσα και γυνη*, to quote Karen's favourite mug. No, that was unfair. Beth had reason to be distressed.

'Other points,' I said. 'I saw Richard Latimer-Brown on Sunday. He's a private collector. Someone had offered to sell him the bull. Richard didn't report the offer to the police because they'd have confiscated the bull and *he* wanted it. And he didn't know it was crucial evidence in Karen's case. I let the matter ride because if the bull's whereabouts could be connected with Karen she'd be in trouble.'

'Oh yes? And how could Karen be connected with this "someone"?'

'Through Peter's Will, though she couldn't have known. Peter owned flats. His Will leaves all his Edinburgh property to Karen. Therefore, his tenants become hers, provided she's not convicted of killing him. The "someone" was one of the tenants. So in principle, Karen is the someone's landlady.'

Beth's arms unfolded again and one hand rose to her face.

'Quite, Beth. She profits big time from Peter's death. Anyway, once Richard told me his story I knew where the bull was.'

'Was that before or after you phoned me?'

I said I'd guessed the truth before phoning her, though I'd visited Richard afterwards. I'd kept quiet about the bull to protect Karen. Beth said it was too late for such scruples.

'I don't agree,' I said. 'Without the bull the prosecution case is weak. And Richard won't tell the police about the "someone". He wants the bull for himself.'

'So how did you acquire the bull from the "someone"?'

'It wasn't an edifying scene.'

She stared at me.

'OK, where is it?'

'In the back of the car.'

'What?'

'It's been there for two days.'

'You mean we've just driven … to … with … Oh, God, I don't believe this! And yesterday, driving in and out of Edinburgh, with the police and … Doug, are you mad?'

'See why I pressed Karen for a way of disposing of it?'

'Doug, you're crazy. *Crazy*!'

She laughed and reiterated 'Crazy.' I didn't find the adjective risible, but she kept laughing until we reached the Edinburgh city bypass. Just before the Lothianburn junction she asked:

'What's a pro form?'

'Property form. A list of items, countersigned by an officer, that a prisoner asks a specified person to provide. Specified person takes the items along with the form and gives them to the visit staff. Or posts them to the prison.'

Her eyebrows lifted. I concentrated on the road.

'You're well informed about prison affairs.'

'I write crime stories.'

Another silence. Then:

'Doug, I was a cow when we left Cornton Vale. You got the full works because seeing Karen had–'

'Upset you. And you've had a horrible week.'

'Why did she have to wear those dungarees? But I shouldn't have taken it out on you.'

I told her we were quits: she'd earthed an electrical charge from my car, I'd earthed an emotional charge from her. She snorted.

'If you're going to be that bloody understanding I'll get angry again.'

'OK, you're an evil-tempered bitch, so while we're walking along the coast I'll throw you into the sea. You'll be OK; witches float.'

'Better. You're an arrogant, self-satisfied git with no idea how to treat other people, so if we walk along a cliff I'll push you over like a partly-cooked Perilaus because it'll be good for you.'

'We understand each other. Any preference for walk?'

'My ignorance of local geography is shameful.'

'The Tyne mouth, then. No cliffs worthy of the name.'

'OK. Can I get to see this bronze bull, please? And the documents?'

I suggested leaving it 'til later.

'Contact with the bull is unsettling, especially when you're upset. Half an hour ago you left a harrowing prison visit, and you were furious–'

'All right. Straight after our walk, then?'

We reached her house at half past three; again, the aroma of spices and fruit. I changed in the bathroom. She emerged from her bedroom in sweater, jeans and boots and fed Harmony. Another tiff threatened: Beth said she had to see the bull so she could describe it to Tom MacIntyre, as she'd promised Karen. I pointed out that hours of daylight were limited. She conceded again; she'd look at the bull later and phone Professor MacIntyre in the evening.

Yes, Beth, I was arrogant, but justifiably. All the characters in this story, including you, are my creations. So I have the right, the duty, to manipulate them in any way necessary for a good literary outcome. A convincing character might rebel against being manipulated but mustn't be allowed too much scope. On the other hand, while I was sharing this world with my characters I was obliged to treat them with respect and acknowledge their right to express their feelings, including feelings about me. It was hard to strike a balance.

By half past four we were walking through Binning Wood to the beach west of the Tyne's mouth. Field maples and birches were replacing summer green with chrome yellow, luminous under the low sun. The beeches were bronzed, oaks and horse chestnuts ochre and russet, sycamores dowdy brown. Beth extolled the colours.

'It's a gorgeous time of year,' she sighed. 'All the pigments you see when the chlorophyll fades. Look at that beech! And what's that? Elm? Gorgeous. And the limes …'

I hummed the *leitmotif* of the *Musical Offering* and redoubled my pace. Beth ran after me.

'Doug, what's wrong? Doug!'

I reached the end of the wood and stepped on the dunes. The Firth was calm, the tide low. Gannets and fulmars soared and dived. Ships passed. Quiet clouds streaked the sky. The sun sank towards the city. I regained self-control but she was now anxious and cross.

'You touched the nearest thing I have to a phobia, Beth.'

'Why didn't you tell me instead of running away?'

'Not much to tell. Let's stroll round the headland. Great view over the mud-flats and Belhaven Bay.'

For several minutes we walked in silence. Late flowers bloomed: rest harrow, some lingering thyme. A pied wagtail hopped over the red sandstone and basalt outcrops. Two distant couples were walking along the beach, otherwise we were alone.

'Binning Wood was replanted during the 1950s, following the eighteenth century design,' I said. 'Originally done by the sixth Earl of Haddington. Or rather the Countess. First area of managed forestry in Scotland. Peaceful, isn't it?'

'Karen said you'd broken up with your partner. Is that connected to your phobia?'

'Mmm.' I watched the gannets. 'I see her at every bus stop, in every crowd, looking out of every window. I hear her voice. Singing. Most nights I dream about her. But I've been too upset about Peter and Karen this past week to think of much else, even her.'

'What's her name?'

It was hard to answer.

'Linda. Linda Piric. Serbian father, English mother. Born in London.'

'So what's the thing about lime trees?'

We rounded the apogee of the little headland and strolled over the grass and heather above the low cliffs. Below us the sea throbbed, rocking St Baldred's Cradle, a susurrus of wavelets on shingle. I recalled the Berwickshire dell where Alison had found solitude. I saw the gate in the hedge, the burn welling from the soft earth, the rough path into the valley, the tree-clad slope where we'd dreamed in golden summer days.

'Linda. Linden.' I shrugged. *Lindenbaum*. Lime tree. 'Any sight of them, any mention of them, stirs it up again. I take refuge in Bach.'

'What happened?'

'She grew apart from me and found someone else. Happens to lots of people.'

'You're the only one who feels your feelings. It might sound corny, Doug, but it helps if you talk. If you found another relationship–'

'I need time. Damn it, why didn't we bring binoculars? Look at those shore waders! Oystercatchers, redshanks, curlews … I've seen greenshank here, and whimbrels, and dunlins and knots and ringed plovers. Twitcher's paradise.'

Beth stared at me and questions climbed towards her lips. Finally she asked: 'What caused the mud flats?'

'The mouth of the East Lothian Tyne is reclaimed land, and the Firth's tidal. The Tyne backs up every full tide and deposits soil eroded from farmland upstream. A twice-daily banquet for birds.'

I pointed out the foothills of the Lammermuirs, carved and deposited by retreating ice sheets, and the ghosts of volcanoes that had erupted when Scotland collided with England four hundred million years ago. She listened. The sun sank lower and daylight began to fade. We completed our tour of the headland and rejoined the path through the darkening woods. On our way back to the car we scuffed up piles of fallen leaves and threw armsful at each other, laughing like kids. There was no further talk of Linda, no further mention of certain trees; nor did I ask why she'd mentioned them when there were none in Binning Wood. When we reached the car she kept her distance until I'd unlocked it.

'Fancy a Chinese?' I said.

'I fancy seeing the bull and the documents. We'll get a takeaway, though. Let's go home and change and I'll phone the order while you reveal the treasures.'

Neither of us doubted we'd spend another evening together.

'I don't want the bull in your house. The documents are fine, but not … No, *listen*, Beth. After I left you last night, Iain McArdle came to talk to me. I don't think the police followed us today but they'll be watching your house.'

'Shit. So how do I get the bull to Tom MacIntyre? Anyway, I want to *see* it.'

'Leave it in the car and I'll drive it to Professor MacIntyre's lab. whenever he says. As for seeing it …'

At East Linton I left the A199, formerly the A1, took the single-track lane past Hailes Castle and parked beneath the overgrown hedge. No traffic passed. I unleashed the case from the sports bag, handed the folder of documents to Beth and stood the bull on the driver's seat. The Toyota's internal light was strong enough to reveal its contours but the shadow beneath it was black. Beth stretched out a hand and then withdrew it again. I put the bull back into its case and returned it to the sports bag. Once again Beth sat rigid, gripping the folder, staring through the windscreen. I drove along the country lanes to Haddington, took the Pencaitland road to the A68 and Dalkeith and returned to Penicuik via Bonyrigg. She said nothing until we were near her street. Then:

'You're right, Doug. It's beautiful, and I suppose it's stylistically correct for a 6th century BCE Sicilian-Greek bronze, but I don't want it in the house.'

Indoors, she recovered her poise but her excitement about the documents was tangible. I showered and changed and she did likewise. We studied the Chinese restaurant menu and she telephoned the order, half her attention on the paperwork. They didn't deliver so I'd have to collect the meal. Beth had to be prised away from the papers to call Professor MacIntyre. He said he'd be in the department at noon the following day and sounded enthusiastic; like most experts past retiring age he liked to be called upon. Beth returned to the documents and started to take notes.

Harmony rubbed against her and climbed on to her lap disregarded. I found plates, put them to warm and set off to collect dinner.

At the front door I almost collided with a tall, skinny, bespectacled man with thinning red hair and a dog collar. His right thumb was hovering beside the bell button.

'Oh– I'm so sorry– I … I was looking for Miss Elizabeth Odombo. Perhaps I've … er …'

'May I ask who you are?'

'Yes, of course, I'm sorry – she e-mailed me last night, most distressing news about my sister, I've come as quickly as I could. Er … Eric Winster. *Is* this Miss Odombo's house?'

16

I hadn't intended to introduce Eric into *The Bronze Bull* until later so I'd formed no clear picture of him. A *clergyman*? I introduced myself and amended the order to the Chinese restaurant. By the time I returned, Beth had answered Eric's initial questions. Our shared distress forged a bond, which the sharing of food reinforced; a ritual dating from the Pleistocene.

'I knew what had happened before I received your e-mail, Beth. A reporter called Emma Menzies phoned. She was seeking "background".'

'Hell of a way to find out, Eric.'

'Yes, Doug, I was shocked.' Eric smiled. 'I thanked Ms Menzies for her interest and offered to pray with her for Karen, and for Peter. It's an effective way of discouraging journalists.'

Beth sniggered. I began to like Karen's brother. He told us he was eight years her senior. He'd been a teenager when their father died, she a child, so he'd become more parent than sibling. He'd graduated by the time Karen entered her teens and had been ordained by the time she started going out with boys. He'd tried not to be over-protective. However, he and Peter had disliked each other.

'Of course Peter was a fine-looking man, charismatic, excellent all-round education. Remarkable drive and vigour. My wife and I understood the attraction. But there was a taint of jealousy; possessiveness. And when we learned of his less ethical business dealings we feared Karen would suffer by association. There was a parting of ways. We've heard little from Karen these past two years.'

I confirmed that Karen loved Peter: both being strong characters they'd argued, but the relationship had been secure. Beth agreed.

'There was a resonance between them,' she said. 'Of course they had disagreements, like all couples, but they never lasted.'

We cleared away the remains of dinner and Eric wanted to smoke. He and I retired to the back garden to share a habit that had degenerated within twenty years from social norm to grounds for ostracism. Beth was anxious to return to the papers so her disapproval was desultory. Harmony scuttled under the hedge.

'Clouding over.' Eric drew on his cigarette. 'The front's moving north. Forgive me if I seem distracted, Doug. It's been a shock. I'm grateful to you and Beth for your kindness to Karen.'

I'd feared some such remark. Once again, needles of guilt stitched my viscera.

'I wish we could magic her out of this situation, Eric.'

'You're convinced she's innocent, aren't you? I wonder why Beth isn't.'

Eric had read Beth's mind. Also, he'd outsmarted Emma. But Emma's search for "background" would continue. She'd unearth schoolfellows, undergraduate acquaintances, boyfriends, colleagues, neighbours, anyone who'd let slip an unguarded word she could quote out of context. Her reports would fuse those infelicities into a caricature of her victim, embellished with fabrication. Any hint about sex would add colour, mainly scarlet. A much-liked and internationally respected archaeologist would be presented to a prurient public as greedy, manipulative, promiscuous, evil and sick. People believe what they read, even when it contradicts their experience, and Emma was good at her job.

'When the police arrest someone,' I said, 'even someone we know and trust, we presume guilt. And ninety percent of murders are committed by someone close to the victim. So you can understand Beth's uncertainty.'

Eric stubbed out his cigarette and lit another, offering me the pack.

'Doesn't Beth's thinking echo that of a member of the jury, Doug? Despite occasional miscarriages of justice, I've always supposed an innocent person has nothing to fear from the law.'

Miscarriages are common in high-profile cases, even in England: the Birmingham Six, the Guildford Four, the Bridgewater Three, the Jill Dando murder. The tabloids increase the likelihood of conviction by keeping the accused in the public eye, and the jury's eye, before and throughout the trial. Karen's case was high-profile, the accused a person of high standing. Also, an RP-speaking English defendant was disadvantaged before a Scottish jury. Moreover, everyone who knew about Peter's involvement in international trafficking of artefacts would assume Karen was complicit, lending her expertise to the traffickers. She'd cohabited with one of them; *ergo* she was involved in crime; *ergo* she was guilty of murder.

'Criminal courts tend to favour the accused, Eric. The prosecution has to prove guilt beyond reasonable doubt, so the defence need only elicit doubt. Indeed, some *guilty* people walk free.'

'You're being kind, Doug, but you're not saying what you believe.'

'Pointless to speculate. The trial's too far ahead. But the prosecution has problems. No witness to the murder has come forward. There's no obvious link between Karen and the murder weapon.'

Eric frowned at the sky and asked about the documents that had commanded Beth's attention. I summarised the bronze bull story without mentioning Jimmy Farquhar, or my inferred reasons for Karen's arrest: the pressure of a high-profile crime on the police, and Iain's need to lay down a marker in the battle against the antiquity-smugglers. I didn't divulge the bull's whereabouts, either, but Eric soon deduced that I had it.

'Er … Doug, you and Beth are obviously close, but I–'

'We met five days ago. All we have in common is Karen's plight. It's forged a friendship that seems deeper than it's had time to become.'

Harmony followed us back indoors. Beth said the documents seemed to authenticate the bull, but she had doubts. She'd e-mailed inquiries to the National Museum of Antiquities in Athens.

We discussed plans: I wondered when we'd deliver the bull to Tom MacIntyre; she was concerned about the state of Karen's flat; Eric had to find somewhere to stay and was anxious to visit Cornton Vale. We soon reconciled our agendas. I rang the *Brigadoon* and reserved a room for Eric for one night. He'd meet Beth at Karen's the following morning and they'd start to tidy the house. Then, with

Karen's permission, he'd move in; his wife and the bishop seemed understanding. I'd photocopy the documents for Karen. 'Don't bother with the *EJA* paper, I can download that,' said Beth. I'd drive Beth and the bull to Tom MacIntyre's lab at lunchtime and take Eric to Cornton Vale in the evening. Beth had amended the visiting arrangements to accommodate him.

I drove back to the hotel and Eric followed in his ageing Volkswagen. His outward calm was commendable; perhaps his recourse to prayer would quiet the demons tearing his soul. I lacked the comfort of faith but I needed to assuage my guilt. I carried briefcase and laptop to my room.

Only two sentences were required to evoke Karen's state of mind, the abyss of despair occasioned by Peter's violent death and her own arrest. It took many more words to restore her reasoning powers and self-command. Too abrupt or absolute an escape from depression would have been absurd; the reader had to be carried through the metamorphosis. I drafted and redrafted sentences, consulting the thesaurus. Midnight had passed before, with a silent appeal to Apollo, I saved the file.

But my guilt resisted the literary exorcism. I lay restless, the day's events gathering to a mental cyclone, the calm waters of sleep far away. Then turbulent dreams sucked me down to depths unplumbed by analysts and hurled me back like a cork to the surface of consciousness. Karen and Jimmy discussed my iniquities, which they'd divulged to the police; my arrest was imminent. Peter delivered an oration to Eric proving that none of the suspects in *The Bronze Bull* could have killed him, so I was perforce the perpetrator. Beth turned her back on me. Then, in the midst of the nightmares, I was making love with Linda. I'd enjoyed, suffered, longed for such dreams night after night after her departure, but lately she'd grown too remote for intimacy. Now my dream passion was overwhelmed by culpability, love suffocated under a mud-slide of blame. How could I embrace another woman when I'd destroyed Karen? How could I have left Jimmy's body untended, like Perilaus on the fanged rocks below the cliff?

I awoke with rain battering the window, reorientated myself and reached for my cigarettes. My hands were clammy. They left a misty, translucent print on the glass cover of the bedside table. The image evoked a shock of realisation.

On the previous evening, Iain had taken our glasses back to the bar. He'd been wearing gloves. He'd returned his own glass but I thought he'd pocketed mine. No wonder he'd looked untidy.

My fingerprints were all over Jimmy Farquhar's flat.

17

I couldn't unwrite what had happened. My World One paranoia had re-awakened in the midst of my World Three pseudo-life, making me hanker after security locks, making me look over my shoulder as I walked. If, or perhaps when, my fictional protagonist arrested me, would an untenable paradox ensue?

This rekindled foreboding made me efficient. Did Y2K have a similar effect on the credulous in World One? I'd showered, shaved, breakfasted and left the hotel before Eric emerged from, I hoped, a better night's slumber than mine. As I drew the maximum sum from the ATM, filled the gas guzzler's tank and photocopied the papers in a newsagent's shop, I felt hooded eyes watching, heard whispers, smelled the excitement of pursuers; but I was focussed. How right you were, Dr Johnson: nothing concentrates the mind like the prospect of hanging. Persistent drizzle and a low grey sky echoed my frame of mind but afforded me camouflage. No more than half the morning had passed before I drove into West Arthur Street and squeezed the Toyota between the perfectly-parked BMW and the obliquely-angled Volkswagen.

The choreography of our first meeting was reversed: I rang Karen's doorbell and Beth answered. She was wearing jeans, sweater, rubber gloves and an expression of dejected anger.

The police search had torn the living room mirror from

the wall, tipped over the chairs and scattered cushions. The chaise longue lay on its back. All the books had been pulled from the shelves and lay in heaps, some open, some upside down with pages bent and spines cracked. The back of the television had been unscrewed. The carpet had been lifted, floorboards examined. The kitchen cupboards had been emptied, packets of dry goods split open, contents spilling over work surfaces. Karen's mug, the present from Peter with the Menander quotation, had been smashed. In the master bedroom, the contents of drawers and wardrobe lay spread across the carpet. The bed she'd shared with Peter had been overturned, the mattress slashed open. Stuffing poured across a pillow from an old teddy bear, a relic of childhood. Eric sat immobile amid the desolation.

'They'd left the door unlocked,' said Beth. 'The police warn us about security but they didn't lock the door. Anyone could have walked in. We did. The fridge was open, too. And look! Every room! What gives them the right to trash someone's property?'

'As far as they're concerned it's just a criminal's property,' I said. 'The level of damage depends on the officer in charge. Neither Iain McArdle nor Bob Williamson was here. Is anything missing, do you know?'

'You're fucking joking. I wouldn't know where to start.'

It wasn't just Karen's home that had been wrecked, it was her life with Peter. The house still echoed with him: his clothes wrenched from the wardrobe, his razor in the bathroom, his scattered CDs. The PCs through which they'd chatted had been taken away. *Anna Karenina*, which he read aloud to her in Russian, lay amid the turmoil, pages like the wings of a shot bird. DVDs they'd watched together, curled up in the same armchair, had been torn from their cases. All symbols of their love had been dismembered.

'We should call the press.' Eric's voice issued from an emotional maelstrom: contrary currents of fury, incredulity and misery. 'Photographs in the papers … the Independent Police Complaints Commission–'

I interrupted.

'The press wouldn't publish the photos, Eric. They give the police carte blanche when a suspect's been arrested. And the IPCC can do nothing about a legal search. We can only tidy up, try to determine what's missing and keep the truth from Karen.'

'Don't the police have to give receipts when they take stuff?' said Beth.

'Everything they take for evidence. Computers, for example.'

But if a light-fingered officer with a wife or girlfriend nicked jewellery, who'd know?

Yet within an hour we'd restored a semblance of order. Righting the carpets and furniture, cleaning up the debris, putting books and clothes away and reassembling the mirror and television made the house less like Bedlam. Framed photographs mocked the desolation: Karen and Peter at the Museum staff Christmas party, laughing together on the beach in Bali, hand in hand outside a coffee house in Vienna.

Karen's hairbrush had disappeared. One hair on the murder weapon would be compelling evidence. In that context, the scullery held an interesting discovery. Peter had kept his tools there. Given his capacity for domestic improvements, why wasn't there a heavy hammer? The argument was convoluted but plausible. When Peter and Alison bought their flat in the Old Town they'd rebuilt it from the inside, doubling its market value. When Peter left to live with Karen he'd taken his tools and other personal possessions, though he'd left everything else for Alison, including the flat. Alison had sold the flat to buy her East Lothian cottage. Her enthusiasm for DIY remained undimmed, yet she'd purchased few tools of her own. When she renovated a house, such – I supposed – as her friend Jan's, she borrowed equipment. At Karen's trial, the prosecution could make Alison testify to the content of Peter's tool collection as it had been when they cohabited; it would have included at least one heavy hammer. The police who'd searched Karen's flat would swear they'd found no two-pound hammer. Add, perhaps, the evidence of Karen's hair on the hammer recovered from The Meadows, and the problem of linking her to the murder weapon could be solved. No one would suggest the police had removed such a hammer from among Peter's tools and added the blood and hair.

Of course, all this was a mere flight of fancy.

Noon approached. Eric had bought sandwiches, which we ate in virtual silence. Then Beth and I drove to King's Buildings while Eric continued the restoration. I parked in West Mains Road, no easy task, and we walked to Professor MacIntyre's lab. A cold wind drove rain and fallen leaves into our faces and the tartan sports bag beat a tattoo on my knee. I wished I'd written better weather. Would the conditions deter watchers? I sensed scrutiny. Beth didn't speak. She was battling against wind and rain, dismayed about Karen's house and wondering what to say to Tom

MacIntyre. But in the lab she reverted to the decisive, vivacious Beth I'd met on Saturday afternoon.

'Delicate situation, Tom. This piece was loaned to Karen; it belongs to a foreign museum. Allegedly pre-Christian, but is it authentic? I've studied the analytical data and I've copied–'

'No, Beth, don't show me. I'd rather work without expectations.' Tom MacIntyre was small and round. A miniature tsunami of white hair broke around his bald pate. His spectacles recalled Richard Latimer-Brown's. 'Discretion needed, eh? Bad business about Karen. Well, let's see the piece.'

I'd no option but to drag the bronze bull from its private darkness into this arena of white coats and fluorescent lights. I could have written the outcome if I'd researched the techniques to be used, even the questions to be asked. The fate of the bull, indeed the novel, rested on this investigation, but again I was unprepared. Tom lifted the bull in his podgy hands, frowned, and settled it on the spotless bench.

'Hmm. How old did you say? *Lots* of verdigris. Hamid! Hamid, will you look at a sample, please? Now, let's see …'

A younger man approached from the far end of the lab. His greeting was civil, his eyes suspicious. He and Tom fell into rapid *sotto voce* discourse; a couple of hours would pass before they could tell us anything. We retired to the coffee room. I asked Beth what Tom and Hamid would do.

'They'll check whether the patina's genuine or artificial and analyse the bronze. Then we can draw inferences.'

Her excitement was back at full strength. She sipped the

dismal coffee and her eyes were distant. My simulation of interest encouraged her. Bronzes intended for different purposes have different compositions, she said. She talked about trace elements and lead signatures, launching into detailed explanations. She soon lost me.

'The lead isotope ratio in a copper ore – its lead signature – is characteristic of the geological age of the deposit,' she explained. 'It helps us identify its geographical origin.'

However, she said, lead signatures were equivocal because of bronze recycling and mixed origins; the copper used to make the bull could have had different sources. Karen's book was considered definitive on such questions. I was regaled with facts and figures about ores from Cyprus, Phoenicia, Syria and Sardinia. Beth had read Karen's book. I hadn't because it didn't exist in World One.

'So Tom's analysis might not tell us the age or origin of the bull after all.'

'Metal analysis can't give unambiguous answers, Doug. Andropoulos and co. included an analysis of the bull in their *EJA* paper and identified the source of copper on that basis. Karen said their reasoning was unsound. Even if Tom gets the same results as Andropoulos it'll still be down to interpretation.'

She went on talking but I only half-listened. When I was planning *The Bronze Bull* I'd sketched a scene like this. I'd made Peter, who was alive and well at that stage, speculate about pre-Roman trade and political power in the western Mediterranean and its relevance to the source of the metal and the provenance of the bull. I hadn't done the research needed to elaborate the idea. No doubt Peter had been repeating what he'd learned from Karen and perhaps Spiro. Now Beth seemed to be explaining what I'd half-planned to put into his mouth, yet I couldn't grasp the details. When you invent fictional experts without re-searching their field of expertise, you stumble over plot developments you haven't actually developed.

I imagined recalling that conversation with Peter. It was hard to remember he'd never existed, almost impossible to accept that Beth didn't exist. I wondered if Tom MacIntyre existed in World One. I hadn't drafted his character in my sketches for the novel.

Beth was still talking about interpretations of metal analyses. I tuned back in when she said: 'But the patina – the verdigris – could tell us something definite.'

'What, exactly?' I asked.

She said natural patina forms slowly on bronze and the resulting verdigris is mainly a thin layer of basic copper carbonate. To make new bronze look old you had to hasten the process. Artificial patina was usually copper chloride or acetate, literal "verdigris", and it was thicker. Chemists could easily tell the difference. You also looked for material such as pollen grains trapped in the verdigris. That was difficult to fake.

I knew I was being watched. I drank the remnants of my coffee, feeling more and more exposed in this open space, struggling to focus on the conversation. I pulled myself together and glanced at my watch. Three o'clock; time we returned to the lab.

Tom and Hamid were ready for us. The patina had proved to be mainly carbonate, but it also contained silicates and organic material, possibly from a clay-rich soil. Hamid had identified pollen grains: certain grasses, and olive.

'Consistent with prolonged exposure to moist air in a subterranean space,' concluded Tom, 'possibly somewhere on the Mediterranean coast with a clay soil. But I'd like to repeat the investigation. Can you leave the piece with me? We'll lock it away securely.'

Tom smiled at Beth. She nodded. So far, so good.

'Anything on the metal, Tom?'

'Interesting. X-ray fluorescence gives copper 91.7, arsenic 3.6, tin 2.4, lead 2.1, plus the usual traces. Arsenic's high, but credible if the piece is ancient. The tin's high for pre-Christian ornamental bronze, though it's well below weapons grade. However–'

'Did you say *two point one percent lead*?' Beth was incredulous.

Apparently this was a hundred times higher than the lead contents of other ancient bronzes. Tin, they told me, made bronze hard but brittle. Lead made it tough but no use for sword edges because high-lead bronze couldn't be sharpened. If the bull was genuine, the high lead content could partly explain its preservation. For a precise replica of a life-size bronze bull designed to support the weight of a man, its composition was well chosen. But the lead content meant the origin of the copper couldn't be traced through a lead signature. Therefore, the data published by Andropoulos and colleagues stank.

Beth and Tom started to discuss techniques to confirm the results. Hamid drew me aside.

'Excuse me, but it is better if you and the lady will leave soon. Tom is growing animated. You know he has heart condition?'

At Beth's prompting, Tom was photographing the bull

from various angles with a digital camera. Indeed, the old boy seemed excited.

'I didn't. I'm sure Beth didn't, either, or we wouldn't have imposed.'

'Please, don't misunderstand. He loves this work. He asks me sometimes to help because I am palynologist. He is good man, excellent scientist, I like to work with him. And he is glad you ask him for this help. But I am worried for his health. You understand?'

'Of course. Thanks for telling me. I'll try to prise Beth away, and perhaps you can calm Tom down.'

Hamid nodded and returned to his microscope. I glanced at my watch again and interrupted the discussion.

'Beth, little though I understand the methods, I can see that Tom will need more time. We should leave. And I need to eat before I take Eric to Stirling.'

She was reluctant but she acquiesced. Within ten minutes we'd left the building, running through the rain to the Toyota, leaving the bull behind.

It was true: I'd need to eat, though perhaps I'd take Eric to Cornton Vale first. Assuming I remained at liberty long enough.

I drove Beth to West Arthur Street and went to the *Brigadoon* to change.

18

My stomach was knotted and I was worried about my blood pressure, but my smile seemed to reassure Eric. He buckled his seat-belt, hands not shaking, and we departed through wet gloom. Late afternoon rush-hour; the city bypass was gridlocked. I tried the radio: something dismal by Arvo Pärt. I switched it off. A gust of wind tugged the steering. The wipers beat.

'I admit to being anxious.' Eric cleared his throat. 'Not sure what to expect. Forgive me for saying so, Doug, but you seem tense, too.'

I muttered about sleep deficit and the week's turmoil. Eric had never visited a prison. I explained about the searches, the visit room, the surveillance, but assured him that many the staff were courteous, and I believed he might find Karen in an improved mental state.

'I trust you'll prove right. Do you mind if I smoke?'

The Toyota manoeuvred on to the M8. Lemming-descended drivers dodged from lane to lane, spray flying from serried wheels. The traffic would cease to be nose-to-tail when we reached the M9. Eric gulped cigarette smoke.

'Early indications are that the bronze bull is ancient and of Mediterranean origin, though the lead content's odd,' I said. 'Check whether Karen's sent Beth a pro form for the documents. And tell her Tom's taken the photos.'

'I will. Beth tried to update me after you returned from the lab. Doug, is the bull safe? Karen will want reassurance.'

'Tom's promised security. No one else will know it's there except his colleague Hamid, and neither of them knows the police want it.'

'Before today I'd have insisted you hand it over to the police. But having seen Karen's flat ...' He sighed and disposed of his cigarette butt. 'Its creator couldn't have anticipated the misery his work would cause. He'd have been distressed. Or gratified, perhaps.'

I took the M9 turnoff, moved into the outside lane and hit the speed limit. Then the mirror showed a police car in my wake. Rain splattered the windscreen and my heart skipped. With one eye on the speedometer I tried to answer Eric, but the knot in my stomach tightened. A small voice of reason said *You're fine, no siren*, but the police car continued to follow.

'Interesting ethical issue about creation, isn't it, Eric? Should the creator be held responsible for what his creations do? Sorry, terrible question to put to a clergyman. I was thinking of technology and maybe art.'

'It's a *good* question. Do you have an opinion?'

'I believe inventors should think hard about applications of their work, but they can't be blamed for *unforeseeable* developments. As for art; during the early twentieth century, young French criminals blamed the influence of André Gide ...'

I was starting to gabble. My voice tailed away. We passed the Linlithgow turnoff. The police car maintained its distance.

'Novels don't excuse criminals, Doug. In technology and art, the immediate purveyors are the moral agents, not the creators or inventors. When you present an innovation or

a work of art to an audience, you can face ethical consid-
erations the creator wouldn't have confronted.'

'And the purveyors don't always acknowledge those con-
siderations.'

Most of my attention was on the police vehicle. I was
hanging on to the conversation by my fingertips.

'Desire for profit, the urgings of vanity, the quest for
celebrity; they're all more persuasive than ethics, Doug.
But weren't you asking about the moral responsibility of
God to His creation?'

Eric was half-smiling. My mind filled with memories of
Jimmy's flat: the knife, the fight, the search for Peter's case.
How long before the siren sounded and the police forced
me on to the hard shoulder? I muttered an apology.

'No offence taken, Doug. It's a complex, fascinating
question. The problem of evil is the oldest chestnut in
theology. It's led to innumerable debates about original
sin, free will and predestination, the testing of faith, issues
about omnipotence and omniscience ...'

The police vehicle pulled into the inside lane and turned
off towards Grangemouth. The relief was so sudden, so
intense, I almost burst out laughing. In that instant came
realisation: there was a simple way of avoiding arrest for
the murder of Jimmy Farquhar. My mind hadn't been
working. It was ironic to have spotted the solution during
a conversation about the ethics of creation, but the lightening of spirit rendered me insensitive to irony. For a
halcyon interval I didn't care about anything, real or
fictional.

'Omnipotence and omniscience? What about them,
Eric?'

'Theologians are like economists: put three of them into the same room and they'll produce six different opinions. Have you read Arthur Peacocke's books?'

I'd never heard of Arthur Peacocke. In my manic condition the name struck me as absurd.

'You'd appreciate them, with your medical background; Peacocke was a biochemist before he was ordained. He argues that "omniscience" denotes total knowledge of past and present but *not* the future. God can't know or determine the future. His interpretation allows for free will, for moral decision-making and responsibility. It reconciles evolutionary theory with Church teachings. Fundamentalists don't like Peacocke because he writes for intelligent readers.'

The jibe allowed me to laugh, which I'd been aching to do since the police car left my tail and inspiration suffused my mind.

'Tut-tut, Eric. Aren't you being unkind?'

'Hardly. Fundamentalism's an interesting research topic for social scientists, but it's a menace to the harmony between faith and reason.'

'I won't argue with that. What has Peacocke to say about omnipotence, then?'

'That's more complex, but it follows once you grasp his concept of panentheism. He has interesting things to say about prayer ... But I mustn't go on. The chief foible of the zealot isn't to kill his enemies, it's to bore his friends.'

How like his sister he was, notwithstanding his frail façade: intelligent, dedicated, enthusiastic, outspoken, critical, self-knowing, but at root sensitive and kind. He and Karen looked alike, too. And I was their creator, after a fashion. But therein lay a question. Eric had developed with little or no input from my laptop, and now he was talking about matters unknown to me such as the works of Arthur Peacocke. So in what sense *had* I created him? And didn't the same question apply to Beth and *The Bronze Bull*'s other characters?

'Eric, I see a problem with Peacocke's argument. Suppose God allows an individual to fall ill, or suffer a crippling accident, or commit a serious crime. If "omniscience" included full knowledge of past *and* future, those misfortunes could be interpreted as part of a Divine Plan. But if "omniscience" *doesn't* include knowledge of the future, hasn't God acted immorally, with unforeseeable consequences? What does Peacocke's view of "omniscience" tell us about the notion of a Divine Plan?'

Concentrating on the road, mind buzzing with my device for evading arrest, I took in little of Eric's reply. The answers seemed to boil down to faith. You could say God was testing us, like Job, or you could blame the Devil ... I think he explained how Peacocke rescued the Divine Plan from my logical bind. But my ears picked up one remark:

'... or you can say the Creator takes an infinitely wider view than we can imagine. According to Peacocke's panentheism, God participates in the world but He's not *of* the world. Therefore, His actions can't be subject to our ethical rules. If you or I were to inflict suffering on a fellow-being we'd do wrong. If God does so, He's not inflicting suffering on a *fellow*-being and therefore can't be said to do wrong. We should view the anticipated end of the world in that light, though theologians debating eschatological matters seldom do so.'

I didn't suppose Eric was talking about Y2K. My mind was on my new scheme, but the discussion had been beneficial, distracting and animating him. However, he was unsettled again when we reached the prison car park. I reminded him of what he must tell Karen. He smoked another cigarette before he trudged towards the visitors' waiting room.

Hungry, I drove into Stirling, bought a fish supper and devoured it in the car. Then I dug out my laptop. Even with greasy fingers I could type quickly. The battery held out and within half an hour my scheme had been implemented. In World One I could have written the same words but they'd have achieved nothing. In World Three they'd teach David Michie a lesson for haranguing me. I'd no longer be arrested for Jimmy's murder. In view of Eric's comments, and Arthur Peacocke's reasoning, could my scheme be deemed unethical?

I drove back to Cornton Vale to collect Eric. He emerged beaming from the prison building. Karen's frame of mind was *far* better than he'd feared. Ah, the power of my laptop! I prayed it would continue to serve me.

'She was angry, of course, and speculating about the identity of Peter's killer. However, she was articulate. She even seemed pleased to see me. And it was easy to switch her attention from the murder to the bull. She was delighted by your news and she's posted a pro form for the documents and photos. She wanted to know all about Tom's findings. I believe I remembered the essential points.'

He could only have learned those points from Beth. They'd established a rapport. I hadn't written that rapport and I didn't intend to. They had no right to it.

'Were you really OK?' I asked. 'It couldn't have been easy after two years. I didn't want to ask you before the visit, for obvious–'

'It was tactful of you, Doug. Thanks. Initially there was constraint and tension, but overall it was easier than I'd feared. Now, before I forget, she told me some names to pass on to Beth, who must consult the literature on her behalf. Let me see … Gale, and Begemann and colleagues, have written about metallurgical matters; there's Ridgway on pre-Roman Mediterranean trade; papers by Giardino, Webster, Smith … I'll write down the names as we travel, if you'll forgive my silence.'

He wrote. Then I let him talk more about Karen. He speculated about the circumstances of her arrest and her safety in the prison, but there were childhood recollections, too. Distant though they'd grown, he loved her.

'It must have been tough for you as a teenager, Eric. I gather your mother started to show dementia symptoms while she was quite young.'

'She was forty when the memory lapses began, a year or two before my father died. I was fourteen, Karen was six. My younger brother had died in infancy. Fortunately, my father's sister and her husband lived nearby and were an enormous help. They're dead now but I remain in their debt. But yes, I had to cope with losing one parent and caring for another, and for a young sister, while I was adolescent. I didn't regain my faith until my final undergraduate year. But the experience granted me an understanding of human sorrow, which with God's help I've been able to use.' He was quiet for a moment and then added, 'My poor mother hasn't had a lucid moment for five years. I

171

remember the last one; she thought she was talking to a nine-year-old Karen. But she spoke to the memory of her daughter with great love, so I believe such recollections as she retains are happy. And she'll never learn what's befallen Karen.' He smiled. 'We shouldn't be too ready to blame God for our sorrows. The Almighty sees a broader picture than we can.'

He'd transferred his distress about Karen to memories of the past. He, too, was a victim of my half-written murder mystery. I was glad I hadn't bestowed close relatives on Peter. A step-sister and her family in Australia were mentioned in chapter 1 of *The Bronze Bull*, but they probably hadn't heard about his death. I hoped they'd remain ignorant until I escaped from World Three. I couldn't have borne my literary endeavours to cast *more* people into misery. Yet even as I formulated the thought I detected hypocrisy. What had I written this evening but further grief for at least one character?

The wind and rain had slackened and no police car followed us into Edinburgh. Perhaps my half hour with the laptop had taken effect.

I drove to Est Arthu, parked in the neat space where Beth's BMW had stood earlier and declined Eric's invitation to supper and tea. I was glad he was there to look after Karen's house. If I'd been in control of the story, as an author should be, I'd have engineered his arrival for that purpose. But would I have made him a clergyman? Why were his intelligence, perceptiveness and kindness tempered with the kind of vulnerability that awakens women's protective instincts?

A need for solitude filled me, familiar from World One.

My *pied à terre* in the *Brigadoon* called. I was glad Beth had gone home. I didn't want to socialise. I bade Eric good night and drove to Newington.

In my room I dropped my briefcase and switched on my mobile. There was a text from Beth asking me to call her. My heart sank but I obliged. She was anxious for news and didn't want to ask Eric in case the visit had upset him. I assured her Karen had seemed more like her usual self, according to Eric; she'd asked him to pass on some work-related messages that I couldn't remember. I hoped she'd ring off and phone Eric but she evinced a desire to chat: there was exciting new information about the bull. I promised to call her in the morning so she could tell me about it.

I bought a bottle of single malt from the bar and made inroads into it before retiring to bed. Whisky was a medical requisite. The radio was playing Shostakovich's ninth quartet, the one with the extended final movement. I made no further attempt to write.

Lying in bed, I wondered why it had taken me so long to solve the problem of impending arrest. Linda would have laughed and called me slow-witted. Peter would have been sarcastic.

World Three had its own momentum, its own programme. I could guide or modulate only certain elements of it by writing. Yet it had been formed and set in motion by what I'd written.

No novelty in that, I supposed. In the beginning was the Word.

19

As promised, I phoned Beth after breakfast and told her I'd been invited out for dinner; old friends. Silence billowed from Penicuik. I asked whether she was free for lunch. She wondered whether I could spare the time.

'You can come round at one,' she conceded, and rang off.

I lit a cigarette. My next phone call was overdue.

'Richard? Doug. About Jimmy Farquhar.'

'He's dead. It was in the paper.'

'I didn't know whether you'd heard. There are implications—'

'Not on the phone, Doug, not on the phone. Can you come out?'

I drove to Abbey House and was admitted. Lydia smiled and handed me a cup of tea. She still couldn't find the sugar. The television was on with the sound muted, as it had been in Jimmy's flat. Richard was frowning, pacing, snapping at Lydia. Then he snapped at me:

'David's visiting a lawyer.'

'Do you know why?'

'I've a fair idea. A fair idea. We'll talk in the workshop.'

He led me downstairs, leaving Lydia to twitter among recipes and Playstation games. Half-completed projects lay on the benches and three drawers had been left open. David had left in a hurry.

Without preamble, Richard announced: 'David's been helping so-called illegal immigrants. Fortress Britain, Doug,

174

Fortress Britain. Can't have the walls breached. Ha-ha! Needs legal advice. What do you know about Farquhar's death?'

'Who killed him, you mean?'

'Do you know?'

'Of course not.'

'Have the police found the bull? That's what matters.'

'We'd know if they had. The papers would be full of it.'

'No they wouldn't. Police would keep the lid on it. You know nothing about police methods, nothing at all.'

I pointed out that smuggling archaeological treasures was big business and Scotland Yard was involved. If Iain McArdle had found the bull, he'd have publicised it so Scotland Yard couldn't steal all the glory.

'Also,' I added, 'it could help him to convict Karen.'

Richard started pacing again.

'Karen Winster couldn't have killed Farquhar.'

'True. But suppose she didn't kill *Peter*, either. Suppose someone in the international smuggling ring–'

'Wouldn't explain how Farquhar got the bull. *Smuggling ring*? Ha-ha!'

I said I couldn't guess how Jimmy had acquired the bull.

'*If* he acquired it. But *did* he, Richard, or was he conning you? And if he'd had it, and whoever killed him took it, what do you infer?'

'I know what you *want* me to infer but there are too many ifs and maybes. Ifs and maybes. Far too many. Farquhar had the bull, otherwise how could he have known about it? You think a gang of interntional smugglers killed him and took it? Ha-ha! Too far-fetched, Doug. Too far-fetched.'

I asked whether he knew about Spiro Andropoulos. He didn't, so I told him.

'So Ibrahim Youssef's a PLO terrorist or something of the kind,' said Richard. 'Nothing to do with the bull. And face facts: Karen Winster killed Peter. Police wouldn't have charged her otherwise.'

'Innocent until proved guilty, Richard. Iain McArdle believes she can be implicated in smuggling. I think he's wrong. In any event the bull's hot property, though it could be a fake. Spiro Andropoulos had a reputation for dishonesty.'

Richard gesticulated, joked about deceptions and coincidences and uttered his hyena laugh; then silence descended. His pacing resumed.

'Bloody shame about Peter. You know, if he hadn't left Alison … He wouldn't have if she hadn't lost the baby.'

'I thought he was supportive after the miscarriage.'

'Of course. Of course he was. Decent young man. But when they told her she couldn't have children it was the end. Remember him at children's parties, juggling, setting up games? Charity fund-raising? He wanted kids.'

As far as I knew, Karen had never expressed a desire for children.

'If he hadn't left Alison he wouldn't have traded in archaeological relics,' I said.

Richard grunted. I'd planted a seed of doubt; investment notwithstanding, he was no longer sure he wanted the bull. Then he said: 'I felt responsible, Doug. Damned silly, but I was twenty years older than them. Brought them together.'

'I thought David made the first overseas contacts for

Peter and was miffed because he never got a cut of the profits. Hardly your doing, Richard.'

'Peter's dealings with David were none of my concern. None at all. And he found that Hermes, the icons from Kiev, the … I meant the day they met. Peter and David and I were talking business. Alison came to see Lydia. Asked them all to stay for dinner. So yes, I brought them together.'

Alison had given me a different account of how she'd met Peter. I'd also heard different opinions about responsibility. And Richard had qualms about introducing two people who'd subsequently separated, but no scruples about buying illicit goods.

I left Abbey House before David returned. Illegal immigrants? Possibly; but my intervention by laptop could have precipitated David's visit to his lawyer. I drove half a mile from Abbey House before I stopped for a cigarette. It was misty. I could hardly see the way ahead.

I cut across country to Penicuik and reached Beth's at ten to one. She didn't want to go out for lunch. She stalked into the kitchen to prepare sandwiches. Silence, except for the soft swish of a knife. No CD playing. I drummed my fingers on the arm of my chair and studied the barometer. A view of her back welcomed me into the kitchen.

'What's wrong, Beth?'

'You know what's wrong. And you didn't try to put it right when you had the chance.'

I wasn't afraid of arguing with her but I feared the potential aftermath.

'I rang as soon as I got your text last night, but I was far too tired to discuss your new information. Much as I wanted to.'

'Oh. And this morning?'

'I said I wanted to see you.'

She put down the knife and turned to face me, arms folded.

'You said you were going out later. You sounded *really* eager. Would you have phoned last night if I hadn't texted you?'

I wasn't disposed to be browbeaten by someone who didn't exist.

'Probably not.'

'Right. So either you'd have left it to Eric to tell me about Karen, or I'd have stewed in a cauldron of anxiety all night and you wouldn't have given me a second thought.'

She'd been rehearsing her lines, whipping up her ire. I hadn't written this scene. I needed to stay calm.

'Eric was happier after he'd seen Karen. You could have phoned him with impunity, Beth. Also, I've had to deal with other matters, nothing to do with Karen or the bull. Don't accuse me of not thinking or not caring about you. As for this evening, the date was arranged some time ago.'

My words glanced off her armour.

'It wasn't just last night and this morning. Yesterday afternoon I was *so* excited about Tom's analysis, but you couldn't get me out of his lab. quickly enough. And you knew what a beastly morning I'd had at Karen's. One day you're all kindness and concern, the next ... I don't know where I am with you.'

I told her if it hadn't been distracted by another major worry I'd have been as excited as she was about the analysis, just less informed.

'And this major worry–?'

'Resolved, I hope. I pulled you away from Tom's because I had to get Eric to Stirling, and also because Hamid asked us to leave. He was worried Tom was becoming over-excited. Seems he has a bad heart.'

She said 'Oh' with reluctant contrition. I pressed the advantage.

'*Did* you talk to Eric last night after I'd phoned you?'

The question rekindled her anger, but then she smiled. Eric had phoned *her*, apologising for the time but eager to tell her how Karen was.

'But you can't blame me for misjudging you. You don't *tell* me anything, Doug. You should have said you'd another worry. Do you think I'm telepathic?'

'Good trick if you can do it. If you leave those sandwiches any longer they'll curl up at the edges and only be fit for a railway buffet. I'm starving.'

'Men. Insatiable appetites.'

We ate in the living room. I brewed coffee. Soon we were laughing; not sure what at. Then our conversation returned to the bull. Tom had e-mailed his photos. Two of them showed the miniature trap door in the model's back and the tiny flutes in the nostrils but the others were blemished; the light must have been wrong. In one, the bull was reduced to a curved sliver of metal, implausibly burnished and surrounded by a crimson halo. Tom had also repeated the metal analysis and confirmed his results, but he still wasn't sure how to interpret them.

'Compare Tom's results with the *EJA* paper, though, Doug. Same tin and arsenic and trace component values, but Andropoulos *et al.* said the lead was less than 0.1 percent.'

Beth's finger guided my eye over the data sheets. Her hands were small and delicate; skin colour aside, they reminded me of Linda's. She was the same height as Linda, too, five feet two or three.

'So,' I said, 'either the analyses relate to different objects or someone's miscalculated the lead content.'

Her laugh was mirthless.

'*Tom* hasn't miscalculated.'

'So the Athens analyst was either incompetent or a liar, and the inference in the *EJA* paper about the copper source isn't worth an arse full of ashes.'

'Goodness, you *are* quick today, Doug. Karen will tear this paper to shreds, along with the principal author's reputation. She has friends on the editorial board. But you think that's bad? It gets worse.'

Beth was enjoying herself; she was leading, I was following. She'd been itching to tell me all this. The National Museum in Athens had answered her first e-mail with the news that the bronze bull was still there in its display case, acquisition number corresponding to one of the labels in the document folder. She'd asked them to check whether another museum had offered to buy it.

'Did you think they would have?'

She lifted a photocopied invoice from the folder.

'Difficult to decipher who's paid, but yesterday evening I went to Karen's office and e-mailed the four museums in Sicily we mentioned. Asked them to reply to me rather than Karen. Two responded this morning.'

'Which two?'

'Paolo Orsi in Syracuse, Regional Archaeological Museum in Agrigento. They've *both* made preliminary payments for acquisition of the bronze bull from the National in Athens and believe they can secure legal title. Both insist it should never have left Sicily. Guess who'd set up the deals!'

I told her I'd need time to think about that, and then asked whether there were leads on the other numbered labels in the folder.

'Jesus, give me a chance! They might prove Andropoulos was trying to set up even more deals, they might not. I'm awaiting another reply from Athens. But I'm getting out of my depth. Thank goodness the pro form's arrived. I need Karen to study this information and direct operations. Just hope she's up to dealing with it.'

'Out of your depth? You've been brilliant. Karen's lucky to have you. I've a couple of dumb questions.'

'Only a couple?'

'Now who's being quick? First: shouldn't the National Museum in Athens analyse the bronze of the bull in their display case?'

Apparently she'd suggested that to the National the previous evening, once again pretending she was Karen and saying there were doubts about the authenticity of the object and the published analysis. 'I assured them of confidentiality, requested a check on the atom spec. results and the patina composition, and asked them to reply to my assistant Elizabeth Odombo, e-mail address supplied.'

I grinned. Beth had initiative.

'Answer awaited? OK. Second dumb question: what were the other bits and pieces in the folder?'

She explained that the Agrigento site had been excavated by a multinational team and the fragments were its various members' contributions to the *EJA* paper.

'So I contacted them. One reply so far, from Ulrike Bauer in Berlin.'

Dr Bauer had confirmed she'd written one of the extracts in the folder, but Andropoulos had performed the analyses of all the bronze finds, including the bull. She'd also conveyed sad news: the team member who'd recovered the bull from the burial chamber, Enrico Fontano, had died in a car accident in Milan soon after returning from the excavation. So the only person who could have provided eye-witness testimony to the find's authenticity was dead.

'Burial chamber? I didn't know–'

'It's described in the paper, Doug. They excavated a single male burial, early Greek; probably in his late twenties or thirties. The skeleton was disarticulated, several bones were broken and there was evidence of partial cremation. He must have been important; rich grave goods. Consistent with what Tom and Hamid found: prolonged exposure to an underground Mediterranean site with a clay soil.'

This kind of mystery fascinates amateurs but probably annoys professionals. It could have made an enthralling television programme. Beth seemed casual but she was excited by the success of her detective work – and by her naughtiness, forging e-mails from Karen's computer. She was more animated than I'd ever seen her. How long since we'd met? A week?

The conversation restored our good relations but Beth's imagination went into overdrive. She was now convinced that the smugglers had killed Peter and Spiro Andropoulos had been the evil genius behind them. After all, she reasoned, if he'd fabricated data to support his claim about Etruscan trade through Sicily, and tried to swindle money from at least two museums, he'd been capable of anything. I pointed out that if Andropoulos had sold the bull to Peter and then killed him to recover it, in person or by proxy, his actions had scarcely been rational.

She planned to have dinner with Eric that evening, since I was going out without her.

20

The Toyota's clock registered 18.50. A high wall capped with broken glass surrounded the garden and I sensed security cameras, but the wrought-iron gates were open, their bolts rusted. A blue Fiat Uno stood in the drive next to Robbie's Saab. I parked behind it and stepped on to the gravel. The drive led me around a rose bed and sundial under the gaze of the portico. I flicked my cigarette end into the bushes and rang the bell. Sounds of drilling greeted me, attenuated by hundred-year-old walls and the evening mist thickening over Cramond. Bare branches dripped. A security light cast shadows and sparkled on the glass crowning the wall. Something scuttled through the shrubbery, making me jump.

Robbie sported a tailored grey suit, elegant shoes and a tie signifying exclusive affiliations. His movements were youthful, belying the styled iron-grey hair and the crow's feet around his blue eyes. Despite my change of clothes at the *Brigadoon* he made me feel shabby.

The hall was festooned with aquatints and silverpoint sketches. A Tracy Butler seascape dominated the stairwell, its muted colours echoing the décor. The drilling continued from the back of the house, interspersed with hammering.

'I infer you've set Alison to work,' I said.

An Oscar Peterson recording played from closer to hand.

'She volunteered. Niall wants stripped pine cupboards. How are you, Doug?'

Robbie ushered me into the drawing room and the door swished shut behind us. Oscar Peterson rose to greet me. The room had all the elegance of upper middle-class Edinburgh: sap-green carpet matching high walls, plaster cornices, white skirting and architraves, soft hidden lighting. It was finicky with china ornaments and antimacassars. A log fire burned to scant effect. A Samisen loomed over the mantelpiece, an early version of his torchlit fishing expedition. The Skene on the opposite wall surprised me; when I wrote the house I'd put the Skene in the dining room.

'Had a hectic week because of the Karen business.' I accepted a glass of Beaujolais. 'I presume Niall's busy cooking while his cupboards are under construction?'

Robbie motioned me to an armchair beside the fire. I took care not to crease the antimacassar. He occupied a matching chair, back to the window. Dark velvet curtains framed his repose.

'It's fortunate one of us can cook. Have you *seen* Karen, Doug?'

'Once. She wasn't good. But she's getting visits. Her brother's looking after her house.'

'Karen didn't strike us as violent. But they freed the tramp they'd detained for killing Peter.'

He sipped his Beaujolais.

'Niall will be able to interview Alison this evening,' I said.
'What about?'

'Background. Life with Peter.'

Robbie laughed.

'We love Alison but we take what she says with a pinch of salt.'

'Known each other since childhood, though, haven't they?'

'Their parents were acquainted. Alison started high school the year before Niall left, so he didn't really know her until she and Peter bought the flat below his in the Royal Mile.' The wine glass brushed his lips again. 'We only met Peter a few times but we liked him. Did Karen know about his illicit dealings?'

'He kept the details from her and she didn't inquire. I think Alison understood Peter's business better than Karen did.'

'How much did *you* know, Doug?'

I smiled back at him. Muted joinery sounds from the kitchen continued.

'Nothing Niall hasn't already learned.'

The chess table was prepared. We started with a standard Sicilian defence. As I drank my wine I asked how Alison and Peter had met. Robbie said it was through the squash club; she was one of the few opponents who'd been able to match him. I inquired about the athletics contest in Berlin. Robbie believed Peter *had* taken her to Berlin, once. He moved another piece and I focussed on the board.

I'd never decided how the Peter-Alison relationship began. It belonged to the past when *The Bronze Bull* opened and was recalled only through flashbacks. Peter and Karen were the established couple from the start of chapter 1. The conflicting accounts I'd heard in World Three must have been floating in my mind. I didn't know how Alison had met Niall, either; irrelevant to the book. Every character in a novel is equipped with an outline CV but I don't flesh out their back-stories if there's no need. Nevertheless I'm often curious about them.

Robbie's position on the board was strong. My mind computed the costs and benefits of alternative moves. The drilling ceased; Oscar Peterson continued uninterrupted. I was studying the board when Alison barged into the room clad in boiler suit and boots. Her spectacles were those of the formulaic pedagogue.

'Don't get up, Doug, for Heaven's sake. Robbie, dear, the chef's begging for a drink and the joiner's desperate for one. Shall I open another bottle?

She deployed the corkscrew. Her muscles bulged and the cork submitted. I took a pawn. Her eyebrows rose.

'Taking *risks*? What did you put in his wine, Robbie?'

'I expected the move,' said Robbie. 'How are the cupboards?'

'Niall seems pleased, though he fears the sawdust won't improve his lobster thermidor. I must deliver this medicine to him before he goes into a decline. Then if I can borrow your spare bedroom I'll change into something more suitable for the dining table.'

'A lobster?' I suggested.

'Beware the claws. Still driving that Chelsea tractor, you eco-vandal?'

Wineglasses in hand she departed. Robbie's grin signified more than the counter-play in his latest move; a private joke.

'Which solicitor is Karen instructing?' he asked.

I moved a bishop.

'Rintoul of Rintoul MacIntosh. They say he's competent, i.e. "expensive". He'll find plenty of holes in the prosecution case if he tries.'

'Karen's arrest did seem premature. From the little I

know about him, DCI McArdle resembles Harold Wilson. You know, intelligent, careful, efficient, but couldn't cross an empty room in a straight line.'

I almost upset the table, then assured Robbie I was fine, just tired after a stressful week. I drained my glass and accepted a refill. We played a few more moves before we were summoned to dinner.

The dining room radiated affluence. The table and chairs were older than the house and in pristine condition. A nineteenth century Highland landscape hung where I'd written the Skene. I couldn't identify the artist.

The meal fell short of perfection. There was no sawdust in the dishes but they were lukewarm. Niall extolled his lovely new cupboards and savoured Karen's arrest. He was a smallish fat man, brown hair a little too long and clothes a little too colourful. He sought Robbie's approval in everything and tried to engage both guests, one an ex-lover of the deceased, one his friend, in talk about Karen and Peter. Alison's face closed. I diverted the conversation to Emma Menzies and her drug-trafficking obsession. Niall tittered.

'Yes, Doug, it's *quite* absurd. Whatever Peter was up to I'm sure it wasn't drugs. But you must *understand* Emma: she's intelligent, but too psychologically damaged to write for a proper paper. And *quite* a drink problem. Her mother died of a heroin overdose, and her father … ahem, least said. The *Record* provides an outlet for her spite and frustration. The police won't divulge what was in Peter's suitcase, so Emma makes guesses. Any ideas about that, Doug? Well, of *course* you have ideas. You were in his confidence.'

Alison's face expressed nothing. A cautionary hand movement from Robbie affected his partner not one whit.

'Peter was careful not to embroil other people in his business,' I said. 'The police believe the suitcase contained an archaeological treasure. They're probably right. He did buy such items from poor countries and sell them in rich ones.'

Robbie poured an excellent Hock. The lobster would have been good if it had been hot.

'Oh, Doug, you can do better than that.' Niall's voice wheedled. 'Whatever was in the case came from a Greek archaeologist about whom *stories* are coming to light.'

'What stories?'

'All rather hush-hush.' Niall tittered again. 'Did Peter *really* not tell you what was in his case?' He tilted his head and smiled. Some of his teeth had gold caps.

'He said he was buying something from a Greek dealer. He'd have wanted Karen to authenticate it, but it seems he told her no more than he told me.'

'Mmm. Well, Karen can't divulge much now.' Niall repeated his grin. 'Her expertise must have been invaluable for Peter. I'm sure you're right, Doug, he'd have wanted her to examine this "item". Any idea where it is?'

'Don't be so fucking stupid, Niall,' snapped Alison. 'How could Doug know that? Does it *matter*?'

'But he knows *what* it is, don't you, Doug?'

'Peter never said. Joinery complete, Alison?'

Robbie gave me a grateful glance. Alison half-smiled.

'It'll need two more rounds of sanding and varnishing. Measure the cupboards when you get a chance, Robbie. You'll appreciate the proportions.'

Robbie's relief was tangible.

'Who else would equate joinery with art and reduce both to numerical ratios?'

'An architect,' I said, 'or an unusually talented interior designer.'

'One with a guide dog?' said Alison.

'Oh, *bitchy,*' said Niall. 'Guess who's had a bad experience with experts so now she does it all herself.'

Alison gave a short, lop-sided smile that reminded me of Linda. Once again, her subdued anger seemed directed as much at me as at Niall.

'You'll never know, Niall. I'm like Doug: forget my bad experiences.'

'Ever so mysterious,' sighed Niall. 'You two have *such* a lot in common.'

Robbie frowned and shook his head. I longed for a cigarette. We ate crème brulée, drank coffee and admired the cupboards. Alison could have succeeded as a joiner if she hadn't been committed to teaching. We retired to the drawing room. Niall put logs on the fire and Alison dispensed more wine. I declined.

'Sure, Doug?' she said. 'Everyone assumes the more alcohol you drink the slower your reactions. I think the relationship's biphasic.'

'Even if you were right, you and I would be over the optimum.'

'If that's a hint I won't take it.'

She relished the hock. Robbie put on a Charlie Parker CD and we resumed our game. We both had reasonable play, but because of the wine, or Niall's provocation, or Alison's presence, or the week's accumulated emotions, I made risky moves. Niall was whispering to Alison about the months since Linda left me, my independent means, my moderate fame. Alison's face was stony. I lost pieces but then my position improved. After a while Robbie offered a draw and I accepted. Either he was being a good host or Niall had embarrassed him; he'd have had the better endgame.

After another hour I left. Alison showed no sign of departing. Robbie saw me to the door. Niall followed me to the car.

'Doug, I know you didn't want to say much in front of Alison, and I *so* admire your tact, but we're alone now. So you can tell me about the item in Peter's case.'

'I can't tell you more than I have, Niall. As for Karen: I'm sure she's innocent, but she'll be convicted if the perpetrator isn't identified soon.'

'Oh, *nonsense*, Doug. You've got a *thing* about our justice system, haven't you?'

'I've seen too many mistakes, including deliberate ones.'

'Scottish justice puts away *far* more criminals than innocent people. The courts side with the accused. Name a country with a *better* system.'

'Choose any that doesn't use juries for high-profile trials. In other words, anywhere in the developed world except England and some former British colonies including the USA.'

'That's absurd, Doug, and you know it.'

I lit a cigarette and inhaled.

'Niall, do you remember Stuart Gair case? Convicted of a murder everyone *knew* he couldn't have committed? Eight separate witnesses he'd named to his QC could have testified he was miles away when the crime was committed, but none of them was called at the trial. All the rent-boys who testified against him lied because the police had threatened them. This was all *known*, but Mr Gair is doing life. And what about T. C. Campbell and Joe Steele? *Everyone* in the prison service knew who'd committed those murders, but T. C. and Joe were stitched up, convicted, and then turned down by one appeal court after another. And what about the guy convicted of a robbery his cousin had committed? Cousin fled to the States, leaving a recorded confession vouched for on oath by two solicitors. But the appeal court wouldn't accept the confession because, quote, "The evidence could have been before the jury at the time of the trial". So yet another innocent party served his sentence although the courts *knew* he was innocent. And must I name the Glasgow drug baron who paid six-figure back-handers to the police and the courts and never got a long jail sentence? And how many cases are *literally* decided on the toss of a coin?'

Niall almost stamped his foot.

'You're arguing from a few anecdotal exceptions and *mocking* our courts. The rule is, justice prevails and is seen to prevail. Are you claiming that most prisoners in Scotland are *innocent*?'

I inhaled again.

'No, they're mainly repeat or habitual offenders who're stupid enough to stick themselves in, or they're grassed. But even *their* trials are often marred by fabricated evidence and lies in the witness box. Scottish justice is corrupt, Niall.'

'It's a free country, Doug, so you can voice your opinion. But you're in a minority of one. You wouldn't convince many *Evening News* readers.'

'And absolutely no *Daily Record* readers. You journalists apply an anti-Socratic triple filter to everything: is it false, is it unkind and is it unhelpful? If yes to all three, publish.'

'Give it a rest, Doug. There's such a thing as public interest. Karen Winster will get a fair trial. If she *is* proved innocent she'll be acquitted. Come on, it's the duty of every law-abiding citizen to support the police and the courts.'

'No, Niall. It's the duty of every citizen to recognise that the fair and impartial rule of law is the foundation of democracy, so when the law abandons fairness and impartiality, democracy starts to collapse. You think I treat Scottish justice as a joke. It isn't a joke. I value integrity. I value democracy.'

I climbed into the Toyota and turned on the ignition. Fog lamps would be needed. I put the vehicle into reverse and glided towards the wrought-iron gates. Niall was still standing on the drive. I wound down the window.

'Thanks again for dinner, Niall. Oh, and by the way, Alison's capable of deciding when or if she wants a new partner. Though I'm sure your intentions were kind. Good night.'

I swung on to the road and left him cocooned in damp mist. I felt my face twist with anger. I'd let the smug bastard provoke me into exaggerating my doubts about Scottish justice, otherwise I'd have punched him or run over him. Robbie deserved better. I switched on the radio: the *Rite of Spring*. Unseasonal, but the mood matched mine. I concentrated on the road and controlled my speed. Given the wine I'd drunk and my state of mind, I shouldn't have been driving. But the roads were quiet for a Friday evening and I reached the *Brigadoon* without incident.

Sleep eluded me. My mind whirled with Beth's discoveries and fantasies, chess positions, Niall Ferguson, Alison's closed face, Karen, Eric, Peter; and, more and more persistently, the bronze bull. *Should I have recovered it from Tom's lab? How could I have left it unsupervised for more than twenty-four hours?*

Perhaps I slept after all and the kaleidoscopic images twisted themselves into my dreams. Certainly the abrupt forcing of my bedroom door at 6 a.m. shocked me. I sat up in bed, wide awake, heart pounding. The visitors were big and grim-visaged and wore suits.

Bob Williamson thrust his warrant card into my face. There was an elderly detective constable beside him. Iain stood in the doorway, his stare unblinking.

Detained under Section Two.

There were more officers outside, some in uniform. Two police cars.

All for one innocuous detainee? Waste of taxpayers' money.

21

Why had my laptop failed in its duty?

To be pedantic, it hadn't failed; I'd been detained, not arrested. But the passage I'd written on Thursday night should have precluded detention, too; it hadn't conflicted with the established story or contradicted the past.

The elderly detective constable's driving was exemplary. Iain swamped the passenger seat. Bob sat beside me in the back. The unidentified senior officer I'd seen outside the hotel travelled with the uniforms.

'You've made a mistake,' I said.

Bob studied his knees and smiled. His suit was well-pressed, not too shiny. Iain's heavy face turned towards me.

'No, Doctor, *you've* made the mistake. Ye've underestimated the police. Senior officers have come to detain ye so ye know ye're caught. We've got ye bang to rights. Save us all a lot of arsing aboot if ye tell us now whit ye've done with the bronze bull.'

'Right enough,' said Bob. 'Ye probably reckon Farquhar had it comin' to 'im. But we need tae get yon bull back i' the right hands, an' ye're the only person can help us dae it. You help us, we'll help you.'

'I can't tell you anything about the bull,' I said.

They tried three more times before Bob sighed, 'Aye, well, jist as ye please.'

The police station stank of stale smoke, imperfect

hygiene and disinfectant. Routine processing: pockets emptied, watch removed, list of property compiled, everything put into polythene bags, fingerprints taken. I declined the offer of a lawyer. I was disorientated and needed coffee. The unidentified officer whispered to Iain. I sensed tension. Bob and a constable took me to a dingy little cell and locked the door while they prepared the interview room. I'd hardly begun to fulminate against my absurd plight when the door opened again and Bob was blocking the threshold, staring at me; a powerful figure, receding black hair, cold grey eyes.

'Listen, Doctor, please tell me where the bull is an' why ye took it. That's all I want to know. Look, there's only me and you here. Nae cameras, nae tape recorder, naebody else listenin'. Nothin' ye tell me the now can be used in court. It'd be inadmissible. Your word against mine. But it'll be a big help if ye'll jist tell me, an' then we'll mak sure the court goes easy on ye. That's a promise. Please.'

I sat on the floor and stared at him.

'How's the stomach bug, Sergeant? Recovered?'

He said we weren't there to discuss his health. He repeated his request and assurance. I told him the bull hadn't been in Jimmy's flat. His eyes flashed; I'd admitted being in Jimmy's flat. Of course I had; pointless to deny it. But if I'd admitted to finding the bull I wouldn't be the only one in trouble. He tried again. He was a good interrogator. He told me I was likely to be charged with murdering Jimmy, but if I helped them find the bull I'd face a lesser charge. I said I admired his professionalism. He was irritated. I was waking up, though my need for coffee was intense.

'I'm concerned about you, Sergeant. It takes time to recover from a GI tract infection. Your dedication to duty is admirable but medically ill-advised.'

He left, locking the door behind him. I'd staved off two rounds of interrogation, and I held a trump card: all these officers were fictional and I'd invented them. If this was revealed during the coming interview, the entire World Three illusion must crumble. I decided I'd reveal it if necessary, though I hoped my knowledge of police procedure would carry me through.

The interview room was cramped and cluttered and dim. I sat on the far side of the table, Iain and Bob facing me. Bob fiddled with the cassette recorder. Iain recited the time. Everyone present stated their names. The unidentified officer, a tall sallow man with heavy brows and stubble, leaned against the wall, arms folded and face impassive; he was a superintendent from New Scotland Yard. Big guns; I was honoured. Bob was given ostensible charge of proceedings, so Iain wasn't sure of me.

I gave my address as the *Brigadoon*. Bob wanted my permanent address. I told him: 17 Blandford Terrace, Edinburgh. Then they started on my background: place of birth, childhood, schools, university, subsequent life. I told them those matters were irrelevant to Jimmy Farquhar's death and the bronze bull. They said they'd decide what questions to ask. I told them I'd decide which to answer.

'I see no point in wasting time. Chief Inspector, when you and Sergeant Williamson questioned me in the car on the way here, I told you I didn't kill Jimmy and don't know where the bull is. And then–'

'Doctor, this interview is being recorded. Lying can only

harm your case. You know fine well we discussed nothing with you after ye were detained until this interview started.'

I feigned astonishment.

'What? In the car, you assured me you had me – what was your phrase? – "bang to rights", and if I told you where the bull was it would save us time. Have you forgotten? And a few minutes ago, when Sergeant Williamson came to talk to me privately in the–'

The Scotland Yard superintendent leaned towards the tape recorder.

'For the record, I was aware of no conversation between Mr Carmichael and any officer here present after he was detained, prior to this interview.'

'Of course you weren't.' My voice was kind. 'You were in the other car. And while Sergeant Williamson was pressing me to reveal the whereabouts of the bull, assuring me I'd face a lesser charge if I told him, you were talking to Chief Inspector McArdle.'

'That's enough, Doctor.' Iain's temper was fraying. 'There are three experienced officers here. We aw ken the rules aboot questioning detainees. Let me remind ye again, the recording o' this interview will be produced in court. Let's get on with it. Bob?'

I suppose they were prepared for responses like mine, but I'd unsettled them. Bob consulted his notes.

'So far, Doctor, ye've refused tae answer straightforward questions and ye've concocted a story about officers questionin' ye afore this interview. Can ye no' tell the truth?'

'So far, Sergeant, you've shown no sign of believing the truth. Indeed, you've denied it.'

He asked me about my job. I described my editing and

teaching work and told him I wrote crime novels. Four had been published and I was writing a fifth.

He asked whether I was married or lived alone. I found I'd told him about Linda. Surname? Piric. No, I wouldn't talk about Linda. I didn't want to talk about Linda.

'Where is she now?'

'No idea.'

No, I didn't have another girlfriend. No, there was no relationship between me and Elizabeth Odombo. No, I wasn't lonely, I was solitary.

Bob moved on to my acquaintance with Peter and Karen. He'd learned from the master who sat beside him: surround the detainee with ropes of innocent admission and then tighten the noose. I said I'd known Peter for years and met Karen through him. Yes, we were friends. Yes, his death had upset me. Yes, I'd visited Karen in Cornton Vale. The bronze bull had been mentioned during that visit. Bob asked how I'd known about it.

'Peter told me. He wanted to keep Karen more or less in the dark about it until he'd got it to her. I told Chief Inspector McArdle this the other–'

'Why do ye think Wishart wanted to keep his girlfriend in the dark, dae ye suppose?'

I pursed my lips.

'Two possible reasons. He never told Karen about dodgy parts of his business because he didn't want her involved. And he didn't want her to have preconceptions about the bull; he wanted her to judge it when she saw it. Of course, it never reached her.'

The superintendent grinned. Iain and Bob gave cynical laughs.

'Aye, right. But it reached James Farquhar? Is that what ye're sayin'?' Bob offered me a cigarette, which I accepted.

'So I was led to believe.'

'Whit led ye to believe it?'

'He phoned me.'

'When was that, like?'

I inhaled smoke and pretended to reflect.

'Let's see … Last Sunday, I think. Late morning.'

'Rang yer mobile, did he? And whit did he say?'

'He had Peter's suitcase and was willing to sell it.'

They asked how I'd known Jimmy. I mentioned fund-raising for children's charities. At which fund-raising event had I met him? When and where was it? Was that where he'd got my mobile number? How long had I had the mobile? I floundered. I was desperate for coffee. The nicotine was good, though.

'Funny thing, Doctor,' said Iain. 'Farquhar made a number o' calls from his mobile last weekend, but there's no record o' one to *your* number. How do you explain that?'

'I suppose he phoned me from his land-line.'

'He didn't have one.'

'Somewhere else, then.'

'So he phoned a lot o' people frae his mobile, then took himself off on Sunday morning to ring ye from somewhere else. Do ye no' think that's a wee bit strange?'

'He might have phoned other people from the same somewhere else. I didn't ask where he was, only what he was asking for the bull.'

'Ye believed he *had* the bull when he … phoned ye from this unknown location, maybe on Sunday morning?' Iain let the silence hang, then continued: 'I wonder why he saw *you* as a buyer. Maybe something ye told him at that charity event ye cannae quite remember?'

I shrugged.

'More likely because he knew I was Peter's friend so he guessed I'd heard about the bull. And he probably knew I'm not violent. And he assumed I had the necessary money. I'm speculating. I don't know.'

'Tell ye another funny thing. When I bumped into ye i' the hotel bar last Tuesday I asked ye about James Farquhar and ye said ye didnae know him. But now ye're telling us he'd phoned ye two days afore and offered to sell ye a priceless archaeological relic. How come ye couldnae remember him or his phone call on Tuesday, but today ye've been able to tell us how ye met him, how he got your number, and maybe why he phoned ye on Sunday mornin' frae somewhere or other on somebody else's phone?'

'I wasn't frank with you on Tuesday. Jimmy was dead and I was afraid you'd believe I was responsible. Which it seems you do. So I denied knowing him.'

'Oh, right, I see. Ye lied then because it seemed easier but ye're telling the truth now.'

'It wasn't a recorded interview then. You called it a chat.'

Iain leaned back and exhaled through his nostrils.

'Are you aware, Doctor, that wasting police time, withholdin' evidence and trying tae pervert the course o' justice are crimes?'

'I didn't waste your time and I didn't try to pervert the course of justice. Quite the contrary. I didn't want you to waste your time imagining I'd killed Jimmy.'

Bob chuckled; Ian snorted; the Scotland Yard man was impassive.

'He phoned ye,' said Bob. 'He offered to sell ye something ye knew wasnae kosher, ye kenned he'd then been killed, and ye telled DCI McArdle nothing aboot any of it – but ye didnae withhold evidence? Aye, right.'

He gave me another cigarette and lit it for me. My head felt light.

'How well did Dr Winster know Farquhar?' asked Bob.

'I'd be surprised if she knew him at all.'

'Would ye, now? Whit about Wishart? Did he know Farquhar, dae ye think?'

'Might have met at charity fund-raisings. And I believe Peter owned the flat Jimmy rented. But I doubt if he recognised him in the restaurant when he bought the bull.'

Suddenly I understood why Iain and Bob had taken so long to detain me. Iain had pocketed a glassful of my fingerprints on Tuesday and then returned home exhausted, only to find himself summoned to London. He'd caught the flight from Turnhouse, forgetting the glass in his coat pocket. Too much on his mind. I smiled. No one shared my amusement.

Bob's questions would persuade anyone who heard the tape that Peter *had* recognised Jimmy in the restaurant, and could have paid him to trail Andropoulos. Hadn't I underestimated their acquaintance, and therefore the likelihood that Karen knew Jimmy? Otherwise, how had Jimmy acquired the bull, if he *had* acquired it?

'Jimmy probably overheard Peter's conversation with Andropoulos. He could have followed *Peter* from the restaurant, not Andropoulos, and stayed on his tail until he trapped him where he could kill him and take the case.'

The superintendent intervened.

'You know that didn't happen. Another person has been charged with the murder of Peter Wishart. Do you think you're writing one of your novels? This is real life, a real police interview.'

Yes, I *was* writing one of my novels, though I seemed to have lost the plot.

'Yes, another person's been charged but she's innocent. James Farquhar killed Peter. He told me so on Monday.'

'Aye, like he'd told ye he'd got the bull?' Bob's sneers were angry. 'But then it turned out he *didnae* have the bull, yet ye still believed he'd killed Wishart for it? Tryin' to mak out ye're stupid, or we're stupid?'

'Ye visited Farquhar's flat on Monday,' said Iain. 'Let's talk about that, shall we?'

Anyone hearing the tape would believe I'd lied repeatedly, which in some respects I had. Now I admitted to visiting Jimmy on Monday; I couldn't recall the time. I admitted I'd fought with him when he pulled a knife. I admitted he was concussed, but I'd left him lying in the hall still holding the weapon while I searched the flat. Iain was sceptical again.

'So he tried to stick a blade in ye, but ye left him lying with the blade still in his hand while ye searched his flat?'

I mumbled about panic and irrational behaviour. I described Jimmy's last moments, omitting only my discovery of the case: the running footsteps on the stair, my slow emergence from the kitchen, my discovery of the body. Iain told the tape that he was now showing me a tartan sports bag. I agreed it was mine. I'd taken it to Jimmy's hoping to put Peter's case into it. Yes, I'd collected it before I left. We went through the same ritual with my coat. And the shoes. Yes, I'd dumped them in a skip so they wouldn't link me to Jimmy's death.

I admitted to reporting the death anonymously several hours afterwards. I couldn't explain the delay. I admitted to the anonymous call from the Museum to police headquarters saying Jimmy had the bull.

Bang to rights. Bob arrested me for the murder of Jimmy Farquhar. He was about to proceed to the charge when the superintendent intervened again. Bob stopped the tape.

'The charge needn't be murder, Mr Carmichael. We know you've got the bull. Whether you took it from Farquhar, or Winster gave it to you, we'll find out later. We need to know just two things for now: where it is, and who you plan to sell it to.'

'Whom,' I corrected silently. Aloud, I replied, 'I don't know where it is and I never planned to sell it to anybody. It belongs in a museum in either Athens or Sicily.'

'OK,' said the superintendent, 'go ahead. We'll try again later.'

The recording was resumed. Bob charged me with the murder of James Farquhar.

End of interview.

22

A uniformed officer relieved me of tie and shoelaces. They put me into a cell. Still no coffee, no food. I was granted a polystyrene cup of water and then they took the cup away. The door clanged shut. The electronic lock clicked. A cover fell over the spy-hole

The cell was twelve feet square, bigger than in television crime dramas. It boasted a small grimy barred window and a metal lavatory with no seat. It stank. Beside the door was an alarm button for emergencies such as a need for nicotine. There was a sunken light; the switch was outside. A thin narrow mattress with a pair of rough blankets reclined on a raised section of the concrete floor, which had once been painted dull red. The rest of the décor comprised chipped institutional paint covered in graffiti, mostly the work of Hibs casuals, who wouldn't have appreciated the floor colour. I wondered how the artists had smuggled writing equipment into the cell but I didn't pursue the question.

I sat on the mattress, studied my laceless shoes and reviewed my confrontation with Niall. Had *he* fed the misleading ideas to the police? It seemed implausible, but Niall and his kind could pan fool's gold from the driest stream and sell it to the gullible. No: Iain was the least gullible character I'd ever invented, and fantasy didn't impress his colleagues.

Niall had angered me yesterday evening, but why? He'd

been insensitive to Alison but that hadn't bothered me. He'd said nothing unreasonable during our argument about the justice system. Maybe I just dislike being contradicted by minor characters.

I'd no laptop, no radio or television, no book, no newspaper, no source of music, no telephone, no way of learning what was happening outside, no means of contacting Richard or Eric or Beth. They say those are the worst aspects of imprisonment: boredom, and the impossibility of conveying or acquiring news. I had solitude but the spy-hole precluded privacy. When I wanted a smoke I'd have to ring the bell and ask the duty officer for one of my own cigarettes and a light from my lighter. I'd manage without.

Why *had* this happened? World Three was supposed to be under my control. But as Siegfried might have observed, man is never master of his destiny even when he forges it himself. What would Siegfried have thought about Y2K? Or about my attempt to transfer blame for Jimmy's death to David?

It was quiet. But this was Saturday. It wouldn't be quiet by midnight.

Unless circumstances changed I'd be there until the Sheriff's Court hearing, forty hours ahead, and then I'd be packed into a cattle-transporter with other livestock and remanded in custody. On arrival at Edinburgh prison I'd go through registration, which is designed to degrade and dehumanise. From what I've been told, bored, mechanical prison officers lock you in a cupboard known as a dog-box until you're processed. You shower publicly. You receive institutional bedding and well-worn institutional clothes.

They decide what personal property you can have in your cell. All other possessions are stored until you're released or transferred to another prison, unless they're stolen in the meantime. You're questioned about drug use and your answers aren't believed. There's a cold medical examination, mostly concerning STIs. They ask whether you have suicidal thoughts. Karen had suffered all this, thanks to me. Now I'd get my just deserts.

My mind was compiling a prospective film-clip from hearsay. Perhaps the reality would be different. I planned to answer 'Yes' to the question about suicidal thoughts. Suicidal female prisoners are given cell-mates; suicidal male ones are locked up alone; under constant surveillance and with restricted facilities, but solitude guaranteed.

I bent my mind to other matters. How could I make sense of a situation that made no sense? Had my laptop lost its power? I wished it were with me. But if it were, what would I write and to what purpose? Could I still trust it?

The case against me was solid. I'd been in Jimmy's flat when he was killed. I'd fought with him. I'd searched his flat. I'd seen no one else. Also, I'd lied about failing to find the bull. The police had made it appear I'd lied throughout the interview. And when the jury heard my English accent they'd have no sympathy with me. My choice was either to direct the police to the bronze bull and get eight to ten years for culpable homicide, landing Beth and possibly Tom in trouble in the process, or maintain silence about the bull and get life.

Even if I'd had my laptop, or a pen and paper, how could I have written my way out of this situation? I lacked the capacity to twist words as Emma or Niall did. Had Emma landed me in here? She might have, since I'd refused to gratify her lust for fabrications about Peter.

I had to *stop* this jitterbugging of thoughts. World Three existed only in my imagination. Niall, and Emma, and Iain, and this cell, were fictions. Deletion of a computer file would extinguish them. If I hadn't started writing *The Bronze Bull* I'd never have met Karen Winster or Jimmy Farquhar, or imagined meeting them. I wouldn't have met Iain. I wouldn't have been accused of murdering Jimmy. So I'd only *imagined* the detention and questioning, the arrest and charge. I only *imagined* I was locked in this Spartan room, cold and bewildered. If I could have stopped imagining I'd have been in the dubious comfort and security of my flat in World One. But imagination was the wellspring of my income. I couldn't afford to stop imagining.

I was doing it again! I'd started to reason about my predicament but then resumed my hunt for scapegoats and my vain quest for World One. *Focus, Doug: review the facts, in the fictional sense of "facts"*. The facts were these: I'd been charged with murder, and I faced a simple but difficult choice.

The case against Karen was equally solid and more high-profile, and unlike me she lacked the culpable homicide option. Her alleged victim had been involved in criminal activity of a kind that whetted the public's appetite. Niall was right: her expertise would have been invaluable to the smugglers, and no one would believe she'd withheld that expertise from her partner. Add the circumstantial evidence, the argument with Peter about the fate of the bull, jealousy of Alison, the terms of Peter's Will, nocturnal walk on the night of the murder, plus her RP accent, and the verdict was guaranteed. Faked forensic evidence such as hairs from her brush on the murder weapon and the absence of a two-pound hammer from Peter's tool-kit would only gild the lily.

Keys jangled and the door opened. A smiling officer offered me food and a cup of tea. There was no facility for washing my hands. I could either starve or submit to eating with unwashed hands and plastic utensils in a foul room containing an open lavatory long deprived of disinfectant. I elected to eat. The food was cold and revolting and the tea was worse. I gagged and swallowed. An indefinite time later the officer collected my used plate and cup and cutlery and locked me in again. He was civil.

If my imagination had created that episode, particularly the tea, I had a psychopathology.

I wondered whether I should press the button and tell them I wished to make a statement. It would have unburdened me to confess the truth about the bronze bull. No: police questioning had induced that urge. I wouldn't land Beth in trouble, fictional or not.

I recalled our conversations. Beth thought Perilaus could have made the full-sized bull *in situ* in Akragas; or had I suggested that? In any event, what applied to the original, if it had existed, could apply to the scale model; if, in this fictitious world, it was authentic. But if the bronze bull I'd taken from Jimmy's flat, the one Peter had bought from Spiro, was truly (in the fictitious sense of "truly") the one removed by Enrico Fontano from an ancient burial site in Agrigento, it had religious significance, otherwise it wouldn't have been buried with the dead. Was it relevant that Sicilian rivers were represented as bulls? That human sacrifices had been offered in Western Sicily? Had a statue of the river god been conflated with memories of those rituals? Had the statue, the implement of torture, existed only in the imaginations of later chroniclers, as its miniature replica, conceivably the motivation for Peter's death and perhaps Jimmy's, existed only in mine?

Andropolous had faked the analytical data to corroborate his hypothesis about early Mediterranean trade. But the hypothesis could be valid nonetheless. Fragments of belief and knowledge and mythology travel along trade routes. Beth had told me about it but I hadn't been listening. I think she'd been talking about Sardinia, something to do with bulls as fertility symbols.

One can choose to believe anything plausible about the world's past, ancient or recent. Or choose not to believe. "Evidence" is whatever you recruit to support your beliefs.

My stomach was rebelling. I concentrated on not vomiting. Whatever the circumstances I needed nourishment. I sat still, swallowed and breathed.

What historical truth lay behind the legend of Perilaus? Or behind the lies to be recounted at Karen's trial, or mine? What lay behind my predicament within a predicament?

I wanted Linda.

I screwed my eyes shut and lay on the mattress and huddled fully-dressed among the blankets. I opened my eyes again and stared at the ceiling. The grimy window was darkening. I tried to sleep. My stomach churned in harmony with my mind. I concentrated on relaxing. I couldn't relax.

The light went on. I turned my face away from the glare and towards the graffiti on the far wall. Muffled voices outside. The door opened. I was half asleep and the other half abominated the prospect of company. I lay on my side, back to the door, and didn't move. Someone entered and stood behind me. *Linda, Linda.*

'Ye know what it's like, being just a tea-leaf away from what you're trying to achieve and no' quite getting the last little bit?' Iain's voice was gentle.

I grunted.

'Aye, I'm sure you can mind bein' there, Doctor. Just like the situation I'm in the now. I wish ye'd just tell me the truth. Ye'd feel better for it and then we could both get a night's sleep. You need it, I need it. You know fine well where the bull is. Why not tell me and get it over and done with?'

'I'd tell you if I knew. Do you want me to *invent* a story, a place, a person?'

Something like hope flickered at the back of my mind. Had Iain and his colleagues left a loophole through which I could slip?

'Ye've done enough of that already, telling us James Farquhar had the bull. He never had it. If ye cannae think up a better story ye're no' as clever as I thought.' He paused. I didn't move, didn't look at him. The pause was so long I thought he'd left. He hadn't. After a hundred heartbeats he resumed: 'Aye, ye're a strange one and no mistake, you and your stories. Ye told us ye'd published novels under your own name. Ye mind that?'

Another glimmer of hope warmed me, but this time I knew the cause.

'Have you read them?'

He sighed. The sound was less regretful than it pretended.

'I've no' had the opportunity and it seems I'm no' going tae. Those books of yours must have gone out o' print. No sign of them in the shops. No trace of them in the records. No evidence they exist, forbye what ye told us. D'ye think ye might have imagined them, Doctor? But I see ye're *planning* to write one. Been keeping a lot of notes about this bronze bull business, haven't you? Interesting notes.' He paused again. 'If ye tell us where it is we'll help you at the trial.'

I'd no answer. Part of my hope faded again. I stared at nothing. Iain said no more. After a while he went away.

An obliquely-aligned graffito on the lower part of the wall before me declared someone to be a fucking radge. I couldn't decipher the name of the person villified. The 'R' of 'Radge' was angular, its closed upper section a rough rectangle, the right-hand down-stroke disproportionate. I wanted to adjust the shape of the letter. It annoyed me. But I seemed paralyzed. The 'g' was oddly shaped as well. In fact, none of the letters was well formed and the entire statement followed a non-linear, one might say crooked, path. The author's literacy was in doubt. Nevertheless the spelling seemed correct. I studied the inscription for some time, trying to read the name, to draw inferences about the author.

What mistake had the police made?

At some point, I fell into a doze and dreamed of Linda.

The noise awakened me a few hours later. It continued unabated until nearly dawn.

23

The darkness seethed with drunken shouts, verbal brawling, cries for help. Rage and frustration gushed from every cell. *Nessun dorma*, to quote Puccini's famous aria: None shall sleep. A writer should have revelled in the auditory panorama of passion, recording details of phrase and intonation, but most of the clamour comprised obscure threats peppered with obscenities, like spoken graffiti. I wrapped the blankets around my clothed body and shut my eyes.

What was Iain's game, pretending my novels didn't exist? He must have known better, but his assertion had disabled any paradox that could have propelled me back into World One. He'd perused the latest sketches for *The Bronze Bull* on my laptop, including my failed device for evading arrest (I wondered what he'd made of that!), yet the glass wall between worlds hadn't fractured.

The suspected error in police procedure ducked and wove through my cluttered mind until at length I snared it and dragged it into the light of introspection. They'd charged me with murdering Jimmy, which I hadn't. However, they hadn't charged me with assaulting him to his severe injury, which I had; or with robbery; or with anything related to the bronze bull. Therefore, once they discovered that someone else had killed Jimmy, the charge would have to be dropped. Of course I could be re-arrested and charged with the real offences, but they'd be more likely to release me and put a tail on me so I'd lead them to the bull. On the other hand, Iain would do something different if he guessed I'd anticipated that ploy.

'A'm needin' a doctor! Git me a fuckin' doctor! Ye're in the shite if ye dinnae git me a doctor the noo, ye fuckin' pig bastards!'

The woman's voice had been reiterating the plea for half an hour with no discernible effect. Our fellow-residents were unsympathetic.

'Shut the fuck up, ye poxy slag!'

'A'll fuckin' doctor ye if ye dinnae shut yer gob, ye cunt!'

'Git tae fuck, ya bam!'

The routine obscenities sloshed from mouth to mouth, monotonous as music by Steve Reich or John Adams, infectious as a yawn. Two detainees were continuing a drunken altercation that predated their arrest. The cacophony intensified. After a while, a duty officer demanded quiet and issued threats. His efforts elicited three challenges to single combat.

I was hungry, queasy, cold, exhausted, angry about the turn of events, alarmed by my prospects, confused and disorientated. Yet the police error afforded hope of a miracle. Miracle or not, I set my mind to determining how I could escape. Then I fell asleep. My dreams were punctured by the incessant yelling.

Breakfast appeared soon after dawn. The building had fallen quiet. Only a few muffled imprecations sullied the peace. The officer was friendly. I negotiated a wash and shave using hard soap and cold water and a disposable plastic razor, but I'd no way of cleaning my teeth. Breakfast was lumpy porridge and a plateful of fatty bacon and gristly square sausage, accompanied by a stale roll and a cup of stewed tea. My stomach rebelled again, but whatever tactic my mind had sought during the night I'd need to keep up my strength.

The friendly officer lent me a book, an old John Creasey thriller packed with cardboard characters and implausible action. I thanked him.

The miracle happened early in the afternoon. There'd been a change of shift. The officer who opened the cell door wasn't amiable; I diagnosed an unwelcome Sunday on the heels of Saturday night. I followed him to the desk. My belongings were laid out in their polythene bags, together with check-list. Why? I knew they couldn't send me anywhere before the Sheriff Court hearing. I scanned the bags from two yards away.

'Right, let's git aw this shite o' yours checked off, then ye can git tae fuck oot o' here.' The officer tried to sound efficient.

'What's happening?'

'Whit d'ye mean, whit's happenin'? Naebody tellt ye? Ye're fuckin' libbed, ye moron! Chairges dropped.'

Half a minute passed before I replied.

'Thanks for breaking the news. What changed the CID's mind?'

He shrugged.

'Some other fucker stuck hisself in. Ye're a jammy cunt, so ye are, so if A wiz you A wouldnae fuckin' worry aboot why nor how nor who. Let's git on wi' this lot, right?'

Perhaps the scheme I'd written after the fish supper in Stirling *had* worked, after a twist and a hiatus. As I kept reminding myself, I was the author, not part of the story. I put on my watch: ten minutes to two. I pocketed my wallet, keys, mobile, cigarettes and lighter together with the small lump of hash, testimony to police vigilance. I recovered my laptop. I signed a document acknowledging the return of my property. The tartan sports bag and the clothes I'd dumped in the skip remain as "productions" even though the charge had been dropped. I wouldn't bother to reclaim them.

Formal charges couldn't be dropped in this manner, so what had happened? I couldn't pursue the question because I couldn't think. I needed a smoke, a cup of coffee or three and something stronger. And a decent meal, once my mind and stomach had settled.

The officer didn't respond to my farewell. Cool sunlight glowed on the police station walls, litter fluttered in the gentle breeze, creamy-white vapour trails ornamented a cerulean sky. I inhaled: fresh October air, petrol fumes, dog shit. I lit a cigarette and walked on to the street. The nicotine hit me and my head began to float. A horn sounded. A silver-grey Mercedes beckoned. I finished the cigarette before I approached.

Richard's mood was twenty-four hours behind mine: agitation, anger, an undercurrent of incomprehension. He asked me to account for myself.

'Tell you later, Richard. I'm tired, confused, short of food and desperate for coffee.'

He started the engine and pulled away.

'You'll get coffee at home. And a meal. Goes without saying. Phone Lydia. Car phone, there. Right, Doug, I want to know what the bloody hell's going on. I want to know why and I want to know *now*. The police have been all over us. Explanation, please.'

He paid scant attention to other road users and none to speed limits. This wasn't good for my nerves.

'You've had the police again? At Abbey House?'

'And David's cottage. Especially David's cottage. Not routine questioning this time, a bloody search with a bloody warrant. You're responsible, so please have the goodness to explain.'

'Responsible for what? I've been in the pig bin since early yesterday morning, Richard. I haven't a clue what's happened. *You'll* have to explain.'

His voice rose.

'Something you told the police made them descend on us like a pack of ravening bloody wolves. What was it?'

'Nothing. Neither they nor I mentioned you or David. Or Lydia. Don't accuse *me*, Richard. I've faced enough gratuitous accusations these past forty-eight hours to last a lifetime. I'm sorry to hear about the search but it had nothing to do with me.'

Which was a lie. If it hadn't been for my scheme for avoiding arrest, David's cottage wouldn't have been searched.

'If it wasn't you then who was it?'

Horns blasted as Richard shot another red light.

'Christ, how the devil should I know? You've had a rough day but I've had a worse one. Get off my back!' I steadied myself. 'Tell me what happened. I'll see if I can throw any light on it.'

He drove in silence for a minute, overtaking in ridiculous places, ignoring give-way signs and angry yells. Then the hyena laugh sounded, brief and bitter.

'Must be quite an experience, being interrogated by the police and locked up. Quite an experience.'

'Sure. Character-building. I'd prefer my character to remain at the planning stage.'

'I imagine David feels the same. Ha-ha!'

The narrative emerged piece by piece. Richard was still talking when the Mercedes screeched to a halt beside Abbey House and he ushered me up to the kitchen, interrupting his harangue only to bark commands.

'Doug needs coffee, Slug. So do I. And food.'

Lydia smiled and twittered among coffee cups and said something about the weather. Richard went on talking until I'd heard the whole saga. David, I learned, had been detained for questioning in connection with the bronze bull and the death of James Farquhar. The police had searched Abbey House and the cottage. They hadn't found the bull but they were sure David had it. Illegal immigrants had also been mentioned.

A twenty-four hour working day must have exhausted Iain. My heart bled.

Then, added Richard, Niall Bloody Ferguson had telephoned asking for information about Doug Carmichael, saying I'd been arrested for Jimmy Farquhar's murder. Therefore, I must have accused David to get myself off the hook. Richard had rung police HQ and learned the charge against me had been dropped, which confirmed his deduction. So he'd driven to the station to greet me.

'I see. No wonder you thought I'd stuck David in. Well, I hadn't. Nor did I kill Jimmy Farquhar. The police would have questioned you anyway because they'd have found your number in Farquhar's phone records. McArdle would have been here three days ago if New Scotland Yard hadn't summoned him.'

Richard took a cup of coffee from Lydia. It misted his half-moon spectacles. He remained seated for almost a minute, then set down the cup and started his habitual pacing. I accepted a large steaming mug.

'Yes. Farquhar's phone records.' Richard scratched his beard. '*He* couldn't have phoned David, though. How would he have known him?'

'How did he know *you*?'

'You know, Doug, we've had an *awful* day.' Lydia smiled. 'Poor David. Though really, you know, some of the things … but never mind, we'll all feel better after a nice meal.'

She plunged into culinary activity.

'I'm a well known collector,' said Richard. 'Very well known. Easy to find my name. David's another matter. Police couldn't have traced him through Farquhar's phone records. I must visit David. Definitely visit.'

His mouth twisted. He sat again and drank his coffee. Lydia stared at him for a long moment, not smiling. When he summoned me down to the workshop I stalled him; I needed more coffee. He left the kitchen and Lydia refilled my mug. Her smile returned but I didn't smile back at her. Richard had no idea that she'd informed the police about David. From his perspective, it had been more logical to blame me.

'I know you told the police about David's dealings with illegal immigrants, Lydia, but what made you grass him for murdering Jimmy Farquhar?'

'I didn't, Doug! Never!' Her shock seemed genuine. 'I'd never *heard* of Farquhar until last night! I only told them about the thing Peter was supposed to have bought for Piggy, you know, that bronze bull!'

I set my coffee mug down with extreme care. My voice remained calm.

'What exactly *did* you tell them?'

'Oh, Doug, it's been awful, it really has, they asked all sorts of questions when they came before, did I tell you, or did Piggy tell you, they were here last Monday? I came back from shopping and there they were, three of them, I saw a car outside I didn't recognise and I wondered whose it was, and it was a police car, you know, an unmarked vehicle. Anyway, they asked *me* what Piggy had bought from Peter, and I told them there'd been nothing since summer, and when they'd gone I made Piggy tell me what it was, and I *knew* they'd be back, and if it turned up here what would happen?'

'Did they search the workshop on Monday?'

'Oh, yes, everywhere, but I didn't know what they were looking for until Piggy told me about the bull. They didn't find it because it wasn't here. Then Piggy said David was searching for it, so I thought if I told the police David was trying to find it on Piggy's behalf, but Piggy didn't *know* he was, then Piggy wouldn't be in trouble even if it *did* turn up. But if Piggy goes to see David and David tells him *I* called the police ... Oh, Doug, what am I to do?'

I considered several answers, none conducive to her wellbeing, and then said that David couldn't have known she was to blame for his arrest. Then I realised she *hadn't* been worried. It had been an act.

'Lydia, I can't stay for dinner. Things to do. Nothing about David or the police. I'll ask Richard to run me back into town. Thanks for the coffee.'

Richard was glad I'd declined dinner. Since I could reveal

nothing more about David's arrest he no longer wanted me at Abbey House. On the drive back into Edinburgh he shot only two red lights.

En route I switched on my mobile. I planned to call Niall and tell him to kill the story of my arrest, and then phone the *Daily Record* with the same message for Emma. But I was distracted by seven text and three voicemail messages.

One text was from Alison. Would I contact her? All the other messages were from Beth. They were frantic. Why hadn't I answered her calls? Something terrible had happened and she and Eric needed me.

The first of her voice-mails identified the terrible something. Tom MacIntyre's laboratory had been raided and the bull had gone.

Tom was dead.

24

I called Beth, explained my radio silence and cut off her questions. I wanted to know about the bull. And Tom. She said she'd tell me face to face. She was at Karen's with Eric.

I collected the gas-guzzler from the hotel car park. Every door in the vehicle was unlocked, keys in the ignition. The police had rifled my briefcase, but finding only sheaves of manuscript they'd left it open, contents spilled. The printed chapters of *The Bronze Bull* were in dog-eared disarray.

On my way to West Arthur Street I bought a copy of the *Sunday Mail,* the Sunday version of the *Daily Record.* Emma's front-page exclusive was about Karen.

DANGEROUS MIXTURE

A museum curator accused of bludgeoning her lover to death was at the centre of an amazing jail blunder ...

When she was locked up in a cell with a German woman charged with threatening to blow up nuclear weapons bases in Scotland.

The jailhouse cock-up was only sorted out when the Record tipped off embarrassed prison bosses.

Now they have split up Dr Karen Winster, 32, and 28-year-old Renate Hertwig.

Winster, of West Arthur Street, Edinburgh, is charged with murdering boyfriend Peter Wishart.

Police are looking into Wishart's business dealings in Germany and elsewhere, which reports say included drug smuggling.

Rumours that Winster was involved in these dealings have not been officially denied.

About 90% of women in HMP Cornton Vale are believed to be drug abusers.

Hertwig, of Leipzig, Germany, is alleged to have conspired to attack the Holy Loch submarine base earlier this year.

Winster was remanded in custody at Edinburgh Sheriff Court last week.

Hertwig was caged in Cornton Vale after her appearance at Glasgow Sheriff Court in July.

Hertwig's dad Klaus contacted the Record after a harrowing visit.

He claimed that his daughter was cooped up in a tiny cell with the accused killer almost 24 hours a day.

He said: 'It was insensitive to put them together. I don't understand why they did this.'

Klaus, a schoolteacher, added: 'It is wonderful news she has been moved.

'But surely, someone in authority should not have put them together.

'If this woman and her lover had illegal dealings in Germany, it makes more trouble for my daughter if she is locked up with her.'

A prison service spokesman said: 'We regret any distress caused.

'It may not have occurred to the prison authorities that these two people could in any way be linked.

'One is on a murder charge and the other is on another charge.'

I phoned Niall, who sounded both contrite and inquisitive, and then called the *Record*. A press room employee said Emma wasn't in the building.

'Tell Ms Menzies there are no charges against me. DCI McArdle will confirm it. Print anything defamatory and I'll sue.'

I'd feel better after a meal but I couldn't have accepted food from Lydia. I smoked two cigarettes.

In Est Arthu I parked behind the BMW. Karen's house was almost tidy, though its erstwhile bouquet of furniture polish was masked by cigarette smoke. Odour aside, Eric and Beth had performed a miracle of restoration. I was obscurely annoyed.

To Beth and Eric, the theft of the bull confirmed the smugglers' persistence. Eric said we should drop the matter because it was too dangerous; Beth disagreed.

'You're ahead of me,' I said. 'Tell me everything in order. What happened to Tom?'

'No, Doug.' Beth was in combative mood. 'First, what happened to *you*?'

I told them what I construed as the truth. Even to my own ears it sounded lame. Then they questioned me about failing to report Jimmy's death until long after the event. Eric was shocked; Beth was amused.

'Anyway, the police have admitted their mistake,' I finished. 'Now, about Tom.'

Someone had broken into Tom's lab during Friday night or Saturday morning, Beth said, and the bull was taken.

Hamid Zaheri had found Tom's body just after nine o'clock. He'd been dead for some time; suspected heart attack. It seemed he'd been working late and the intruder had surprised him. He was a widower. His two daughters had been informed.

'How did you find out?' I asked.

'Hamid rang me about eleven o'clock Saturday,' said Beth. 'Found me in the directory. Asked me to contact you because he couldn't find your number.'

A shock phone call around eleven o'clock Saturday?

'So Hamid told you the bull was missing. What had he told the police?'

'We didn't ask.' Eric sighed. 'The police had only just finished questioning him. He was distressed.'

So Eric had been at Beth's on Saturday morning and they'd spent Friday evening together. Damn it, he was married, and a clergyman! I wanted another cigarette. Eric offered me his pack. My hands shook as I lit it. Beth wrinkled her nose.

'Did you get Hamid's number?'

They did. I suggested Eric make the call; Hamid would trust him. Eric demurred.

'Does he know you're a clergyman?'

'I think so.'

'Yes, he does,' said Beth. 'It was mentioned when he phoned.'

Hamid's news must have upset Beth, so Eric had consoled her. Hamid had overheard him, so she'd have been obliged to explain who her companion was. What mattered was that Hamid knew Eric was a clergyman.

'Why would it help?' said Eric. 'I presume he's a Muslim.'

'He'll trust a man of God.'

I explained what was needed. Eric was reluctant until Beth supported me. Then he spoke on the phone and his voice resonated with care and concern. He asked whether Hamid's friends or family were with him, whether he needed to share his distress at Tom's death. When at length he posed my questions, Hamid answered. Beth paced the room adjusting books and ornaments. I smoked another cigarette. Eric smiled *au revoir* and ended the call.

'It seems the uniformed police entered Tom's laboratory first,' he said, 'then a forensic team and the CID. Hamid told the senior officer the only item he knew to be missing was a piece that he and Tom had been asked to analyse. They asked him to describe the piece but he'd hardly seen the bull; just taken patina samples to examine.'

What senior CID officer? Iain and Bob had been interrogating me.

'Did he tell them who'd brought the item to the lab?'

'He told them Tom examined items for many people. He didn't keep track of ownership.'

On the face of it, this was reassuring. But someone in the CID could still have added two and two and derived an answer implicating Beth and me. And perhaps Hamid had told the police more. Who'd raided the lab and stolen the bull? I could guess, but I hadn't written it. I offered to take us all out for dinner. Eric went to collect his coat.

'Beth,' I said, 'if the police question you, tell them you'd nothing to do with Tom.'

'Lie to the police?'

'Yes. Remember what they did to Karen's flat. If they

push you, tell them *I* took the bull to Tom and you didn't know until later. I can handle them. Recent experience.'

'Yeah, experience of being locked up.'

We walked through deepening twilight to a Chinese restaurant in South Clerk Street. The scene at the table became dream-like. My mind repeated random phrases that might as well have been incantations in a lost language. I'd been charged with murder and released again. David had been accused instead. Abbey House has been searched. Tom MacIntyre had died, possibly of a heart attack, probably during the raid. The bull had been stolen. And an unintended relationship was blossoming between Beth and Eric.

'Does Karen know about the theft?' I asked.

'We haven't told her.' Eric sounded soothing. 'It would have been unavailing and unkind.'

'I think you've misjudged. The worst aspect of imprisonment is lack of news. It's best to tell a prisoner *everything*, however painful. Even trivial things if they'll keep her in touch with normality.'

They weren't persuaded but perhaps they'd reconsider. Beth's visiting rota would have to be changed; for the following few days it allocated time to people who knew nothing of Tom or the bull. Our conversation turned to the smuggling ring. Beth leaned forward.

'I've made further inquiries. Ibrahim Youssef, you know, the guy who shot–'

'Yes?'

Starters arrived. I attacked the wun tuns. Beth continued between mouthsful of chicken and sweetcorn soup.

'Ibrahim Youssef is a curator in the Iraq Museum in

Baghdad, responsible for some of the early Mesopotamian collection. Parts of said collection that went AWOL after the War include a black diorite statue of Entemena, the ensi of Lagash, discovered at Ur and dated to the mid-third millennium BCE. Any archaeologist would recognise it; the head's missing but Entemena's name is inscribed in cuneiform on the back and shoulder. And there's a three foot high sandstone statue of a male priest with an inscription on the right shoulder mentioning the goddess Ninshupur. Every museum in the world knows about those thefts so nobody will touch them, except unscrupulous private collectors.'

I'd never heard of Entemena or Ninshu-whatever and I didn't know what an ensi was. Archaeologists might have recognised the treasures but, like the rest of Joe Public, I wouldn't. I'd little idea what ancient Mesopotamian statues looked like and I couldn't read cuneiform.

'So what do you infer from the shooting?' I asked.

'Two possibilities.' Eric was conspiratorial. 'Youssef was either part of the smuggling ring and believed Andropoulos had cheated him, or an honest man who took the law into his own hands. I believe the latter. Beth believes the former.'

'Why?'

Main courses arrived. I helped myself to beef with black bean sauce, sweet and sour vegetables and char siu.

'Whoever stole those items knew their value,' said Beth, 'and where to find them. So the thief was an insider with expert knowledge. Like Youssef. I think he shot Andropoulos for trying to cheat him.'

I told Beth her reasoning fitted Eric's opinion as well as hers, but it had little to do with the bronze bull's disappearance. Eric shook his head.

'No matter who's right about Youssef, this smuggling ring is well-organised and dangerous. And Beth's surely right about the smugglers dealing mainly with private collectors.' He insisted we now let the authorities search for the bull; we lacked the necessary skills, resources or experience.

'Where would that leave Karen?' demanded Beth. 'The police believe she killed Peter and she's involved in the smuggling ring. It isn't in their interests to exonerate her. But if we discover who took the bull from Tom's lab we'll prove Karen *wasn't* involved. Then we might convince the police a smuggler killed Peter.'

I let my companions argue; this was my first edible meal for forty-eight hours, and Friday night's lobster hadn't been special. I spoke no more until my plate was empty.

'You're right in principle, Eric, but we can't talk to the police without implicating ourselves. Beth, I see your point, but if a smuggler had killed Peter he'd have taken the suitcase. The person who took the case didn't smuggle archaeological treasures. He was a small-time heroin dealer.'

'Is *that* who killed Peter?'

'He denied it, for what it's worth. But there's something of more immediate concern.'

'What?' Beth looked angry.

'Karen probably has a new cell-mate. Regardless of your rota, Beth, *we* need to visit Karen again and try to persuade Cornton Vale to change the arrangement if necessary.'

I showed them the *Sunday Mail*. Beth climbed out of her seat and read over Eric's head, one hand on his shoulder.

'This is outrageous!' shouted Eric. 'The innuendo! Is it *legal* to publish such trash when a case is *sub judice*? If potential jurors read it—'

I nodded. 'That's the intention.'

Klaus Hertwig had come to Scotland, I explained, to learn what had befallen his daughter. He'd gone to her lawyer and the police, and the police had advised him to talk to the *Daily Record* if he was unhappy about Renate's custody. They knew the *Record* would seek to influence Karen's trial. The *Record* often paid prisoners and prison employees for titbits about high-profile inmates, but a prisoner's parent was a better source and cost nothing. Klaus was an educated man who knew nothing of such tabloids. Even at their worst, German newspapers were barred from instilling prejudice among potential jurors. So, intending no harm, he'd followed police advice and phoned the *Record*.

'Great.' Beth's voice was brittle. 'How are we supposed to get justice?' She glared. 'You could help, Doug. Peter had promised the bull to a private collector, so we have a prime suspect for the theft and for Tom's death. *And* for Peter's.'

There was a faint sheen of perspiration on her face; the beef dish was spicy. Eric tried to restrain her with vague hand gestures.

'I know who arranged to buy the bull from Peter,' I said, 'but Richard isn't a ruthless villain. He's a respectable citizen, albeit eccentric. Therefore, knowing his identity does *not* give us a prime suspect and does *not* tell us who stole the bull. As it happens, he doesn't have the bull and I believe he no longer wants it.'

Beth grew icy. I didn't react. Eric tried to restore harmony and insisted on paying for the meal. I was too tired to argue.

I drove back to the hotel, leaving them to make whatever arrangements they pleased. I was overdue a long, comfortable sleep.

25

Under my bedroom door at the *Brigadoon* lay a misspelt hand-written note from Mr Merriman. It smelled of lavender. His office was in darkness. The barman replied to my question with a shrug and went on drying glasses. I drank two measures of whisky and went to bed.

I dreamed of Peter, and Blandford Terrace, and Alison, and Linda, and the bronze bull. Then a half-waking nightmare returned me to the police cell and I awoke with my pulse-rate over a hundred. I showered, shaved and dressed. On my table in the dining room was another note; Mr Merriman's spelling hadn't improved. After breakfast I cleaned my teeth, sent a text to Alison and walked into the manager's office.

Mr Merriman essayed a businesslike frown, but his face was too youthful, his hair too curly and his desk too mass-produced to carry conviction. He cleared his throat and asked me to settle my account and leave the hotel, citing my detention by the police as his reason. My eyebrows rose.

'You know I haven't been charged, Mr Merriman. The police have apologised to me.'

'Maybe, Dr Carmichael, but they ransacked this hotel.' His tone groped for assertiveness and settled on abruptness. 'Ransacked it. Looking for some bronze thing they said you'd hidden. Questioned everybody. Including me, like. Spent most o' Saturday putting everything to rights. Now, it doesnae matter to me–'

'I was wrongfully detained. I've instructed my lawyer to compile a compensation claim. Anyone who treats me unjustly will face consequences.'

'That's your business. Mine's running an orderly hotel. Yer presence has caused this orderly running to be disturbed, so I'm wantin' ye to leave.'

Not a bad little speech. I restrained the urge to applaud.

'You haven't understood me, Mr Merriman. I said anyone who treats me unjustly will face consequences. The police disturbed your hotel; I didn't. Therefore, if you demand I leave, you'll be treating me unjustly. Take my point?'

He attempted a fulminating glare. I relented.

'I'll leave before the end of the week.'

Perhaps the compromise persuaded him he'd won. He said nothing as I left the office.

There were more important matters to consider. The bull had vanished, I knew not where. Tom MacIntyre was dead, perhaps through natural causes, but it was another tragedy to lay at my door. Karen faced life imprisonment. Beth intended to hunt smugglers. David was in prison; the fault was mine, not Lydia's. And I couldn't elude Iain in World Three.

Sunlight sparkled on windows and frosted branches. Leaves crackled underfoot. I checked the Toyota's fuel gauge: three quarters full. My watch said it was twenty to ten; plenty of time for reflection. I locked the car and walked to Blackford Hill and up to the observatory, sharing the park with young mothers and pensioners with sedate dogs. The cold air cleared my head but didn't clarify my thoughts. After two hours I returned to the *Brigadoon*'s car park and drove towards Longniddry.

A week earlier, the view from the foreshore opposite the Gosford estate had been grey, a world wrapped in tissue paper. Now, all was revealed. Beyond the shining Firth the Fife coast was sharp against the pale sky. I could see upriver to the bridges. Young men and women jogged over the shingle, breaths steaming; an overweight beagle waddled after one of them. An old man in a tweed jacket and flat cap stood beside his Vauxhall Astra, puffing a pipe and staring out to sea. A bus grumbled along the road behind the buckthorn hedges. I didn't have to wait long; today, I was expected.

'We can't go on meeting like this,' she panted, pulling on a sweater.

'Cliché. Niall's influence?'

'Needed ear-plugs. Not going to drive me to school in that thing again, are you?'

'Not if you'd rather walk. You summoned me. Your word is my directive. Shall we stroll or find somewhere to sit?'

'Stroll, if you can after smoking those lung-rots. I've got half an hour. I want to talk.'

We set off towards the bents. I smoked a lung-rot and didn't meet her eyes. The jogger with the waddling beagle preceded us. Cockenzie power station foreclosed the vista. The silence stretched.

'I wanted to see you yesterday,' she said. 'We could have talked for longer.'

'I was unavoidably detained. Dinner tomorrow?'

She shrugged.

'Nice of you to try to shut Niall up on Friday, but you were drinking wine and playing chess with Robbie while he was being a *real* arsehole.'

Why did that make me feel guilty?

'I was Robbie's guest, Alison. You were busy with the cupboards and Niall was cooking. What did you expect me to do?'

'You know something, Doug? You're fascinated by other folks' troubles, you mouth the right words, you get people to divulge *their* feelings, but you dodge questions about yourself. And what do you ever *do*?'

This was the kettle calling the pan black. Maybe she'd resented my questions when we met a week earlier. But she had a point: Peter had been a man of action, but when *I* acted the consequences were infelicitous; witness my visit to Jimmy Farquhar.

'You think there's something I should have done that I haven't? The police believed I *had* done something I *shouldn't*.'

She stopped, wide blue eyes level with mine. Her face held none of her sister's affected ingenuousness, only a world-weariness reminiscent of Iain's. Her voice was brusque.

'What? What did the police think you've done?'

'Killed someone.'

She mouthed *Oh my God*, gesturing as though her hand sought to encompass mine. She'd have crushed my metacarpals if it had succeeded.

'Who? Who did they think you killed?'

Whom.

'He was called James Farquhar. You didn't know him. And before you ask, I didn't.'

Her nascent harangue was derailed. She walked distracted among dunes and buckthorn, questions splintering. I kept pace.

'The police knew I'd visited Jimmy near the material time so they supposed I'd killed him. I enjoyed thirty-six hours of their hospitality before the killer confessed and I was evicted. As I said: unavoidably detained. The adverb was dubious, the participle precise.'

She pounced.

'That's *exactly* what I meant. Something dire happens and you joke about it and reveal nothing. And when you're not joking, you're using other people's troubles to hide from your own.'

The accusation concealed guilt or self-doubt, transmuting me to a projection of *her* reluctance to confide, as though I were a character she'd created or imagined, an *alter ego*. The irony didn't amuse me. She plunged on:

'When people ask you about Linda you describe her physically, you talk about her job, but you never say what she's *like*. Niall's right: you're not trying to get over her. You convey nothing about her yet you remain obsessed. It's unhealthy, Doug.'

How could anyone grasp the ineffable qualities of the Linda who'd shared my life? Her skin had the taut smoothness of a younger woman's. Only in a small area beneath her throat, an inverted triangle around the suprasternal notch, was there significant darkening and wrinkling. It evoked tenderness. Would Alison, or anyone, consider that relevant? At work, Linda was a political Jeeves, her attire conservative, her manner impeccable, her responses to demands courteous and measured; and she knew how to delegate. The Director of the Scottish Prison Service relied on her. Home from work she was cynical and witty, seeking refuge in vodka, music, theatre, horror films, pornography, imaginative love-making. At the ballot box she was an old-fashioned socialist. None of that was anyone else's business.

'What did I do to earn this accolade?'

'Doug, for Christ's sake, I'm a friend! Or trying to be.'

Involving herself in my troubles in order to hide from her own? She glanced at her watch and turned back towards the Toyota. I followed.

'I never heard you talk much about Peter.'

'I did when I had to, but you were the *last* person I'd have talked to, except my spiteful little sister and her past-his-bloody-sell-by-date boyfriend. You hero-worshipped Peter, applauded everything he did, as though he was everything you wanted to be and weren't. You encouraged him to go off the rails whether you meant to or not, so I couldn't keep him on the straight path and he ended up with that bitch from the Museum. It was hard to go on liking you.'

Her tone was an amalgam of contempt, bitterness and misery. Wind from the North Sea ruffled the Firth and shook the dead grasses. She quickened her pace. A few strands of blonde hair settled across her forehead. I wanted to stroke them back into place.

Her words had shaken me. Was this why I'd had to drink myself into a stupor in order to write chapter six of *The Bronze Bull*? Because I was killing the man I wanted to be?

'Why now, Alison? Why wait so long to tell me?'

'What a bloody stupid question from an intelligent man. Think about it.'

I was thinking.

'Something else has distressed you. I don't think it's anything to do with me, but you believe I could ... No, you'll have to tell me.'

She didn't answer until we reached the Toyota. She climbed into the passenger seat. Goose-bumps swathed her legs.

'I had an almighty row with Iddy yesterday morning.'

While I'd been in custody. I started the engine, turned the car round and glanced at her profile. She stared through the side window as the landscape panned past her.

'She'd grassed David Michie for helping refugees into the country. You knew, didn't you, Doug? Knew he was helping frightened, persecuted people into a country that could protect them if it had the political decency?'

'I'd gathered. I saw Lydia yesterday afternoon. I'm afraid it's worse, though, Alison. It was David who confessed to the murder I was accused of.'

She squeezed her eyes shut and bared her teeth. Her breathing grew ragged, her face mottled. I concentrated on the road and said, 'I know you admire David. He was a good friend to Peter once.'

He'd given Peter the contacts he'd needed to start smuggling art treasures, which Alison wouldn't consider friendly. But Peter had never shared his profits with David. Nor had he engaged in people-smuggling. Their mutual suspicion had evolved into animosity.

'Jesus,' she muttered. 'The whole bloody world's falling apart. I don't know how much more I can take.'

Y2K; my foreboding; Eric's eschatological ruminations; and now Alison's despair.

'I'm going to visit him this afternoon. Will you come?'

She shook her head. To visit an old, estranged friend in prison was beyond her capacity. And she had classes to teach.

'Dinner tomorrow?' I invited.

'Don't think so, Doug. Thanks, though.' She uttered a short, brittle laugh. 'Don't bear grudges, do you? After the way I spoke to you, most men would have socked me on the jaw and driven away. *You* ask me out for dinner.'

'I wouldn't have dared.' I wasn't joking. 'You're wrong, Alison, I do bear grudges. And I sometimes act, though not always as I ought. But you're right about my reticence. As Niall so subtly observed, we're two of a kind.'

'I hope that wasn't a chat-up line.'

'Fear not. Alison, I'm sorry about David.'

'Me too. Hell, Doug, I've waited two years to take my anger out on you. Waited 'til you no longer deserved it.' She sighed again. 'Maybe I *can* visit him. Not today. I'll see.'

I pulled into the school yard. Children squealed and galloped, immune to cold.

'Will you be OK?' I asked.

She unfastened her seat-belt and opened the door.

'Fine. Shower, change, teach my second years about the quadratic formula … Life's full of roses, Doug. Whole rose bushes.'

She grinned and didn't peck me on the cheek. I watched her cross the school yard, kick a football along a curved trajectory into the top left hand corner of the goal chalked on the wall, and disappear into the building to a torrent of applause. I lit a much-needed cigarette, switched on the radio and drove away. Mozart's clarinet quintet; second movement. I returned to Edinburgh, driving with care. Nicotine and music allayed my disquiet.

I bought sandwiches for lunch and drove to West Arthur Street. The Volkswagen sat outside number 9 but no one answered the buzzer. I parked along the road, caught a bus to the centre of town, walked to George Street, stepped into Waterstone's and examined the shelves.

Then I inquired at the desk. Computer screens were examined. Heads were shaken. The response was adamant and negative.

My novels didn't exist. Douglas Carmichael was no longer a published author in World Three. Was he still an author in World One? Would I ever find out?

26

The Toyota drove my body to Holyrood Park and sheltered behind Samson's Ribs. My mind followed it, surveying the vista beyond Duddingston Loch: the 1960s eyesores of King's Buildings, the Braids golf course, the Pentlands clear against a heartless sky. Nearer at hand, mallards quit the water and wandered the hillside with lugubrious industry. A gleeful child in a red anorak and matching Wellingtons pursued them under fond parental scrutiny. Carrion crows gathered. The desultory wind picked at leafless scrub.

The car radio was playing a quick opening movement I didn't recognise: oboes, bassoons, open horns, rushing strings. Emmanuel Bach, perhaps, or Johan Stamitz. Confident in its elegance, it was underpinned – so hindsight, or hindhearing, suggested – with uncertainty, groping towards an unknown future. It straddled two worlds and belonged to neither, rejecting the symmetry of Bach but only hinting at Classical sonata form. Polished and poised, it evoked insecurity.

My novels no longer existed. I'd never accounted myself a literary giant but I was proud of those books. How could they have been there one day and gone the next?

Depression presents differently in different patients, and Alison and Karen were different. Karen was under care, more or less. Alison wasn't.

A half-distant siren cut across the music. Blue lights punched their rhythm behind my eyelids. I turned on the ignition. Monday: last visits to remand prisoners began at half past three but visitors were supposed to be there forty minutes earlier.

I told people nothing meaningful about Linda because everything meaningful was untellable: elusive musical phrases, evanescent images, inimitable caresses, a fleeting perfume that slipped through the gaps between words and left no trace. Sometimes I saw her lips curl without obvious cause, conveying who knew what emotion. One side of her mouth flicked upwards and then downwards, smiling and disapproving. In the immediate aftermath, she swallowed. The gesture was unconscious, but I always loved that half-smile, half-grimace. No one else would have understood the desideratum. It could have conveyed nothing about Linda except to me.

Seen through Alison's eyes, Peter must have comprised a comparable constellation of irresistible, inexpressible attributes. She claimed to have talked about him after they'd parted, but what could she have said? The inconsequential fragments constituting our memories of loved ones resist imprisonment in the cage of language. We can capture only fragile, imperfect simulacra that disintegrate under the scalpel of utterance. Alison hadn't talked to me not because she couldn't forgive me, but because her words would perforce have missed the point.

More plausibly, she hadn't talked to me because the past of World Three didn't exist in World One. When she'd separated from Peter she'd been in no place of being or becoming. She, and Peter, and Karen, and the bronze bull, had yet to be created. Now, in World Three, she'd upbraided me for actions or inactions inhabiting both worlds. I could have upbraided her in return: after the miscarriage she'd locked and barred her emotions beyond reach of visitation, unable to weep themselves on to Peter's shoulder. She'd made herself inaccessible to him, which was, to cut a long story short, why he'd left her. But I was glad my recriminations had been left unspoken. They'd have boomeranged.

The drive to H.M.P. Edinburgh took half an hour. The waiting room was opaque with smoke. Visitors trickled in, many carrying "parcels". In prison, "pass the parcel" isn't a party game. It denotes the transfer of contraband from visitor to inmate unseen by staff or security cameras. There's a second stage, in which the prisoner transports the contraband back to her or his cell without being caught. The percentage success rate owes much to skill born of practice and experience.

At length the visit was called. David hadn't expected me. He marched to his place and sat upright, arms folded, staring me in the eye. Lydia had been right: he looked younger without the moustache, but the military posture and hardness of feature remained. Even if he'd been real we'd never have been friends.

'Well well. To what do I owe the honour?'

'Your irresistible charm, David. I've come to ask whether you need anything I can legally bring or send to you.'

'I want nothing from you.'

'I'm glad we've cleared that up. But perhaps I need something from you.'

'And perhaps I won't provide it.'

'I can but ask. Why did you confess to killing Jimmy Farquhar? The police had nailed *me* for it.'

He gave a bark of laughter.

'Nailed *you*?'

'They'd charged me. They dropped the charge only when you confessed.'

He looked away, exhaling through his nostrils, then stared at me again.

'You think they had evidence to convict you?'

'I was in Jimmy's flat at the material time. We had a fight and I kicked him unconscious. My fingerprints were everywhere. When I found him dead in the hall I ran. Several witnesses saw me. I threw my bloodstained clothes into a skip; the police found them. Hours after his death I rang the hospital to report it, then I rang the police and they recorded the call and matched my voice. So yes, they had evidence.'

His expression was almost pitying.

'You bloody fool, they bluffed you. Farquhar was stabbed to death with his own knife. Were your fingerprints on the knife?'

I scratched my head.

'No, I didn't touch the knife. I left it in his hand when–'

'When you kicked him unconscious and searched for the bull. So you left your fingerprints everywhere in the flat except on the knife you used to stab him. What were you supposed to have done, waited 'til Farquhar recovered consciousness, *then* put on a pair of gloves, *then* took the weapon off him and stabbed him? The police were trying to con you into telling them where the bull was. I'm amazed you resisted. I'd have expected you to crumble like rotten plaster.'

My mind underwent a gear-shift: the "charge" against me had been a bluff. The tapes, the charge sheet, had never been lodged.

'No, I didn't tell them. *You* knew I had the bull, didn't you?'

His grin was mirthless.

'Richard finally told me where it was. I went to Farquhar's flat and found he'd been beaten half to death. Half his attention was on me and half somewhere else. There was an empty sports bag in the hall; not his. I guessed the visitor who'd battered him was still in the flat. I demanded the bull. He tried to stab me. *My* prints were on the knife.'

So World Three *could* rationalise retrospectively. I'd written David's confession days after Jimmy's death, so, unless there'd been an almighty coincidence, my laptop had changed World Three history. David hadn't fabricated his story; he couldn't have concocted fingerprint evidence by lying. His account was more detailed than what I'd written but essentially the same.

'Then you ran down the stairs and away,' I said.

'I ran down the stairs and hid. I wanted to see the visitor. Four minutes and fifty seconds later you came down carrying the sports bag. It wasn't empty, so you'd found the bull. After that I watched your movements.'

'You followed me and traced the bull to Tom MacIntyre's lab. You broke in during Friday night and took it. Taught you to steal in the army, did they?'

For a moment he glared and said nothing. Then:

'I hadn't expected anyone else to take the bull from Farquhar. I'd intended to wait until the visitor left, then go back and find it. You made me change the plan.'

'How gratifying. But if you knew or guessed I had the bull when I left, why didn't you tackle me there and then?'

'Why don't you engage your brain? I'd just killed a man. It was self-defence, so the murder charge won't stick. I knew a jury would buy my story. But if I'd taken the bull from you outside the flat and you'd blabbed about it, the jury would decide I'd killed Farquhar in cold blood and then menaced you to get my hands on it. I don't make stupid moves.'

'Confessing to killing Jimmy strikes me as stupid.'

'Does it? The police detained me for questioning about so-called illegal immigration. Took my fingerprints; routine. So it was only a matter of time before they found the match with Farquhar's knife. Confession to killing in self-defence was the best option.'

Calm in a crisis, cool under fire. There's much to be said for military training. David made rational choices where I'd have panicked. He and Peter had much in common. He'd do time for culpable homicide, but with no previous convictions, an exemplary military record and a plausible defence, it shouldn't be a long sentence. However, if he was such a meticulous planner, why hadn't he worn gloves when he went to Jimmy's flat?

'You haven't denied taking the bull from Tom's lab. Where is it now?'

Again the bark of laughter.

'Beyond your reach, beyond the reach of the police, beyond the reach of anyone except the person it's intended for.'

I shook my head.

'When the police questioned you about Jimmy they knew you'd searched for the bull, so they asked you about it. Did you tell them *I* had it?'

'I told them it wasn't in Farquhar's flat so I'd been mis-informed. As far as they're concerned I never had it.'

He'd told almost the same lie that I had.

'Tom MacIntyre died in the lab the night you took the bull. Won't your fingerprints be at the crime scene? Hair samples? DNA evidence?'

The news startled him, but only for an instant.

'I wore a forensic suit. The old boy came into the room, saw me and passed out. But he was breathing when I left.'

'He was dead long before morning. Suppose I tell the police what you've just told me. Alternatively, you could tell me where the bull is. What's your rational choice this time, David?'

He laughed.

'The police won't believe a bloody thing you tell them, and it would be your word against mine. And what use could your information be? The bull's safe. You'll never recover it.'

His *sang froid* verged on the pathological.

'You killed Jimmy in self-defence and you killed Tom by accident. But someone killed Peter Wishart on purpose and someone took the bull from him. When people learn all those elements of the story they'll make connections.'

For once, his reply was disingenuous.

'Karen Winster killed Wishart. She's been charged.'

'Iain McArdle no longer believes she did it. Better watch your back, David.'

A slow, hard smile curdled his mouth.

'Trying to scare me?'

'You've handled the bull, you've hidden it, and it's not just Iain McArdle who's–'

'Dearie me, cue dramatic music. Scotland Yard have no more hope of finding the bull than McArdle has. Or you have. End of conversation.'

He stood up to terminate the visit.

I quit the prison and drove back to Holyrood Park. The weather was still dry. I decided to climb Arthur's Seat. At the old triangulation point on top of the hill I sat and smoked a cigarette, turning my back on Duddingston Loch and the south-west wind. Beyond Portobello and Musselburgh the southern shore of the Firth dipped inwards past Port Seton and the strand where earlier today I'd walked with Alison. Then it curved round to Aberlady Bay. Beyond the bay stood the improbable cone of North Berwick Law. Somewhere over there was Binning Wood and the mouth of the Tyne, where an aeon ago, one afternoon last week, I'd walked with Beth. She too had interrogated me about Linda.

I was cold but unwilling to move. The sun began to dip over the city, the castle back-lit by the reddening sky. Where had David hidden the bull? Somewhere out there in the city, or beyond the sea? I started to shiver. The wind brought a foretaste of the dark time of the year. The vista began to fade.

I stumbled back down the hill. It was a relief to reach the car and drive a few yards into Duddingston for a pub dinner. I wished I hadn't been driving; I needed alcohol. At least the pub was warm and for a while I could relax and drink coffee, but damned pop music invaded my ears. People are afraid of silence.

I watched the television in the bar. The fires of introspection were damped but continued to glow, subtle but consuming.

27

Back at home in the *Brigadoon* I drank. Like an earthquake zone I'd suffered aftershocks. I doubted whether my cannabis supplier existed in World Three. Stocks were low but the urgency was great, so I rolled a joint and switched on the radio: the first of the Beethoven Razumovsky quartets.

David had no wish to exonerate Karen, though he knew the charge against her was implausible. So who *did* kill Peter? David was an unlikely suspect, though the bull was a motive and he'd followed Peter to Loki's. But Jimmy, not David, had taken the bull from beside Peter's body. However, if David had told the truth, he'd had the forethought and self-control to let me escape with the bull from Jimmy's flat, knowing he'd recover it later. By the same token, suppose he'd anticipated Jimmy's intervention that fateful Saturday night. His calmness under pressure could have led him to kill Peter but leave the case, watch, follow Jimmy home, and then lie low until the media spotlight had turned away from the murder. The scenario seemed far-fetched, but David said he'd learned about Jimmy's phone call from Richard and then traced the address. However, when I'd first visited Abbey House, Richard hadn't intended to tell him about that call. And even if David *had* acquired the information that way, how had he the located the flat, unless he'd followed Jimmy? Or had he followed *me* that Monday afternoon? On the other hand, would he have challenged me the evening after Peter's murder if he'd already known where the bull was?

Fogged with whisky and cannabis, my ruminations grew random. What would determine the outcome of my story?

I closed my eyes and concentrated on the music. Beethoven wrote that slow movement after his brother died. It evokes a weeping willow over the grave. Yet to my ears it always seems tranquil, not sad. Each of us interprets what we observe in our own way.

Where had David hidden the bull? Again I'd no clues. But if I couldn't find the answer, how would I finish the novel? Only David knew the truth and he wouldn't divulge it.

I waited until the quartet reached its end, switched off the radio, went to bed and fell asleep. I didn't dream.

During the night the weather turned. The morning dawned grey. The wind had veered to the north and drove thin cold rain. Yet at breakfast I was cheerful. All my worries seemed distant: Karen, Alison, David, Beth and Eric, the bull, the disappearance of my novels, the problem of returning to World One. A detached ego once more, I planned a day's writing. Fed and watered, I needed only a cigarette to kick-start my creativity. I'd return to the story and take control.

I mused in my room for twenty minutes. Rain spattered the window. The radio played the *Tristan* prelude and Dvorak's violin concerto. My mind wove shreds of plot around scattered images. I started to formulate sentences. With the finale of the concerto I began to focus. What was David *likely* to have done with the bull? His aim was to add it to Richard's collection, but he wouldn't have placed it in or near Abbey House; too much police activity. So he'd put it somewhere that was inaccessible to everyone, yet Richard would be able to retrieve it when the time was ripe. Where might that be? Considered in those terms the answer was obvious. If David believed it would elude me he'd underestimated me. But he'd claimed the bull was beyond my reach, not that I couldn't deduce where it was.

I'd typed half the relevant passage when my mobile rang. Beth.

'Where are you?'

'Hotel room.'

'What's going on? We couldn't get your phone yesterday, so we rang the hotel and the manager said you were leaving.'

'I'll be here 'til the end of the week. I was out yesterday; people to see.'

'About the bull, or anything concerning Karen?'

'Indirectly. I'm working on an idea.'

'Want to share it?'

'Yes, when I've thought it through. How're you doing?'

'Day off, and *I* have news about the bull. And we've elbowed other visitors out of the way so we're going to see Karen this evening. Coming?'

'If I won't be intruding. How about lunch?'

'Indian in Forest Road again? It's only a few minutes' walk for me.'

'You'll get wet.'

'Maybe I'll grow. What time?'

I suggested 12.30. It gave me two hours to develop this passage and draft more of the story. But my concentration was unsettled. What news did Beth have? Surely she hadn't located the bull?

She hadn't, of course. We sat at the table we'd occupied

the day Karen was arrested. Her confidence had returned, but it was undershot with unaccustomed grimness. Eric had stayed in the house to phone his wife. We placed orders.

'What's this news, Beth?'

'Yours first. Have you thought your idea through?'

I told her David's story: how he'd watched me take the bull from Jimmy's flat and shadowed my movements, and subsequently stolen it from the laboratory. She shook her head.

'The conclusions don't make sense, Doug. If he followed you from Farquhar's flat then he knew the case must be in your hotel room or your car. So why didn't he take it when you weren't looking?'

'More risk of being caught breaking into a locked car or a hotel room than a university building. And maybe he wanted to see what I'd do with the bull. If I'd given it to Richard he wouldn't have needed to act.'

'Ah. He works for *Richard*. Is he in with the smugglers? Could he have killed Peter?'

Food arrived. Beth was hungry. Perhaps she and Eric had been too busy for meals.

'He *could* have killed Peter and let Jimmy take the case away, intending to recover it once the hue and cry subsided. Unlikely, though. Involvement with the smugglers is unlikely, too. David put Peter in touch with foreign dealers, but he was more involved in people smuggling. For altruistic reasons, I'm told.'

'Convincing or what? Sounds a shady character. Didn't care about Tom, did he?'

I told her David had been in no position to summon help for Tom. But Beth wasn't interested in David. She wanted to know where the bull was.

'You said *you* had news about it.'

'Yes.' She devoured another mouthful of lamb Madras. 'But not its whereabouts. I'm waiting for *you* to tell *me*.'

I explained my deduction. She frowned.

'So how do we get hold of it?'

'We don't. For now, no one does. The authorities could obtain a court order but it would take time. Anyway, it's only my guess. Or to rephrase, my only guess. Now, over to you.'

She kept me waiting until she'd finished lunch and ordered coffee, and then she told me about the latest e-mail from Athens. They'd analysed the bronze bull in the National Museum.

'It has the composition of United States government bronze: 88% copper, 10% tin, 2% zinc. And the patina's largely copper acetate.' She smirked.

'Transparent fake.'

'Expert on bronzes now, are we?'

I reminded her that *she'd* told me fake patinas were acetate not carbonate, and she and Tom had explained that high tin bronze in the ancient world was reserved for weapons, not ornaments. She conceded the point.

'And since their bull's a fake,' she concluded, 'ours is genuine.'

'That doesn't follow. Could be more than one fake.'

'You're being picky.'

Spiro Andropoulos had been an expert on ancient bronzes, I argued, so he'd have known a copy of the bull in U.S. government bronze wouldn't convince anyone. Therefore, he'd *meant* us to know it was a forgery. Maybe he'd been in a hurry and had to make do with inadequate materials, but he could have made a second and better forgery with the intention of selling both that *and* the genuine article.

'Remember he'd made preliminary deals with *two* Sicilian museums. So: is our bull the genuine article, or the better forgery, sold to Peter in order to get one over on Karen?'

'Rubbish, Doug. Not even Andropoulos could produce that good a fake: the patina, the pollen grains, the–'

'Tom said the patina was *thick*. Didn't you say artificial patinas tend to be thick and natural ones thin? And the contradiction between the lead content Tom found and the data in the paper–'

'Common sense says we've got the genuine bull. Or had. It needs to be back in Athens.'

'Or Agrigento, or–'

'Yes, Doug, let the museums argue the right to title. It ought to be back *somewhere*.'

'Returning it would make Peter's death pointless. *If* he was killed for the bull.'

'His death was pointless anyway. Returning the bull won't change that.'

'This is all academic. We can't return the bull if we can't recover it. Or locate it if my guess is wrong.'

'Should we ask Karen?'

She was asking *me*? Yes, I believed we should discuss it with Karen. But that should be for Beth, and Eric, to decide.

The rain had eased when we left the restaurant but the wind snickered cold and malevolent down George IV Bridge. We hurried on to Chambers Street, returning with unspoken accord to Karen's house. So much for my afternoon's work. But it seemed more urgent to talk to Karen, and I needed to speak to Eric first.

'Didn't you bring your car, Doug?'

Did it alarm her to walk past the Museum or did she want to escape the weather?

'If you were going to walk to the restaurant, so was I.'

'A masculine amalgam of righteousness and stupidity.'

'Do you make sexist comments like that to your father and brothers?'

'What's sexist about describing a man as masculine?'

'The way it's done. I don't drive everywhere. I climbed Arthur's Seat yesterday after I'd visited David. On foot.'

'Wow. I'm impressed. You're out of breath now, though. You shouldn't smoke. As I don't need to tell you.'

'I received a similar rebuke yesterday. From a woman, of course. The nagging gene is activated by Y chromosome deficiency.'

'Pathetic and contrived. Four out of ten and that's generous. I only wanted a lift to Karen's.'

I managed to light a cigarette. I needed to buy more but it could wait. I'd scrounge from Eric in the meantime.

He greeted me with his customary politeness and brewed tea, but his manner betrayed an undercurrent of agitation.

'What's wrong, Eric?' said Beth.

'Mmm? Nothing.' He proffered cigarettes. I accepted one.

'Trouble at home?' Beth persisted.

'No, not at all. She's missing me but she understands why I need to stay here. And the bishop has allowed me extended leave. We have a good young curate.'

'What, then?'

I sighed.

'Whatever's on your mind, Eric, Beth will give you no peace until you share it.'

Beth stuck out her tongue at me. Fragment by reluctant fragment, Eric divulged his reflections on Karen's situation and state of mind. His thoughts were dizzying his soul.

'Obviously I don't want her to be unhappy, but her predicament *entails* unhappiness. She has to grieve for Peter, for herself, perhaps for a failure of justice. Even to feel bitter. The night I arrived, Doug, you said Karen was clinically depressed. But Karen wasn't miserable or un-communicative when I visited. You said she'd be better, but ... *that* much better? I was relieved, of course, but I was also unsettled by her *lack* of misery. I've now talked about it to my wife. But she's far away.'

He drank the rest of his tea.

Carmichael's anti-Midas touch again! Guilt at Karen's plight had impelled me to mitigate her suffering. I'd written her out of the abyss of depression, not for her peace of mind but for mine. My intervention had robbed her of her right to misery, precluded the fulfilment of her duty to grieve. By the same token, it had upset her brother. Since then, my literary skill had landed David in prison. Yet I continued to write, to forge the fates of my characters. What further ill might my morning with the laptop have wrought?

'The course of clinical depression differs among patients,' I said. 'Maybe you misread the signs, Eric. I don't believe Karen's ceased to grieve; she's just made herself appear normal again. To herself, mainly.'

Beth scolded him.

'I don't understand why you're blaming yourself, Eric.

Surely it was a visit from her brother that pulled Karen out of the pit and made her responsive. Doug and I couldn't get a word out of her before you arrived.'

Honest and supportive but mistaken.

She went to the kitchen and prepared a snack. Eric and I smoked; he seemed mollified. My cloak of clinical objectivity concealed disingenuousness. I couldn't tell either of them the truth. I choked down a sandwich. Beth glanced at her watch and cleared the plates.

'We've things to tell you about the bull, Eric,' she said, 'but we must go. Doug can tell you while I drive.'

Beth, it seemed, trusted her driving more than Eric's.

'I'll keep it brief, Eric,' I said. 'We'll have to repeat it all to Karen.'

I reclined in the back of the BMW and recited David's story, explained my guess about the hiding place, and declared the bull in the National Museum in Athens to be a fake. I suggested our bull might be a subtler fake; Beth scoffed. Inner torment notwithstanding, Eric was a good listener. By the time I'd finished we'd reached the Stirling slip road. The rain was steady. Beth started to explain more about the analytical evidence but broke off in mid-sentence.

'What's wrong?' I asked.

'I don't wish to sound melodramatic, but we're being followed. Check the car behind, Doug. Tell me whether you recognise the occupants.'

The car behind was a black Ford Sierra. The occupants became intermittently visible as the wipers passed to and fro. The driver was Bob Williamson. The passenger was Iain McArdle.

Why were they following us this time?

28

The Sierra disappeared along Fountain Road. Beth drove on to Cornton Vale. Rain sheeted down.

'They could be visiting Stirling for reasons unrelated to us,' said Eric.

'Yeah. There might be mermaids.' I was rattled. I'd expected Iain to follow me, but not so blatantly. What was his game?

'Why would they follow *me*?' demanded Beth.

'I was in the back seat. Why did they want us to *know* they were following us?'

I scanned Fountain Road. No loiterer on the opposite pavement studying a soggy newspaper. No workmen, no parked van. Of course, there were security cameras.

We dripped over the waiting-room seats until the visits were called. Karen was pale, stressed and volatile. Her mental agility and articulacy had returned but her poise hadn't. When I mentioned her former cell-mate she shrugged and waxed loquacious.

'Renate's bright but obsessive, incapable of small-talk but burdened with an inexhaustible stock of the larger variety. Better to be locked up with than most of the women here but she's a bloody bore. I now have the company of a shop-lifter and part-time prostitute called Jean McIvor, who smokes fags, which is a bastard, and heroin, which is scary. *She* talks about herself all the time, too, but she's amusing. Her stories are embroidered, but as a window into an alien order of society they exert morbid fascination. Mind you, I wouldn't trust her further than I could hurl a Steinway.'

Eric was horrified: his sister was housed with a drug addict! Karen shrugged again: near-certainty, she said.

'I could buy most illicit substances here within five minutes. No, Eric dear, not the slightest intention. But if I'd led the kind of life they lead I probably would.'

I'd written her out of depression without intending its sequela: garrulous hysteria masquerading as jollity, intellect and sleight of tongue varnishing over the cracks. This wasn't the self-assured Karen of *The Bronze Bull* before Peter's murder but a human battlefield on which bravado wrestled with despair. Beth asked whether she felt isolated or endangered, since she was different from those around her.

'I get flak for "talking posh" but I'm respected for killing my partner … No, of course I didn't, but no one believes you if you protest innocence. Everybody denies or minimises her own crime. Rumour throughout the jail makes me a domestic abuse victim who hit back, so I'm a heroine in the eyes of many. Also, Beth, helping semi-literate women to write letters and complaint forms guarantees cupboard-love. So yes, I'm isolated, I'm lied about, but I'm not at risk.'

I marvelled at the speed with which she'd established coping strategies. I hadn't written this. It now seemed disconcertingly easy to converse with her. Eric mentioned her solicitor, Rintoul. She said there'd been little progress with the defence because the PF's office hadn't yet released the forensic evidence. Witnesses were being sought, though in vain. Perhaps; but from everything I'd learned about high-profile trials in Scotland, prosecution witnesses could be conjured up at little notice or expense.

I recounted recent developments regarding the bull. Karen was excited about the analyses, cynical about the news from Athens, horrified by Tom's death, infuriated by the theft from the lab, stunned by David's involvement.

'Somewhere safe from whence his darling Richard can recover it when he chooses?' she mused. 'Bank deposit box. Must be good pals with the manager or he couldn't have spirited the bull into the bank on a Sunday morning.'

'My guess, too.' I nodded. 'So how do we get it back?'

'If you're right,' said Eric, 'this *must* be left to the police.'

Karen disagreed, either because her brother had suggested it or because she mistrusted the police. Beth sided with Eric: if the bull *was* in a deposit box in David's bank, Karen couldn't have put it there, so the case against her failed. Karen said she'd discuss it with Rintoul.

She wanted to talk about the bull, not her personal situation. She'd studied the photocopied documents and confirmed Beth's interpretation. The two women discussed the data and debated the rival claims for Sardinian and Cypriot copper, Etruscan trade, factors affecting the properties of bronze. Karen's eyes shone. Eric and I listened with intermittent comprehension. I picked up random phrases: a recent exhibition in Oristano, wherever that was; metal processing in Etruria; a copper mine called Su Fruscu; something about Arab settlers and the origin of the word "Saracen"; the Sardinian bull cult. Karen seemed to be repeating old lectures. It was probably doing her good.

'Beth, you should read Lilliu on pre-Roman relations between Sardinia and Etruria.'

'How do you spell it? What's his first name?'

Karen continued her quasi-lecture.

'... so Spiro was talking through his arse; to say nothing of his fabrication about the lead, the bastard. I'm sorry I ever gave his address to ... I like your idea about the bull cult entering Sicily, Beth. Lilliu might offer evidence.'

I returned to Lucian's story.

'Beth and I talked about this the other day. We wondered whether Perilaus made the original bull, the full-sized one, in Akragas itself, and maybe the model as well.'

Karen burst out laughing. All eyes in the visit room turned to us.

'Perilaus, indeed!' She shook her head. 'Don't fall for Lucian's satire, Doug.'

'I don't see the joke, Karen.'

'Don't you?' She giggled. 'Look, suppose you wanted to tell a story demeaning the Scots. You might invent a nasty, twisted, subservient character and call him, say, Robert Bruce or William Wallace.'

'I wouldn't tell it in the pub. You mean there was a Greek hero called Perilaus?'

'There were *several* Greek heroes called Perilaus. According to the Orestes myth, Perilaus was the noble son of Icarius and Periboea. He was the guy who accused Orestes of murdering Clytemnestra. In the tale of Jason and the Argonauts, Perilaus was the son of Ancaeus of Samos and the demigoddess Samia, hence a grandson of Poseidon. Herodotus tells us about a brave Syconian general called Perilaus who fell in battle against the Persians. You don't find the name in Pindar's account of the Bull of Phalaris, or Aristotle's. Greek writers wouldn't have used it. Lucian wrote for educated Romans who knew about Greek culture, legends, history … He called his villain "Perilaus" to amuse his audience by demeaning Greeks.'

She burst out laughing again. The myth makers had let me down. I'd wanted Perilaus the metal-worker, the creator of the Bull of Phalaris, to have existed, a historical figure in World One as well as World Three. But here was a conundrum: could an argument by a denizen of World Three, however intelligent and informed, affect the historicity of a figure in World One? Perhaps it would if I decided to incorporate Karen's speech into *The Bronze Bull*, and if the novel were published in World One, and if anyone read it. But were *any* of my novels still published in World One?

The visit ended. We'd brought Karen up to date, omitting to tell her that Iain had followed us to the prison. Did he imagine the bull had been hidden in Cornton Vale?

The rain had stopped. Beth's BMW gleamed. Eric insisted I take the passenger seat and I complied, relaxing beside Beth while she drove. We discussed Karen's improved state of mind and her renewed interest in work; we declared ourselves glad. What Karen was feeling, back in her cell with Jean the junkie, we couldn't imagine.

There was no sign of a police pursuit. As we reached the city bypass Eric remarked, *à propos* of nothing identifiable: 'The moral and the aesthetic needn't coincide. If Perilaus existed and made the bull, he did wrong, even by the standards of a cruel age. Yet his creation was beautiful.'

'*Very* profound,' snapped Beth.

By the time we were back in Karen's house her good humour had been restored. Eric brewed tea and produced biscuits; the archetypal vicar. Talk returned to the bull's whereabouts and our hopes of recovering it.

'Karen reached the same conclusion as you, Doug,' said Eric, 'and since you both know David Michie you're probably right.'

'Maybe,' said Beth, 'but it doesn't help us.'

'*Petit à petit, l'oiseau fait son nid*, as they say across the Channel. Excuse me a moment.' I dug out my mobile. 'Richard? Doug. Have you visited David?'

Beth and Eric sipped tea while a four-minute harangue filled my ear. No doubt Lydia had been battered with a longer version. Finally I contrived to express concern about David's bank account: did it need to be closed, or frozen pending developments? Richard hadn't thought about it. It was now easy to offer my services and elicit the address of the branch. Beth grinned.

'Neat, Doug, but where does it get us? You can't walk into a bank and demand the contents of someone's private deposit box.'

'Doug might be able to establish whether the deposit box exists, Beth,' said Eric. 'As he says, a step at a time.'

'Tomorrow morning's organised, then.' I placed my cup and saucer on the coffee table beside the chaise longue. 'Thanks for tea and nibbles, Eric. Must go. I'll report after I've visited David's bank.'

'I need to go, too,' said Beth. 'Work tomorrow. I'll give you a lift, Doug.'

Eric saw us to the door. He waved until we turned into St Leonard Street and then disappeared from the mirror. His faith would sustain him.

Beth stopped some distance from the *Brigadoon*,

switched off the engine and stared at the windscreen. After a minute she murmured:

'Doug, I don't want to be on my own tonight.'

I didn't respond. If she'd wanted company, why hadn't she stayed with Eric? She turned towards me and her eyes pleaded.

'I can't, Beth.'

'Why not?'

'Because of Linda.'

Tension gushed out of her with a whimper. She slumped over the wheel, face resting on her hands. After half a minute she sat up.

'OK, I understand. Good night, Doug.'

'Good night, Beth.'

She drove away without looking back.

I walked to the hotel through renewed wind and rain, drank a third of a bottle of whisky, went to bed and dreamed about a tiger catching fire in a castle banqueting hall. I'd had a similar dream the previous week. As the vision evolved, the walls and roof of the hall crowded in to enclose the burning creature. The floor rippled beneath it. The tiger's body metamorphosed to glowing bronze, its form to that of the bull. The floor became a heap of blazing papers, or a book. I should have known better than drink whisky before bed.

29

Wednesday morning, cool and cloudy, didn't go according to plan. My hangover not being conducive to driving I decided to take a bus to Portobello, but before I reached the bus stop a car halted beside me and in a trice I was surrounded by Iain and three of his colleagues. I clutched my briefcase.

The London superintendent started the verbal bludgeoning: given a false address, liable to face further charges, many years in prison, better start cooperating. Bob Williamson and a massive constable crowded against me. Passing drivers and pedestrians drew each other's attention to us. Iain allowed the softening-up to continue for five minutes.

'I think Dr Carmichael understands, Derek.' His voice stilled the superintendent's aggression. 'He'll maybe talk, but the whole four of us is a wee bittie overpowering. Best if there's just two.' His smile was almost benevolent. 'Visited a few prisons lately, haven't ye, Doctor? Getting a preview of life inside?'

'You've put one of my friends and one of my acquaintances in jail so I've visited them. Incidentally, the superintendent's mistaken. I didn't give a false address.'

I handed Iain my driving licence. He nodded.

'Aye, we've seen it. But yon address disnae exist, so I'm interested in where ye got this document and yer reasons for carrying it. I think there's no need to go back to HQ for our wee chat, though, Derek, unless we're forced tae proceed with charges. Let's see how forthcoming Dr Carmichael is over a cup of coffee, eh?'

To my surprise, the superintendent agreed, and he and Bob departed. Accompanied only by the large silent constable we crossed the road to a café and sat at a corner table. The angle of the walls sheltered my back.

'For a senior officer who plays it by the book, this is unconventional,' I said. 'Thanks for the coffee.'

'Ye're welcome. It's an unconventional case, Doctor.'

'Laying fake charges on me *was* unconventional.'

'Aye, but you know why. And as my Scotland Yard colleague said, there's plenty else we can charge you with.'

'Or I could sue you for false arrest. I still don't know where the bull is.'

'Ye don't, eh? By the way, yer prison visiting's been noted.'

He handed me a copy of the morning's *Daily Record*. I was on page 2: Dodgy Doc Dodges Murder Rap. I'd been arrested for the murder of James Farquhar but later released, then visited the man who'd taken my place, ex-commando David Michie, 45, who was now in Saughton jail. I'd given the police an untraceable address so they were hunting for me again. A spokesman said they needed to question me about certain matters. I'd also visited jailed museum curator Karen Winster. Winster had been charged with murdering her lover Peter Wishart. Some reports said Wishart had been an international drug dealer. Possible links among Carmichael, Wishart and Winster were being investigated. *Etcetera*. The photo of me was abominable. I returned the tabloid to Iain and wiped my hands on a napkin.

'The night we first met, Doctor, you said Dr Winster would need analytical tests to check if the bull was authentic. Ye've visited her twice. Seemingly she engaged the services of Professor Thomas MacIntyre for work o' that nature. The late Professor Thomas MacIntyre. Did ye know him?'

'Met him once. I heard he'd died.'

'Aye. In his laboratory. Something he'd been working on was stolen. Our informant couldnae say what the something was except it was made of bronze and had been buried in a Mediterranean country. So we can make a guess, dae ye no' think?'

'Depends how reliable your informant is.'

'Good point. Informant's an asylum seeker. Your pal Captain Michie helped get him into the country, and then he worked for Professor MacIntyre. He shouldnae have been doing paid work while his asylum application was being considered. But there seemed no advantage in reporting him tae the Home Office, unless he failed tae help us with our inquiries, like. So we believe our informant's reliable.'

Poor Hamid. What impression had he received of Scotland?

'I understand that army officers below the rank of major aren't known by rank after they retire, Chief Inspector.'

'Being a wee bittie pedantic, aren't you? I'm trying to be polite and you're trying to change the subject. I wonder why. Ye still don't know where the bull is?'

'I'll tell you if I find out, as I promised.'

'I wish I could believe ye. Why did you go tae see Michie along in Saughton?'

'He confessed to the crime you'd mock-charged me with, so I owed him a visit.'

'Did he no' tell you where the bull is?'

'I asked him. Like me, he thought Jimmy Farquhar had it, so he was disappointed when he went to Jimmy's flat.'

The constable was itching to handcuff me.

'You were quick to learn it was Michie who'd confessed and got ye out o' jail,' said Iain. His weary unblinking eyes stared into mine. 'Mighty quick.'

I stared back at him. He waved the constable away. Finally *tête-à-tête* with me, he lowered his voice.

'Wondering why I brought you in here, why you've no' been dragged down to headquarters again and charged wi' everything short o' stealing the Crown Jewels? Well, there's something mighty strange about you, and although ye've been a lot less honest than I'd wish, I doubt the strangeness is altogether criminal. Maybe if I can get to the bottom o' this strangeness I'll have the answers. If I can't we'll do it the hard way and proceed with charges. Real charges. So it's in yer interests to start telling me the truth at last. Got it?'

I nodded. 'Cooperation will suit me. I need answers too. But I've had good reason … Let's say the truth would challenge your professional scepticism.'

'So ye've no' been telling the truth because it's too far-fetched, is that it? Well, it's just you and me now. So try me. For starters, how did ye know about Michie's confession afore he confessed?'

'Ah. You read it on my laptop. There's the answer: I wrote it, so it happened.'

'Aye, right. Things only happen if you write them

aforehand, is that it? Or ye foresee things and then write them down?'

'Foreordaining, not foreseing. And it doesn't apply to everything. For example, I didn't write Tom MacIntyre's death. But I wrote Peter Wishart's purchase of the bull, and his murder, and its theft. I wrote them two Fridays ago at home in 17 Blandford Terrace. To be precise, I wrote the murder three and a half hours before it happened. Twenty-four hours later I couldn't find Blandford Terrace. Which is why I'm now living in a hotel room and you can't trace my real address. I wrote your involvement in the case, too.'

He leaned back and studied me. His coffee grew cold. I drank mine.

'Can ye no' dream up a yarn a jury might believe?'

'I don't expect anyone to believe it. That's why I've lied. But now you've given me no option. I have to tell it like it is.'

Behind the unblinking eyes, his mind was working. The world didn't split open. Even this crisis hadn't translated me back to World One as I'd half hoped, half feared. I'd no idea what to say or do next. My heart raced. I expected Iain to summon the constable, arrest me, take me to head-quarters and charge me. But he didn't.

'Did ye by any chance write a postmortem report on Wishart after ye'd written his murder?'

'Yes.'

'What did it say?'

I took the laptop from my briefcase, opened the file containing the abbreviated PM report and turned the screen to face Iain. His face struggled. He'd seen an identical report, a confidential report, which I couldn't have accessed. This information hadn't been in the papers. He finished reading and scrutinised me again. He was forced to suspend unbelief now. I shook my head to expel Linda's voice: that song, that infernal song. Pain stabbed my right temple. I jumped and shuddered.

'Whit's wrong?'

'A rat. Ran across the floor. There.'

I pointed. He turned to look. No rat.

'Yer eyes are playing tricks, Doctor. If ye wrote the murder then ye wrote who the murderer was and who stole the case and the bull.'

'Two different people. But events have moved on. I'm no longer sure …'

'Ye'll need tae explain. Names would maybe help.'

'Jimmy Farquhar stole the case, but … Look, Chief Inspector, I've lied, but I think you now understand why. The truth is–'

'The truth is, if Farquhar took the case from Wishart, and you and Michie went to get it from Farquhar, one of the two of ye went away with it and took it to Professor MacIntyre's lab. Whichever of you didnae take it from Farquhar's flat nicked it from the lab later. Which was which?'

I said that if David had killed Jimmy he'd probably saved my life. I admitted to taking the bull to Tom's lab; and yes, it was Karen who'd said if I got my hands on the bull I should take it to Tom for analysis and then turn it over to the police.

'I don't know who took it from the laboratory,' I added. 'I didn't write that. I sent Tom's analysis data to Karen and photocopied the documents from the case for her. She's studied the information and believes the bull could be genuine. The copy in the National Museum in Athens is a fake: modern bronze, artificial patina.'

His eyes blazed. He was angry with me for concealing information, but he was angrier with himself because he knew now he'd charged the wrong person with Peter's murder. Unless he could recover the bull, his contribution to dismantling the smuggling ring had evaporated.

'Karen never saw the bull,' I said. 'She expected it that Friday night but Peter was killed and the case was stolen. *She* didn't kill him.'

'Aye, very good, very good, ye smug lying stage-magician bastard, very fucking good. So who the fuck did kill him, then, you whit *wrote* the whole shebang?'

'I had someone in mind when I drafted the story but events have moved on. Jimmy seemed an obvious choice. Recent revelations have made *David* a likelier bet. Have you identified the owner of the hammer?'

'Whit hammer?'

'Come on, Chief Inspector. Peter was killed by three successive blows to the back of his skull with a two-pound hammer, which your officers found two hours later on a seat in the Meadows beside a tramp called Seamus Goldstein. None of which information has reached the press.'

His face was beetroot-coloured.

'Maybe it'll amuse ye to know a two-pound hammer's missing frae Wishart's tool kit and the only other person wi' access tae it wis Karen Winster. Did ye write *that* on yer fucking laptop? Yer pal Winster's no' out o' the shite, mister, whither she got her hauns on the bull or no.'

His accent thickened in proportion to his ire. But he'd lose interest in Karen if he couldn't link her to the bull.

'I didn't write anything about Peter's tool kit. But I hardly need tell you that such evidence requires scrutiny.'

He pressed his clenched fists into the table top and stared at them, breathing heavily until he regained his self-command. I didn't envy his subordinates when he lost his temper.

'All right. Suppose, fer argument's sake, I believe what ye've telled me. Just suppose it. I can't make any manner o' sense of it, and I dinnae think you can either if the truth be told, which it seldom is. But there's plenty o' things in this world make scant sense. All this came about because ye were writing one of these non-existent novels of yours, right?'

'Two of my four published novels were on sale in Waterstone's the day after Peter's death. But on Monday I checked again and you were right: they'd gone, just as my car's gone and my home's gone and the street it's in has gone. I can't explain any of it.'

He shook his head to and fro and said if it weren't for the evidence I'd given and the bizarre circumstances surrounding the case I'd be certified insane. I couldn't disagree.

'But for aw you've told me today, for aw ye say ye've written, you cannae tell me who the murderer is or where the bull is now. Right?'

'I have ideas but nothing to back them up. And I'd rather not tell you those conjectures because if they're wrong you'd charge me with wasting police time.'

'We've enough to send you down several times over for withholding information and trying to pervert the course o' justice.'

'It isn't perverting the course of justice to withhold conjectures, is it?'

The ghost of a grin haunted the corners of his mouth. His jowls shifted. His unbelief was only partly suspended but he'd hit on a way of testing me. His face betrayed malicious pleasure.

'Whit would happen if ye wrote these conjectures down? For example, what if ye wrote the whereabouts o' the bull and an explanation of how it got there? Would it make yer idea come true?'

'Such was my plan for today. But before I could get to the bank in Portobello to execute it, you interrupted me.'

He devoted another minute to silent thought. He took two deep breaths, then said:

'Bank, eh? Safety deposit box? In whose name?'

I explained my thoughts, my scheme for the novel's culmination. He whipped a phone from his pocket.

'Derek? Iain. We were right. Carmichael's just telled me. Will ye get Bob to pick up the sheriff's order, pronto, and come and join me afore ye get on to London? I'll keep ye posted … Aye, right, cheers.'

He pocketed the phone and grinned without humour. He was getting ahead of himself, ahead of me, and he knew it. I hadn't written the requisite passage, let alone verified the outcome.

'Ye called it "unconventional", bringing you here for a chat,' he said, 'but sometimes unconventional works. Maybe we're better informed now, though I'll never be able to use the information. Then again, maybe ye've fed me a load o' bull manure. I hope for your sake you havnae.' He paused, then continued: 'Anyways, I'm about to do something unconventional enough to land me in deep shite if it disnae work. I mean, if it disnae work because *you* let me down. And if I land in deep shite, you're going to land in deeper shite. Understood?'

'Perfectly.'

'So ye'd better no' let me down. Right, I'm going to let ye go. Get yerself out o' here, go to the bank or wherever ye're going and write what ye can write as quick as ye can. And then bring whit ye've written straight back tae me. Make a run for it and ye'll be in the jail faster than ye can say "laptop". We're watching you.'

'I don't think I can write the identity of the murderer for you. But the whereabouts of the bull? No promises, but I'll give it my best shot.'

'Ye'd better, pal. Remember, ye're on the leash. Bolt and ye're throttled.'

30

During the twenty minute bus journey to Portobello I deployed my laptop. I'd written half this scene before lunch the previous day but now I had to finish it, rapidly. *Its success will be in the laptop of the gods.* My snigger was a little hysterical.

Phalaris had intended the Bull as a gift to Apollo, whose intercession I now craved. Since even my dialogue with Ian had failed to return me to World One, divine intervention seemed my only hope. I should have discussed it with Eric. I saved the file, closed the laptop, put it back into my briefcase and alighted in Portobello High Street.

The cash machine didn't recognise my card. I walked into the bank and asked the teller for cash. The computer told her my account number didn't exist. I asked to see the manager. I was admitted to the sanctum and gave my name, date of birth, home address and account number. None of that information could be found in the bank's records. The manager's hand twitched towards the phone. I suggested that if he was calling the police he should ask for DCI McArdle, who knew me. His hand hesitated.

'Speaking of Iain McArdle,' I said. 'He and I wondered whether a deposit box has been registered here during the past few days in the name of Richard Latimer-Brown.'

'Good gracious, I can't reveal information of that sort!'

'Not even to Mr McArdle when he brings a sheriff's order? We believe the box contains an item for which the police are searching. I'm not accusing Mr Latimer-Brown of wrongdoing, though.'

The manager donned a well-bred mantle of indignation. He'd render all possible assistance to police officers if they presented the appropriate documents, but not to a stranger with a fake bank card and fabricated personal details. As he ushered me out of his office with more haste than courtesy we collided with Iain and Bob.

'Mair trouble?' Iain grinned. 'I told you to report straight back to me.'

'My bank account has gone the way of my novels, flat, car and street. A few days ago I drew two hundred from an ATM, but now neither my card nor my account number is recognised. Hence the delay. However, I believe a deposit box has been registered here during the past few days in the name of Richard Latimer-Brown. What you seek is in that box. I should emphasise that Richard knows nothing about it.'

'Whit's he on about, sir?' asked Bob.

'You've *reason* to believe this, dae ye, Doctor?' said Iain.

'Yes.'

'Let's hope ye're right, eh?'

The manager demanded enlightenment. Iain and Bob produced their warrant cards and the sheriff's order, which must have been ready-prepared; so Iain, or the superintendent, had reached the right conclusion before I had. Bewilderment dented the manager's dignity. He dispatched two minions, each bearing a key, to the depths of the building.

'It's not sensible to store articles of intrinsic worth in a deposit box,' he fussed, 'but Head Office advised me to accommodate a valued customer. Of course, I'd no idea–'

'Bad luck about yer account, Doctor.' Iain oozed insincerity. 'But if ye've got this right ye've struck gold. Bronze, anyways.'

'Ye mean the bronze bull's bin here a' this time?' Bob was furious. 'An' ye kenned aboot it and didnae tell us? Is that whit this sheriff's order's aboot?'

I started to tell him the bull had arrived here recently and circuitously, but belated realisation stilled my tongue. David said the bull would be beyond the reach of anyone except the person for whom it was intended, but he'd known I'd deduce where it was. Given the technical skills he'd acquired in the army …

Before I could issue a warning the fire alarm shrilled. There was confusion, then panic. Customers and staff fled for the exits. Displays advertising low percentage loans and holiday finances took flight, forms cascaded in showers of pink and blue and white like elephantine confetti, plastic pens crackled underfoot, computer screens fell and office chairs spun. The manager tried to impose order but no one heard him. Smoke poured from a door behind the tellers' desks. There was a stench of charred paper. The door burst open and the minions leapt out, coughing and dishevelled.

'Where's the fire?' shouted the manager.

'Deposit box,' yelled one of the youngsters.

He and his companion rushed to the street door. The cloud of smoke issuing from the depths had started to thin.

'Incendiary!' Iain bellowed. 'Switch that fucking racket off, somebody!' He grabbed a fire extinguisher and headed for the source of smoke. Bob swallowed his demand for explanations and followed. I tagged along. The manager fiddled with the alarm system. As I passed through the doorway he found the switch and deafening silence fell.

No, not silence. At first I thought the alarm was still ringing in my ears, but it wasn't. A faint, high-pitched wailing rose from the smoky darkness. Even Iain stopped in his tracks. For several seconds we didn't move. I was reminded of pan-pipes but the sound was higher, distant, ghostly. Hairs rose on my neck. Bob's face paled.

'Whit the …?'

Iain crept forward again, extinguisher at the ready. Bob and I tiptoed after him. Behind us sidled the manager. As we reached the foot of the stairs the wailing faded and died. Iain deployed the extinguisher. The vista cleared and the epicentre of the disturbance was revealed.

Several deposit boxes were damaged but one had been blown wide open. The twisted remnant of its door lay against the opposite wall. Within what remained of the box was a pile of burned paper. In the middle of it stood the bronze bull.

'Don't touch it,' I said. 'It'll be hot.'

'Ye don't say,' murmured Iain.

He couldn't take his eyes off the prize. His contribution to dismantling the smuggling ring was assured, and he'd done it without his Scotland Yard colleague.

'What on earth's happened?' The manager scanned the devastation.

'We'll let the fire brigade's forensic team tell us,' said Iain. '*I* want to know where yon weird noise came from.'

'From the bull, Chief Inspector,' I said. 'There are flutes in the nostrils. When it's heated it plays tunes. The full-sized version did that when it had an occupant …'

Bob and the manager stared at me. I shifted my feet.

'Details can wait,' said Iain.

He still couldn't take his eyes off the bull. He asked the manager to confirm the owner of the box and the manager retired to his computer terminal. I wandered away; they no longer needed me. Iain probably wanted to forget about me and return to routine procedure. I went upstairs, left the bank and stood on the pavement.

Events had more or less finished my novel for me but there was little comfort. My head throbbed. I couldn't find my way home to World One. Apart from the remnant of cash in my wallet I'd no money and now I'd no means of obtaining any. Once the car was out of petrol I'd have no transport. I couldn't pay the hire charge. Or my hotel bill. I wouldn't be able to buy food or cigarettes or top up my mobile. I wondered whether Richard might give me a job, David being in prison. However, I hadn't written or even considered Richard's future. Or anyone's. Iain no longer cared about Karen, so although he knew she hadn't killed Peter he might allow Scottish justice to take its natural course, aided by Emma Menzies and her conspecifics. It would be his easiest option. My books never had satisfactory endings.

'Doug? What brings you here?'

It took me a moment to identify her: Alison's colleague, Jan.

'Oh, hello, Jan! Sorry, miles away. Not at school?'

'Free period, so I'm using lunchtime to get my messages. Have you seen Ali?'

'Couple of days ago. Why?'

'She's not at school or at home, though her car's gone. I

rang her sister but *she* doesn't know anything. I think they've fallen out. Wasn't it terrible about Peter? But God forgive me, I believe he brought it on himself. He dumped Ali while she was recovering from losing the baby and then he took up with that Winster woman, and she's killed him. Papers have been full of it. Any idea where Ali might be, Doug? It's unlike her to be off school. I'm worried.'

Yes, I'd an idea.

'No, but try not to worry.' I smiled. 'If I find her I'll ask her to call you.'

I took the bus back to town. My thoughts raged and billowed; my head pounded. I returned to my hotel room and closed the curtains and lay down. World Three would no longer accommodate me so I had to leave it, but how? Had my tormentors not tired of their game? Hadn't the charade been played out?

After a while I fell into a doze. The bull had grown to mountainous proportions. It glowed fierce and red. From the gigantic pipes in its nostrils poured a melody I should have recognised. I floated upwards, past its hot massive flanks, over its burning shoulder, above the scorching bronze musculature of its back. The trapdoor was open, a huge boiling space towards which I moved without volition. I stared into the fiery depths. There, an infinite searing distance below, stood the miniature figure of Peter. He looked upwards, saw me hovering far above, cupped his hands to his mouth and called. I heard only echoing vowels.

'WHAT?' I yelled. 'I CAN'T HEAR YOU, PETER!' My voice bounced from the boiling bronze surfaces and melted into silence in the vast space beneath.

Peter cupped his hands to his mouth and called again. And again. Slowly, the sounds took shape:

'CALL … THE … FERRY … MAN …'

'Mr Merriman!'

I started awake, gasping.

'Mr Merriman!'

A woman along the corridor was outraged about her accommodation. I heard the manager's footsteps on the stairs and landing, his placatory tones, a door closing. I sensed continuing acrimony but couldn't hear the words. I sat still until respiration and heart rate returned close to normal. My head still ached. I needed food.

In a small café off Mayfield Road I bought sandwiches and tea. My stomach didn't want the intake but the rest of my body needed it. My mind started to function again. A pattern began to form in the vortex of disconnected thoughts. There were loose ends, which must somehow be secured.

I returned to the *Brigadoon* and collected my belongings. The Toyota's fuel gauge read half-empty but I made myself believe it was half-full. I smoked a cigarette and drove to Abbey House. A hint of sunlight penetrated the sky.

Richard nodded a curt greeting as I stepped out of the car.

'I presume you've had another visit from the police,' I said.

'You know perfectly bloody well we have. Perfectly bloody well. At least there was no search warrant this time. They only wanted what that damned McArdle fellow called a "wee chat". For an hour and a bloody half. About David registering a bank deposit box in my name. Stuff and bloody nonsense.'

An abrupt movement summoned me indoors and up to the kitchen. Lydia smiled as though happy to see me. I gave an edited account of the morning's events, omitting the disappearance of my bank account. Richard wasn't impressed.

'You seriously suggest David registered a deposit box in my name without telling me? He wouldn't dream of it. Wouldn't dream of it.'

'I deduced it from what he said when I visited him, though I realised you didn't know about it. Iain McArdle was all set to accuse me of stealing the bull so I had to tell him. I thought he'd get off all our backs once the infernal thing was in his hands.'

Richard shook his head. Lydia wondered whether I'd like a cup of coffee. I asked to look at their yellow pages; and there, at last, was the entry I wanted. My heart leapt. I noted the number.

'In the end they accepted it was none of our doing,' said Richard. 'McArdle had a photo of me; *Telegraph* magazine, probably. Interview a couple of years ago. Nobody at the bank recognised it. Said somebody else had registered the box: fellow with a moustache, clean-shaven fellow, anywhere between five-nine and six-three, accent Scots or Southern English, age twenty-five or mid-forties … Security camera tapes were fuzzy. I told them it couldn't be David, whatever he looked like. I suppose you'd told them it was.'

'I didn't.'

I drank the coffee.

'I *do* wish they'd leave us alone,' sighed Lydia. 'It's so *worrying* when none of us has done anything wrong.' She smiled again. 'Anyway, they've gone now.'

'The deposit box business wasn't the most worrying part,' said Richard. 'Did you tell them there was something missing from my workshop, Doug?'

'*Is* there something missing?'

Disingenuous again, Doug. The police hadn't spotted the absence on their previous visit because they'd been looking for the bull. You don't find what you're not seeking.

The familiar foreboding of doom returned, more personal than Y2K.

'I'd no idea,' said Richard. 'Bloody McArdle went snooping around the workshop with that big sergeant. Called me down and asked me what belonged in a space on the wall I hadn't noticed. Amazingly, Slug knew. Didn't you, Slug? Just as well. Ha-ha!'

'Oh, yes!' Lydia was excited. 'I told them straight away. You see, a few days ago, I went down to the workshop to get a small screwdriver, Thursday I think, or Friday, the fuse had blown on the iron and I needed to put a new one in, and I noticed this gap among the tools. It seemed funny because David always has them lined up along the wall like soldiers on parade, and it must have been something quite big, and he wasn't using any big tools just then, and neither was Piggy, and they both put things away ever so carefully. So I asked him. "David," I said, "What's missing from there?" He said, "Two-pound hammer, I don't know where it is," and carried on with what he was doing, and then I remembered. I don't know how I could have forgotten! So I came back upstairs with the screwdriver and mended the plug and got on with the ironing–'

Richard's smile was almost fond.

'Damned if I know why they were interested in a bloody

hammer but they started asking where David had put it. I told them straight: if David had used it he'd have put it back again where it belonged. Ha-ha! So they started interrogating *me*, as though *I* knew where the bloody thing was! Slug to the rescue again. Told them what had become of it. They left quicker than you could say Jack Robinson.'

I put down my coffee cup. My hand was shaking.

'So *you* knew where the hammer was, Lydia.'

'Oh, yes. It was two Saturdays ago, when Hibs were at home to Aberdeen, Ali called on her way into town, she was putting up some shelves or something for a woman who lives – where does she live, Piggy, that skinny Jan woman, can you remember? – anyway, she teaches at the same school as Ali, and you know what Ali's like, never has anything she needs when she's doing joinery. She said could she borrow a hammer, and Piggy and David weren't around, so I took one out of the workshop, and do you know, I couldn't remember having done it until last Thursday, or Friday, or whichever it was, when I went down for the screwdriver and asked David! I should have told Piggy when he got home that Ali had borrowed it, but I forgot. But it'll be all right, Ali always makes sure things come home to roost.'

I had to cough before I could speak.

'Glad there was a simple answer. Lydia, thanks for the coffee. Must run. Richard, sorry you've had more police trouble but Lydia's right, they'll leave you alone now.'

I took the stairs three at a time, like Richard, and spun the Toyota out of the courtyard. It was designed for speed over rough tracks. It sped over asphalt roads, too. My foot was on the floor.

31

They say we always return to the place; in this case, a place in a photograph facing my bedroom wall in 17 Blandford Terrace. There was the gate in the hedge, the burn welling from the soft embittered earth, the rough track, the tree-clad slope where we'd dreamed sweet dreams, the trunks on which I'd carved words of love. Always it drew me, in joy and sorrow. It mocked me while I slept, telling me I'd find rest there. Now, in this dark night of the soul, in the world's darkness, I'd have preferred to pass it by. With my eyes closed.

But the Land Cruiser nosed through the gate and down the track. No sign of pursuit. Yet.

The blue Fiat had skidded at the final bend and buried itself in the bole of a massive oak. The engine housing was wrecked, the bonnet lid sprung, the windscreen smashed. The driver's door hung open like a dead mouth. Cooling metalwork ticked our lives away. I edged past the wreck, stopped on the rim of the clearing, alighted and walked forward.

She'd crawled across the grassy space and she was leaning against *that very tree*. The great John Muir once said he'd never seen a discontented tree; they grip the ground as though they like it. That one was an exception. She stared and grinned, in acknowledgment of my arrival, or in pain. Her injuries hadn't robbed her of the power of speech; worse, the power of song.

'*Am Brunnen von dem Tore*
Da steht ein Lindenbaum;
Ich träumt in seinem Schatten …'
'Stop it, Alison. Shut up.'

Her voice wasn't as resonant or as melodious as Linda's but her capacity to hurt was no less. She laughed.

'Thought you liked that song, Doug.
Ich schnitt in seine Rinde
So manches liebe Wort …'

'I said *shut the fuck up*. I came to get you out, not to hear you singing–'

'Get me out? Because *we're two of a kind*?'

I edged towards her. The singing had stopped but inside my head it went on and on and on. The trees wept their last leaves, covering the earth with mourning. My feet dragged through them, heaping them into piles of russet and gold. I watched one leaf, chrome yellow, settle on her lank blonde hair.

I focussed on practicalities: broken tibia, probable pelvic damage, maybe abdominal injuries. Right clavicle had gone. How she'd crawled so far I didn't know. More to the purpose, how would I move her?

'How long have you known, Doug?'

'Long enough.' Since I'd started drafting *The Bronze Bull*, as a matter of fact. I'd made Alison the murderer from the outset. Now I understood why. 'The police know you had the hammer. They're coming.'

'It was only a matter of time. This is where I want them to find me. And you.'

'I don't want them to find either of us.'

'You can't stop them.'

'I might. How long have *you* known, Alison?'

'I suspected from the outset. Your aversion to lime trees was so sudden, so exaggerated. Is this the place?'

'Right where you're sitting.'

Rains had cleansed the trunk, leached the washings into the soil where I'd buried her beneath the dying remnants of summer. The physical past had been recycled but the memory, or its simulacrum, wouldn't fade. I was standing in a photograph I couldn't see without suffering, couldn't throw away.

Alison stared upwards. The sky was as grey as her face; the hint of sun was mockery. Daylight was dwindling. I imagined she was lying on the bed of the burn, gazing towards heaven through a curtain of water. Her voice was little more than a whisper.

'After he'd gone I tried to avoid him. Even the thought of seeing him hurt. It was about half two in the morning when I left Jan's. I'd been drinking. I shouldn't have driven but the traffic was quiet. The Pleasance was deserted, except for him, striding along the pavement, suitcase in hand. Going home. To her. If only I hadn't noticed … I stopped because I couldn't go on driving. I could scarcely see, scarcely breathe, my heart was in my throat, I was shaking. He saw me and gave a … a friendly nod, as though I were an acquaintance he quite liked. When I got out of the car I didn't know I was holding the hammer. I don't know what I said. He told me to go home. Said he too was going home. I remember his voice, the look on his face. Dismissive; kindly contempt. Then he turned and walked away. There was a loose thread on his sheepskin coat. She never looked after him properly. I hit him and then I dropped the hammer and jumped back into the car and drove. I was half-way down Dalkeith Road before I noticed how fast I was going. I trod on the brake and then drove the rest of the way below the speed limit. Didn't realise what I'd done until I heard the news the following morning. Maybe not even then.'

Robbie had said they took everything Alison told them with a pinch of salt. Her account probably contained *post hoc* reconstruction: the act dissociated from the path of life and memory, fixed in history yet fictionalised by its essence; the body acting without volition, or in seeming obedience to an inner voice that isn't one's own. The full truth can't be told because it's never apprehended. At the moment of commission the senses dream and the memory circuits are overloaded. We may invent such details as we please, what history we please. I concocted an empathetic reply.

'Undying love is the romantic ideal. It's Aphrodite's blessing even if it's unrequited. But if it's encouraged and then ceases to be reciprocated, it's Aphrodite's curse, and there's no defence against a capricious goddess.' I sat beside her, considering splints. 'Peter was callous but he never misled you. He was open and straightforward. But I was deceived. Linda asked me to bring her here one final time so she could explain and we could both move on. Here. A place with such meaning.'

'Yes. We're two of a kind. Let's wait together, Doug. I've had enough. I hoped the crash would kill me. I can't live any longer with the memory.'

'Yes you can. Remember Eliot? "The awful daring of a moment's surrender that an age of prudence can never retract; by this and this only we have existed." What each of us did was wrong but it doesn't make us evil. It makes us human.'

'Convince yourself. For me, it hurts too much.'

Finding branches that were straight, firm and not too heavy was difficult in the failing light. Tearing my shirt into strips was harder than I'd expected. I hadn't attended fractures in years and never in so makeshift a way. She was passive, drifting into haunted half-sleep. Her eyes closed. I recalled my condition after I'd abandoned Jimmy's body.

'Did you meet Jimmy Farquhar, Alison?'

'Who?'

'The man who saw Peter die. I told you about him. He stole the suitcase and then took the hammer to the Meadows and put it beside the sleeping tramp.'

'He did what?'

'You never heard from him?'

Her head shook. The binding I'd placed around the broken shoulder held firm. I believed her this time; she hadn't known Jimmy. He hadn't blackmailed her. Yet he'd seen her kill Peter.

Jimmy Farquhar's motives became plain. Like many career criminals he'd had a twisted sense of chivalry. For a man the rule is "do the crime, do the time", but women must be protected from the forces of law. He'd seen a woman kill Peter. He hadn't known who she was but he'd known she was a woman, so he'd altered the crime scene to protect her. Perhaps he'd thought his rectitude, the ethic of the underclass, somehow compensated or justified the theft of Peter's case.

My arrival at the dell had been greeted with a siren song.

Now I heard distant sirens. My train of thought slammed into the buffers.

I manoeuvred the Toyota beside Alison, opened the passenger door, and tried to lift her. She was a big woman, heavy-boned with an athlete's muscle mass, and I wasn't strong. The passenger seat was high above us. Both physically and emotionally she was incapable of helping. And I had to take care with her injuries. The sirens were approaching. How long? Minutes, if I was lucky.

'I can get us out of here, Alison. Trust me. I'll keep you safe.'

She scarcely responded. She was drifting back into half-sleep: physical pain, emotional anguish. Another siren sounded. Terror gave me strength. Appealing to the gods for aid, I struggled, struggled again, and brought her half-upright, braced my foot on the floor of the vehicle, lifted, twisted. I felt my grip slipping. I put my knee under her back and lifted again. The sirens were closer; they knew where we were. Another surge of panic, another concerted effort.

Somehow I hauled her into the passenger seat, dreading what further injuries I might be inflicting. The exertion pulled a muscle in my shoulder. My eyes watered. She flopped like a broken doll. Panting, I regained the driver's seat and half-straightened her and managed to secure her seat-belt. Then I put the vehicle into gear. The fuel gauge said quarter full. How accurate was it? Ignoring my shoulder I pulled out of the clearing and started to climb the track.

Too late.

Blue lights flashed. A white police Land Rover nosed

towards us. It paused; they'd seen the wrecked Fiat and summoned an ambulance. Then it advanced again.

The speed of reaction didn't surprise me. Iain was in his element now; no need to be unconventional. Once he had the information, he only needed to activate the machinery of Lothian and Borders Constabulary and then choreograph the routine. Finding Alison neither at home nor at school, her car missing, it had been a simple matter to elicit and broadcast details of the vehicle and summon the force.

I switched to four-wheel drive, turned sharp left, burst through the edge of the track and tried to ford the burn. The wheels spun in the mud on the far bank. I changed gear and cut the revs. There were shouts behind me. We'd been spotted. I heard running footsteps.

If I managed to get Alison out of this, what would Iain do? Admit he'd failed to apprehend Peter Wishart's killer, or let Karen take the rap? How honest, how honourable, *was* my protagonist?

I pressed the accelerator. The wheels spun again. The Land Cruiser lurched sideways. Sweat ran into my eyes, as it had in Jimmy's kitchen. Same eyes, same stinging sensation, same terror. Not the same sweat, though; time had moved on. You can never step twice into the same river. Now time was standing still. I reversed a couple of yards, slammed the vehicle into second gear and accelerated again. We mounted the bank and bumped on to the rough pasture beyond. Pain lanced my shoulder. Alison moaned and, I thought, fainted.

They were following. Trained police drivers were more skilled than I. Gritting my teeth against the agony in my shoulder I went up a gear and rammed my foot down. The landscape yawed and pitched ahead and around me. Tyres squelched through swamp. Alison flopped to and fro in her seat. I realised she might not survive this journey. She needed emergency care. I headed uphill.

How many vehicles had they brought? How many were waiting in the lane? Where were they? Probably not many; to organise a full-scale hunt at short notice would have stretched even Iain's capacity. But they'd be optimally deployed. At least there was no helicopter. One might have been on the way, though. I'd have to trust to Luck. I wouldn't insult the Lady but she seldom smiled on me.

I checked the mirror: oscillating images of wood and sky and brown wet pasture against which I saw flashing blue lights, white Land Rovers. Two were converging, one following my path, one coming from further up the track to cut me off. They were gaining. I looked ahead. A hawthorn hedge divided me from the lane. Beyond it would be a ditch. Between me and the lane the gradient was steep. Two hundred yards ahead, a field gate interrupted the hedge. It looked stout but it was wooden; traditional five-bar gate, locked and chained. I changed down to second, turned the nose of the Land Cruiser towards it and floored the accelerator. The engine roared. The vehicle gathered speed.

They'd soon divine my intent, shout into their radios, alert their colleagues in the lane and at headquarters. I glanced along the hedge. No sign of blue lights, but so what? How quickly could they set up road blocks? I knew nothing about the logistics of road blocks. What appalling ignorance for a self-styled crime novelist. Why didn't I do better research? No wonder my books received lukewarm notices. If they existed.

The view through the windscreen was full of five-bar gate. I shut my eyes. The crash was felt rather than heard. The seat-belt almost cut me in half. My shoulder howled. What the impact had done to Alison I hated to think, but, thank Asclepius, she was still unconscious. The engine screamed, the offside headlamp and indicator disintegrated in showers of plastic and I heard metal bend and tear, but the vehicle kept going. The windscreen was cracked but not shattered or frosted. Rocking to and fro, we were in the lane.

A police car bore down on us. I manoeuvred to the wrong side of the road, switched my surviving headlamp to main beam and drove straight at it. I saw the determination on the driver's face metamorphose to bewilderment and then fear. He started to turn the wheel to the right but I was a millisecond ahead of him. He saw me veering across his nose, overcorrected to avoid the collision and landed his nearside front wheel in the ditch. The rear of his car jack-knifed and struck a glancing blow on the flank of the Land Cruiser. The driver's door buckled towards me. I almost lost the road; the heavy Toyota fishtailed and I wrestled with the steering, my shoulder protesting. Then I was on course again. I changed into top. Behind me, enraged sirens screamed in pursuit.

Then it was down to knowledge of geography. They'd have maps. They'd see where they could cut me off. But Linda and I had driven those lanes in happier times so I knew them. I switched off my surviving headlight, and in the thickening dusk I turned right on to a single-track through the trees. The sirens performed a Doppler shift behind me; they'd gone ahead. I slowed down for safety and drove another five minutes. Then I put the light on again. Gradually my muscles relaxed and my heart-rate began to settle. My shoulder throbbed.

The logical move would have been to cross the border into England. That would have slowed the pursuit because exchanges between police forces take time. Anticipating this tactic, Iain would have deployed officers to stop me. Or, I wondered, did he know me well enough to foresee the improbable? I decided to take the chance. There was a faint hope of success, provided the torn metal below the wrecked headlamp didn't rip the front tyre. And provided I didn't run out of fuel. The gauge still read quarter full. Was it exaggerating? If so, in which direction?

Alison moaned and stirred. I murmured something and she went back to sleep. Then I started to negotiate the network of narrow winding memories linking the present to the past, the borderland to the hub of the story's action. Soon it was dark.

I made my way north-westward over the Berwickshire hills towards East Lothian. Alison half-woke, muttering in delirium, then slept again. How long before Iain realised he'd made the wrong guess?

At Cranshaws there was a moment of panic; a uniformed police officer emerged from his parked patrol car, stepped in front of me and held up a commanding hand. I had to choose between running him down and stopping. I stopped. My heart was in my boots.

'This your car, sir?'

I licked my lips but they stayed dry. My tongue was like sandpaper.

'Hired. We've had a crash. Obviously. I'm a doctor, Constable. I have a badly injured patient here. I need to get her to Edinburgh Royal. Delay could be fatal. As soon as I've dealt with her I'll put the car in for repair. I know it scarcely looks roadworthy but I've already driven from near Hexham–'

'Taken a funny route from Hexham, sir. Can I see yer licence?'

'I got lost. I don't know this part of the country.' I handed over my licence. He registered my lack of shirt. 'Yes, I had to use it to deal with the patient's injuries. Please, Constable, this is an emergency.'

He shone his torch on Alison, grunted, noted my name and address and the Land Cruiser's details, returned my licence, and lectured me about driving a vehicle that contravened the law. He started to radio a report but I'd driven on. He'd be in trouble before the night was over. As soon as I was out of his sight I picked up speed. The fuel gauge dropped, dropped again.

Through East Lothian I kept to country lanes as far as I could, emerging on to the A68 south of Dalkeith. Driving through Dalkeith was a nightmare; traffic lights stopped me, the wrecked Land Cruiser drew attention and I expected the police to pounce at every moment. They didn't, but the fuel warning light came on. Praying to any god who might be listening I drove on towards Edinburgh. I turned off the A68 before Little France, stopped and took out my mobile.

'Acheron Taxis? Good. I'm at–'

'I know where you are, Douglas Carmichael. Out in the sticks. You wish to be taken to 17 Blandford Terrace.'

For a long moment I couldn't find my voice but the ferryman was patient. When I could speak again my words were a hoarse whisper.

'Yes. But there's an injured woman with me.'

'Each of you will pay the fare.'

The line went dead. I sat, shaking, legs refusing to function. At length, after repeated efforts, I contrived to unfasten Alison's seat-belt, force open the buckled door of the Land Cruiser, step on to the road and go round to the passenger side. I was exhausted, and my shoulder injury meant I wouldn't be able to lift her out without dropping her. I needed help and the ferryman wouldn't provide it. Any passer-by intent on a good deed would serve, but there was no one except a tramp swaying along in an alcoholic haze. He was rangy and big-boned; no sandwich board. Once upon a time he'd been strong but years of self-abuse had ruined him. Recognition dawned. I called:

'Seamus! Seamus Goldstein! Here, I've got something for you.'

I took out my wallet and extracted one of the few remaining notes, a fiver. The sound of his name drew a fraction of his attention; the sight of money drew the whole.

'Ah, God bless ye, sarr, God bless ye, 'tis a kind heart ye have–'

'Little job to do first. This lady's hurt. I need to get her out of the car without hurting her any more. A taxi will come for us.'

His attention was on the five pound note. I had to repeat the request, with explanatory gestures, before his mind registered it. Even then he could provide little help. However, the little sufficed. An exhausted man with an injured shoulder and a brain-damaged alcoholic contrived to manoeuvre a wounded killer on to the pavement. She leaned against me, less than half conscious. Seamus grasped his money. Then he noticed Alison's condition.

'Aaaahhh! Blood! 'Tis blood over me hands! Blood! 'Tis death! They said I struck him. They said. But never, never. I never saw de hammer before, never in me life, God be my witness!'

He broke off, howling, and staggered away clutching his fiver. He was still howling when the taxi appeared and I pushed Alison into it and flopped beside her. We drove away with the cries of Seamus Goldstein receding in our wake.

She regained consciousness on the journey but didn't speak. When we reached Blandford Terrace I handed over two copper coins. The taxi departed.

I stood beside my own door. My home in World One. With no shirt beneath my jacket I shivered in the frosty air. Alison leaned on me.

I was home. All the memories I cherished were here; books, photographs, CDs, diaries. Even my Ford Capri was parked where I'd left it. Linda and I had been happy in this place until she began to drift away. I'd clung to her, but to no avail. Around me now, the familiar terraced walls, the asphalt, the lawns, the privet, all echoed with her, chiming through the icy dark, mourning the transience of earthly things. Sorrow welled up from the depths of my being. My eyes shed tears.

It had taken a journey through a work of fiction to find myself and confront what I'd done, what I was. And now I was home.

Somehow I contrived to guide Alison into the flat and on to my bed. I closed the door on her and retired to my living room or office. I unloaded my briefcase, transferred the files from my laptop to my PC and switched on the printer.

While the files printed, page after page, I opened a bottle of Glenmorangie. By the time the night was over I'd drunk most of it. But *The Bronze Bull* was finished. World Three was a memory consigned to typescript and computer files.

I was home. I faced an old, or a new, reality.

32

I felt the hangover before I was awake. The whisky bottle had fallen under my desk and lay like a corpse. I must have dropped asleep on the sofa after I'd finished the final chapter. The computer still hummed. Print-out covered the desk and carpet. I groaned. Everything hurt, particularly my head and shoulder.

I sat up and the whisky bottle rolled away from my foot. My fingers picked up a half-smoked joint and lit it at the fourth attempt. Stockbridge traffic noise penetrated the room and rain pattered on the window. Early morning light crept dull and lifeless through the yellow curtains. I inhaled smoke. It hurt. I seemed to have pulled a muscle in my shoulder.

Linda's portrait stared, enigmatic. I sensed the upward and downward curl of her lips and looked away. After tidying the print-out I staggered into the bedroom, rid myself of my sticky clothes and lay down. The bed was cold. I shivered under the duvet and shut my eyes. There were half-dreams about *The Bronze Bull*. Its characters still seemed real.

I dozed until mid-morning and then dragged myself into the shower. Ten minutes under the hot downpour left me feeling, if not better, then a touch less worse. I decided against shaving; I never take unnecessary risks. However, I cleaned my teeth; my mouth had become the quarters of a hibernating creature with low standards of hygiene. I put on clean clothes, stumbled to the kitchen and made a cup of coffee, which I sweetened with fructose; as good a hangover remedy as I know. Some day I'd have to clean those mugs properly. Linda would have nagged me about them. I needed to eat, but the thought of food wrenched my stomach.

Coffee in hand I returned to the living room or office and put on a CD of *Dido and Anaeas*: a period instrument group conjoined with innocent voices untrammelled by grand operatic gestures. Purcell's simplicity, wit and technique invariably sooth and please, while the characters's emotions shine through the formal Baroque gestures and animate them. The witches always raise a smile, but sadness has seldom been portrayed as it is in Dido's lament. The closing passage elicited tears: *'When I am laid in earth … Remember me, but ah, forget my fate'.*

As the final chorus faded the telephone rang, making me jump. I lifted the receiver and snapped 'Hello'. It was seven minutes past eleven.

'Hello? Doug? It's George. I don't know whether you've heard, but I'm afraid there's very bad–'

At first I didn't recognise the voice, yet it seemed familiar: baritone, Scottish, cultivated.

'George?'

'George Mitchell.' Verging on the indignant. 'That *is* you, isn't it, Doug?'

Of course. George and Sally. Warrender Park Road. I needed to visit them. I'd been invited for dinner to meet their neighbour, Guy, and his sister, whose name I couldn't recall. George had phoned to remind me.

'I … Yes, this is Doug. Sorry, George, not at my best. Heavy night.'

'Have ye heard the Scottish news?'

'Not this morning. Why?'

He took two deep breaths.

'I'm afraid it's a wee bit of a shock. I'm no' just sure how to tell ye this.'

I knew what he was about to disclose. My mouth went dry.

'You'd better just say it, George.'

He paused. Seconds ticked past before he found his voice again. My eyes scanned the room for an anchor of hope. In vain.

'Doug, they're sayin' Linda's dead. They've found her body, like. The reports aren't detailed, but …' He broke off.

It had only been a matter of time: a chance walker hunting for mushrooms, children digging beside a late-season picnic, a pet mongrel scrabbling, or a police search with tracker dogs.

'But what, George?'

'This isnae easy to say, Doug, but … well, they say they're treatin' it as murder.' He paused again. The question screaming in his mind made it hard for him. I didn't respond. At length he continued: 'I know. We were stunned as well when we heard. I can't even start to imagine the effect on you, mate. Doug, ye'll no' want to hear this, but the polis will be wanting to question ye. Ye've got to understand, it's inevitable. A murder inquiry; they'll need to talk to–'

'Of course, George. They'll need to talk to partners, past and present. I'll be here. Thanks for letting me know. I appreciate it.' I swallowed, not without difficulty. 'Are you and Sally OK?'

They were. They'd never liked Linda, which is why I'd relied on them after she left. George asked whether I'd like them to come round, or perhaps go to stay with them for a day or two. I was grateful but I declined. This was where I belonged. My home. Linda's home, if she'd chosen to stay. I like solitude. I thanked George again and ended the call.

I lit a cigarette and made another cup of coffee. My stomach was beginning to recover. Even my headache was lightening, though my shoulder still hurt. I felt as though a discord had been resolved, a cadence completed. Waiting with dim hope and grim expectation is worse than receiving definite news, however ill.

After Linda had left, I'd invested time and money in surveillance systems. My computer couldn't be hacked, my telephone couldn't be tapped, and no one could gain access to the flat unless they were very patient and technologically sophisticated. It paid to be careful about privacy. I was happy to stay within my Stockbridge fortress, writing books, listening to music, sometimes watching the news or a film, venturing out to the shops or for a walk. For the rest, I only wanted to be left in peace. But for some there could be no peace, no rest. Soon the telephone rang again.

I listened, answered and replaced the receiver. I switched off the power points and ensured everything in the flat was safe. I emptied the ashtray and washed it, rinsed the coffee mugs and made the bed. Then, mechanically if clumsily, I shaved, put on jacket and tie, checked that wallet and keys and smokes and mobile were in the customary pockets, donned my raincoat, picked up my briefcase, set the alarms, left the flat, double-locked the door and walked downstairs.

The late morning was dull and damp. Blandford Terrace was quiet, as usual on a Thursday, and its normality mocked me. Someone was cleaning a window with a bright yellow cloth, bucket of soapy water beside her, and chatting to a passer-by. Three children played among the parked cars; the two older ones should have been in school. A couple of women returned with the day's shopping. A cat stalked timorous movement in a privet hedge. An ageing crow pecked at the pavement. There were no trees. I wished there had been trees. Just not lime trees.

A young couple aglitter with piercings, clad in trainers and jeans and combat jackets, were leaving the house with the 'For Sale' notice. I supposed they were purchasers. I watched them saunter down the terrace hand in hand, tinny pop music oozing from the plugs in their ears. A yellow chestnut leaf from an unknown source descended upon my hair. Its touch was a caress. A distant dryad whispered. Perhaps it was whispering to me.

I lit another cigarette. I smoked it standing beside the wet road, waiting for the pain to leave me, for the end of the world.

About the Author

 After he retired from a career in medicine and university teaching, Mark Henderson moved to the Peak District of Derbyshire, England, where he started to write fiction and to collect and tell local folktales.

Mark's previous two novels, National Cake Day in Ruritania and The Engklimastat, met with critical acclaim and the former was a contender for the Republic of Consciousness literary prize.

Mark has many publications to his name, long and short, covering many genres, including a collection of 62 traditional Peak District stories and a collection of performance pieces, Cruel and Unusual PunNishments.

Mark is secretary of his local creative writing group. He regularly performs at storytelling gigs and is in demand for his talks about his work and life experiences.

Printed in Great Britain
by Amazon